WHAT WE RE(

Noa Sl

Production by eBookPro Publishing
www.ebook-pro.com

WHAT WE REGRET MOST
Noa Shalev

Translation from Hebrew: Zoe Jordan
Editing: Danielle Nagler

Contact: noashalev01@gmail.com

ISBN 9798335893039

WHAT
WE
REGRET
MOST

A Novel

NOA SHALEV

1

"Fishman, what's taking so long? We have a meeting. You taking a shit or what?" Weiss pounds his fist on the bathroom door. The stall's rusty latch shakes with every blow.

This is the only bathroom stall on the floor. The tiles are broken, the toilet tank leaks, and when you flush, the weak flow is sometimes insufficient. Good thing I'm not taking a shit.

"No!" I call through the door. "I have my period! You want updates on how heavily I'm bleeding or do you think you can leave me alone for one minute?"

"Oh ugh, that's so gross! Why do you have to be so vulgar?" He shouts, then clears his throat and says, "Oh hey, Pinto."

"What's with the shouting?" I hear Pinto's calm, gravelly voice.

"Ah, well, I'd like to make a complaint about a hostile work environment," says Weiss.

"What now?"

"Fishman just started telling me about her period out of nowhere. I practically sprouted breasts just listening to her."

Weiss's chest is bigger than mine—and firmer too. Whenever he has free time he disappears to the gym to "get his pump on," as he puts it. His workouts are two hours on average, and include thirty minutes of cardio, thirty minutes of weights, fifteen minutes of abs, and forty-five minutes of admiring himself in the mirror. His girlfriend of three years

5

must be very open-minded to permit the intensive romance he seems to have with himself. Post-workout, he wolfs down two cans of tuna straight from the tin, and audibly gulps down a protein drink that fills whatever room he's in with a distinct banana scent.

"If it bothers you so much, maybe you shouldn't stand outside the bathroom when she's in there. Come with me, I wanted to discuss something with you before the meeting anyway." Pinto saves me, as always, getting Weiss away from the door.

Their voices echo farther and farther down the corridor. I take a deep breath and wipe away the makeup smeared under my eyes with coarse paper towels. The last thing I need is for Weiss to catch me crying. Whenever I get irritated with him, (which happens every half hour or so) he calls me hormonal. I am not hormonal, he's insufferable.... Fine, maybe I am a bit hormonal.

When I get to the meeting room, everyone is already sitting around trays of pastries, and Pinto is standing and speaking passionately, wearing cargo pants and a T-shirt despite the cold. It doesn't matter what he's talking about: Pinto always speaks passionately. He could have been a great preacher. He peppers his cascade of speech with data, shooting names and dates into the air like a commander briefing his men before battle. He stands with his back to the white wall and the presentation is projected onto his face, full of tables, data and pie charts, and when he moves, the names and numbers across his forehead change. The sheer volume of data could be intimidating, but Pinto does not refer to it nor bother to change the slides.

One of the criteria for which department heads in our office are assessed is the length of their presentations. It's not only length that matters, of course. Incorporating humorous videos with so much as a passing connection to the topic at hand is not insignificant. Gross, head of logistics, once got a comment from his boss about his choice of font. But Pinto is not your average department head. They didn't recruit him from the naval commando unit to fill out forms and write minutes, which is fortunate because he's dyslexic. All of his presentations are based on the original slideshow which he received from his predecessor three years ago. The only thing he changed was the floral background, which he made gray, and before every meeting he asks Gidi, his bureau chief, to change the date, the subject and to add a slide summarizing the meeting's central items.

"Good of you to join us," he smiles warmly at me, drawing everyone's attention to my tardiness and his tolerant tone with me. People tend not to be late for Pinto, but if they dare, he reprimands them in a cold, restrained voice, sparking fear that his estimation of them has plummeted. Nobody wants to lose Pinto's esteem but I'd rather endure some scolding and concern for my reputation than be punished by the constant suspicion of nepotism.

Pinto and my brother were best friends in the naval commando unit. When Shahar was killed I was thirteen and Pinto was twenty. He was at our house for the entire week of mourning, all day every day, like the rest of Shahar's crew, and kept coming afterwards, and was always nice to me, even when he hardly said a word. On weekends, when he left the base, he would board the train from Atlit to Tel Aviv, catch a bus from there to Givatayim, where we lived, and knock on the door with flowers and the sesame bagels that he knew I liked. Only after visiting us would he go see his own parents in Yavne. He played speed and checkers with me and tried to teach me chess, too, but I never got the rules. He introduced me to "The Princess Bride," and we would hum "as you wish" together before Wesley rolled down the mountain, and I would duck under his arm when the giant rodents attacked Buttercup. Sometimes he took me out into the dark night and pointed out the North Star and Ursa Major. On my parents' birthdays he'd call, even years after

Shahar was killed, and on my birthday he would make special visits and bring me huge gifts. When all of my friends were obsessed with Justin Timberlake, I was in love with Pinto. Pinto, unlike Justin, was real and I knew that I could count on him. He was a bit of dry land during a time when all of my ships sank. When he came to visit us, the house would fill with life and I felt that the air, thick with sadness and my mother's cigarette smoke, would clear up a little, and for a moment you could breathe easy. When I came to work here, Pinto set it up for me to work with him and took me under his wing, so that instead of living just in Shahar's shadow, I now worked in Pinto's, too.

"Ok, so in a nutshell," Pinto's voice brought me back to reality, "our objects, Ali Mansour and Mustafa Aziz, are two high-ranking Hezbollah operatives. We intercepted an email that they sent to two known operatives in Rome, and it appears that they are planning some kind of attack in the near future."

Weiss interrupts, "How near?"

"They bought tickets for next week."

"Who'll wait for them at the airport?" I ask.

"You two," Pinto looks at me, eyes smiling.

"Why do we have to wait for them at the airport?" Weiss asks.

"I assume we don't have details regarding their accommodations," I say. "We'll have to tail them when they get off the plane."

"Exactly," Pinto says, and some of the others smile, but not Weiss. He narrows his eyes at me and bites his upper lip, which is unflattering, and when Weiss makes an unflattering face, it means that he is thoroughly displeased. I can no longer hold back a smile, but Weiss does not give in so easily, saying, "This concerns the assessment from Brussels intelligence that Hezbollah plans to carry out an attack in Italy in the next few months."

"Precisely," Pinto is pleased. I am not. "So," he continues,

"Weiss and Fishman will leave one week yesterday, Saturday night, to Rome. You'll join the crews already there on the ground tracking the two operatives known to us—Ibrahim Shakir and Rushdi al-Saadi, who have been there for some time already, deep undercover as students, gathering intelligence. Gidi will get the organized material containing additional information to you after this meeting." Gidi nods without looking up from taking the minutes and Pinto continues to verify various points with those in the room and then concludes, "Okay, kids, we're done for today. Weiss and Fishman, we need to tie up some loose ends; the rest of you are dismissed."

I have two minutes until the room empties to process everything that has been said. On the one hand, this operation is a great opportunity for me to stand out, show what I'm made of and quiet the critical voices; and on the other hand, with all of the pressure and stress in my life right now, I feel that traveling with Weiss will not do me any good. I can act business-as-usual at work and streamline operations like a pro, but I always pay a mental price for intensive time spent in Weiss' company, and in my present circumstances the mental cost is higher than usual.

"Umm, Pinto," I say after the last of those leaving the room swipes a final pastry and returns to his office. Pinto looks up at me with dark eyes and long eyelashes. He stands close to me now, and I smell his Turkish coffee scent and notice how I'm always overly self-conscious around him. "So," I begin, and he bends toward me. I am a little muddled and pause. Weiss pulls up a chair and sits down beside us.

"Just so you know, I feel good about having my best people on this operation," says Pinto, who has moved away from me. "Isn't that right, Weiss?" He turns to Weiss who is leisurely poking between his teeth with a toothpick.

"Sure," Weiss smiles with the toothpick in his mouth, "Fishman is the hottest chick here, which could be critical to the operation's success." He pauses to pick the remaining pastry crumbs out of his teeth with small clicking sounds, then adds, "not that there's so much competition around here."

"You see what I have to deal with every day?" I say to Pinto. "This kind of talk drives me crazy."

"Oh sweetheart, I know that I drive you crazy, but you must control yourself: You're a married woman," Weiss narrows his eyes at me.

"Hey, are you sure that Weiss is necessary for this operation?" I address Pinto.

"Are you sure that you're necessary in this department?" Weiss shoots back.

"Okay, enough," Pinto silences us both, "Fishman, I'm sure that you can handle a few unfunny jokes."

"It's way more than a few unfunny jokes," I say in a voice of contrived calm. "It's damaging to my work environment, and to me on a personal level."

"That's a period thing, she's hormonal, everything gets her on a personal level right now," Weiss winks at Pinto.

"I said that's enough, Weiss," Pinto stands up and Gidi, who has just entered the room, hands each of us a bound booklet. "Alright, guys," Pinto becomes matter of fact. "Read this thoroughly," he gestures at the booklets, "and don't forget to return all of the materials to Gidi when you're finished." He pats me gently on the shoulder and gives Weiss a friendly blow across his broad back. "We're basically done here," Pinto concludes. "But I wanted to tell you before you go," both of us look up at him as his speech slows, "that this will be our last operation together."

"Weiss finally realized he's not a good fit?" I smile sweetly at Weiss.

"You wish," he smiles back.

"Weiss stays. I'm leaving my position," Pinto says as casually as if he was announcing that he's popping out for a smoke.

I have known for a while now that Pinto is supposed to vacate his position in the foreseeable future, and I even see myself as a leading candidate to replace him—which only further compounds the tensions between me and Weiss—and still this nonchalant announcement turns my stomach. I don't know this office without Pinto. Sure I'm plenty confident in my professional ability—which might be the only thing in my life that I feel secure in, and don't torment myself with questions and doubts—but this is precisely the reason that I don't want to find out that all my confidence comes from the safety net that Pinto spread beneath me from day one, that Weiss is right, and without Pinto I wouldn't have gotten where I did.

"Where to?" I ask, trying to hide the tremble in my voice.

"Up," Pinto smiles. "I'm a candidate for head of the division, Shabtai's position. I wanted you two to be the first to know."

I look at Weiss and he looks at me, pleased. He probably thinks he's got this one in the bag. Let him think that.

We gather our things, leave the room and retrieve our cell phones from their lockers where we stored them before the meeting. Weiss' phone rings and the words "Do Not Answer" appear on the screen. Weiss rolls his eyes and silences it, "Some people can't take a hint."

Pinto and I exchange glances and Weiss starts talking about Arsenal and Barcelona's last game. I find myself walking a little behind, feeling like my eyes are stinging again. I'm sad that Pinto's leaving, and excited by the possibility of promotion and also afraid of it, and irritated by Weiss and stressed and anxious to go home, and all of these feelings swirl in my belly and form a lump that rises up in my throat and forces me to admit that Weiss is right: I really am more hormonal than usual. Not because of my period, but rather because of the hormones that I am taking. And I really am especially sensitive, not because of Pinto, but because the period that came made it clear to me that this month, yet again, I have not got pregnant.

2

Jonathan is in the kitchen washing the dishes in his financial advisor uniform—black pants, slim cut button-down shirt and a line of bitterness around his mouth. He still has not noticed me entering the apartment, but from his sharp movements, which threaten to scratch the plates, I can sense his resentment because he is washing the dishes that I promised I would wash. He'll probably also be mad at me that his shirt is wet.

I dream of getting a dishwasher, but Jonathan prefers tightening our belts and saving up for an apartment. I am in favor of loosening the belt when I get home from work and not spending forty-five minutes scraping dried avocado off a fork. I stand beside him, take the sponge from his hand and start soaping a large pot.

"I'm mostly finished," he says without looking at me.

"I know. Sorry."

Dalit, the couples' therapist we've started seeing, told us recently that there's no shame in apologizing. On the contrary, it's a show of strength. But I think it's a problem if one side is always apologizing and the other is always right, always justified. I married a man who is always right. He's right that we need to save up for an apartment because we can't live in a rental forever; and right that it's not economical to sleep with a comforter *and* the air conditioner on; and right that I look better with my hair up; and right that I need to rest more; and that work should not come at the expense of our relationship; and that we haven't gone out, just the two of us, for almost a year now; and that it doesn't seem to bother me too much.

He's still scowling at the pan in his hand and I figure that this is not ideal timing to tell him that once again, we're not pregnant. Or, "we failed," as Jonathan puts it. Everything is either success or failure to him. Like in his work where there are ups or downs, victory or defeat, but I'm tired of these battles. He accuses me of no longer wanting a child, that I'm not making enough of an effort, that I don't take care of my body, even though I do way more exercise than he does. He even makes comments about my runs. He makes me green parsley smoothies and disgusting black bean stews because his naturopath says that they promote fertility, and then he gets offended when I don't want them, ignoring the fact that it's his sperm that's defective. Well, he's not completely ignoring it. Following the naturopath's advice, he eats a clove of garlic every day and also makes himself fertility-promoting shakes. Maybe they're working, but it's hard to tell because we hardly sleep together anymore. The insemination treatments have relieved me of the burden of sex.

When I finish with the dishes, I take off my shoes and sit down in the living room but refrain from putting my feet up on the sofa: I know Jonathan hates that. He's sorting mail by the front door and I know that the credit card bill will only make his mood worse and his tolerance for bad news nonexistent, so I call him over to sit with me. He pauses for a moment, as if considering it, then sits a small but perceptible distance from me. I feel a spasm in my abdomen, maybe it's stress or maybe my period. I want to hold Jonathan's face and turn it towards me, so he'll look at me, so he'll see me, but the thought of that admonishing, disappointed look of his makes me want to get up and run out of the living room, or out of the house, or to a parallel reality in which there are no fertility treatments, and no expectations and no disappointments, and everyone just lives their lives without missing everything they don't have. Maybe it's our past that I want to escape to, or maybe it's our future as I dreamed it. I used to dream. I'm sobered now.

As I search for the right words and the courage to speak them, he turns on the television and is sucked into reports about sanctions in the hospitals. I ask him to turn the TV off.

"Just a sec, there's an item on housing prices coming up that I wanna see," he replies, not taking his eyes off the screen.

"So mute it for now," I insist.

He looks at me. "What?" he asks, matter-of-factly.

"I got my period," I say and shrink in anticipation.

He slowly closes his eyes, then opens them and breathes audibly. I observe his face, he probably blames me, and I want to say that it's not my fault, that I'm following instructions, I *am* taking care of myself, I even stopped running, though Dr. Plotkin said I can. But he doesn't say a thing, just takes another deep breath, then looks back at the TV.

"Say something," I try to bring him back to me.

"What is there to say?"

"What are you feeling? What are you thinking? Are you mad?"

Why would he be mad? What does he have to be mad about? Why do I always feel guilty about everything? I tell myself to talk about that with Dalit, but I already know what she'll say. It's about my mother. Everything with Dalit comes back to my mother and my need to remain her dutiful daughter. I was a biology major like she was; I had the same job in the army as she did; and when I was considering placement in a residential base, she began talking more and more about how lonely she was, how God only knows what she would do if I wasn't by her side, and it was clear what I had to do. My family was like a dilapidated building where moving one pillar would make the whole structure collapse, like a house of cards, or a pup tent poorly-secured in the ground. I knew that any minor move on my part could topple my mother who leans on me, and my father who leans on her. But I'd made one mistake. In a triangular structure each side rests on another, but I had no one to lean on.

"I'm not mad, I'm disappointed," Jonathan answers.

"With me? Are you disappointed with me?" I cross my arms over my empty belly.

Why do I put ideas in his head? Why should he be disappointed by me? But he doesn't answer, nor deny it, nor reassure me; or take me in his arms and promise that it'll be okay and eventually we will get pregnant, and even if we don't it'll be okay. I no longer believe that it will be okay, no longer really believe that this pregnancy, even when it does finally arrive, will be able to fix what has broken between us, and bring us back to ourselves again. It feels like we're in separate boats, each drifting on a different current, and though I'm sitting beside Jonathan and feel the heat of his thigh on mine, I am alone.

My question hangs in the air, like a soap bubble hovering over us, taking much more space than I meant it to. I wait for him to respond, to reach out one small finger and pop it with an invisible splash, but he lingers and lets it grow.

"I'm not disappointed with you, Vishi," he finally sighs and looks away from the TV, "I'm disappointed with the situation. But yes, since we're talking about it, I think you could take better care of yourself."

"How exactly?" The flinch rises from my belly and fills my throat, "What more can I do than what I am already doing?"

"You could, for example, take the sick days they offer you after each insemination."

"Oh come on, this again?" I raise my voice without noticing, then lower it. Jonathan hates when I raise my voice. "You know I can't just take sick days at my job. I still go to work when I have a fever—now I'll just start taking days off because someone suggested it? Dr. Plotkin herself said it wasn't necessary."

"I expect you to do everything possible. You promised me you'd do whatever it takes. If there's any chance that resting would help, even if it's only psychological, why not do it? Why not rest?"

"Because I have a job!" I cry.

"Exactly," he says as if he just won the argument, encouraged by a sense of victory.

"Exactly what? What do you expect me to do? Quit? Is that what you want?"

"I can't tell you to quit," he says, but I also hear what he doesn't say.

"You knew about my job and my ambitions from the beginning," I feel my pulse quicken in my neck, "It doesn't come at the expense of building a family, it just affects the pace." He rises to respond, but I go on, "And to tell you the truth? I think that's precisely what bothers you. My lifestyle and all my trips abroad don't suit you, you're worried that you'll be the one staying home with the baby when I travel, that I won't be like your friends' wives who took a year-long maternity leave and cried when they sent the kid to daycare."

"Wow, that's bullshit," Jonathan says.

"What did you think would happen?" I continue, "that I'd get pregnant and start working from eight to three and the rest of the time I'll be barefoot, kneading dough and raising babies? You know that won't happen."

"So who's going to raise the kid?"

"Us. Together. Remember how we used to do things together? Remember how I was your partner?"

He looks at me and his expression gradually softens. "You're still my partner," he says and the pressure in my belly that has accompanied me since morning eases a little.

I grab his hand, squeeze it in mine and lean my head on him, not letting him break away, and we sit like that for a few moments.

"Maybe we could do something when I get back from Rome, just the two of us?" I touch the top of my head to his shoulder. "Maybe we could go to that hotel you wanted?"

He doesn't reply, but leans his head on mine, sighs, then brings his face closer, beams and says, "Let's start with dinner?"

"Deal. Wherever you want, even if all they serve is buckwheat and mung beans," I hug him.

"It's good for the sperm count," he kisses my neck.

"Sure is," I murmur against his lips and breathe him into me, and reach a hand under his buttoned shirt, and his skin is warm, and I get goosebumps.

For a moment, everything is natural and easy, and we are as we used to be, present and able to hold onto the moment without letting the past or the future or the doubts or the hurt and disappointment tear us away. His rough fingers flutter on my back, and I let my muscles relax and the tension in my shoulders release. The soft TV blanket caresses my cheek, Jonathan's day-old stubble scratches my skin and his breath travels over my body, warming and cooling intermittently. His weight presses me to the couch and I wrap my arms around him and pull him to me.

Afterwards, Jonathan picks the clothes up off the floor, we get dressed and he reminds me to refill my prescription. I promise that I'll get back from the upcoming trip in time for the insemination and that I'll ask Pinto to take me off operational trips as soon as possible. But I can't actually imagine that conversation, especially not now when the promotion, which I still haven't mentioned to Jonathan, is up in the air.

3

He's known to be pretty level-headed, the kind of guy that's hard to irritate, or at least hard to tell when he's irritated. He can control it, relaxing his facial muscles to the point of apathy. He's been working on it for years, it only looks like it comes easily. It's all in the cheeks and the forehead: You have to imagine that they're heavy and that gravity is pulling them down. Emptying the mind of thoughts helps, too, a bit like delaying an orgasm. Like tantra for the face.

Still, Weiss' anxiety ahead of the routine polygraph is hard to miss. He's sweating through his black polo shirt, despite the cold, rainy weather, and his heart is beating hard.

He looks at the people walking past him in the lobby, wondering if they notice something, though he knows they don't, nobody sees what's going on inside him and nobody knows, only Weiss, and sometimes even he manages to forget. Still, he raises his chin higher and slows his steps, only breathing remains difficult, and he has trouble swallowing the stubborn lump in his throat.

He takes the elevator up, his image reflected at him in its three mirrors, replicated over and over and all around him. He is surrounded, ambushed by himself.

He usually enjoys looking in the mirror, examining his white teeth up close, his straight nose, his prominent cheekbones, his square jaw, then taking a step back to marvel at the harmony with which all the pieces fit together. Sometimes, when he's alone, he'll lift up his shirt and inspect the definition of his six-pack. He even likes the long scar on his cheek. He thinks it makes him look dangerous, like ripped jeans, enhancing his appearance, and doesn't tell anyone that it's from getting scratched climbing a barbed wire fence as a kid.

Now he's trying to avoid his image in the mirror, but wherever he looks, there he is, he can't escape, and the ultra-modern elevator, meant to be fast as a terrifying amusement park ride, is taking forever to reach the twenty-sixth floor.

The polygraph is the only thing between him and the promotion, that's clear. He's the most suitable candidate to replace Pinto, the most versatile, the most strategic, the sharpest. Sure he might not have Fishman's connections, but he has skill, which is almost as crucial. He trusts Pinto to make the professional choice. It'll all be okay. As long as he passes the lie detector.

When the doors finally open he exits the elevator of mirrors, waves his employee badge in front of the security cameras, and the heavy steel door opens. He hands his phone over to the security guards at the entrance and sits on one of the couches in the waiting room, where Israel Today newspapers and Israeli flags are scattered around in equal number. There are young men waiting next to him, and he can smell the army, engine oil and youth on them; and Weiss breathes it in, allowing himself to be intoxicated by it, just for a moment. They are all good-looking, noticeably shaved ahead of the test, but with short stubble both to emphasize the toughness that is a job requirement, and to hide their anxiety. He smiles cautiously, lest it be misinterpreted, and makes small talk with two candidates for security positions, giving them last minute tips, reassuring them, calming and reminding himself how much he has to offer.

"Is there a Gal Weiss here?"

His heart leaps. He makes an effort to smile and stands

slowly. As he walks, he holds his elbows out as if making his way through a crowd. In the training course, they'd tried to work on his walk, telling him it would be hard to blend in in a crowd, but the elbows remained. He waves his employee badge and wishes the young man luck before disappearing down the hallway.

The examiner does not introduce himself by name, but from the notice he was sent, Weiss knows that his name is Alon. He had a classmate named Alon in elementary school. He was short, thin and fast, and he once moved Weiss's chair before he sat down. Weiss fell with a thud and the whole class laughed. Alon was also the one who came up with the nickname "Gallstone Weiss." He was heavier back then. Unfortunately, it caught on in a way that "Galvanize," Weiss's attempted substitution, never did. Since then he has hated the name Alon.

Alon the examiner sits in a big, soft brown leather executive chair. Behind him is a view of North Tel Aviv which only makes Weiss dizzier. Alon's expression swings between joking and hostile as he asks about Weiss's health and anything that could interfere with the exam. Weiss answers in the negative. He sits with his legs spread, his broad body sprawled in the simple office chair. Alon asks him to stand. He bends over him, encircling him with his arms, and Weiss smells nicotine and the sharp scent of aftershave. Alon attaches straps to his chest and right arm, lightly pinching his left-hand fingers with the electrodermal electrodes. He activates the polygraph machine and the needle immediately comes to life and begins to scribble lines on the page.

Alon begins with general questions, and Weiss carefully provides his home address and number of siblings. Once the device is calibrated, they move on to questions concerning information security, contact with foreign elements, drug use, financial and criminal entanglements, extortion and threats. Weiss feels his muscles clench even though he is not moving.

With each answer comes a tiny, involuntary jump and twitch at the corner of his mouth, his stress made manifest. Alon does not respond, just watches the needle, wrinkles his nose and pinches it between his thumb and forefinger. He continues until he has covered all the topics, then asks Weiss if he's concerned about anything else or hiding further information. Weiss responds in the negative and feels the sweat stains at his armpits and in the middle of his back merging into a huge, singular spot.

Alon is quiet, examining the machine's output, then looks up and Weiss shrinks under his gaze. He rises and exits the room, letting the door slam quietly behind him, leaving Weiss alone, strapped to the chair, frozen in the same upright position as though if he moved, the needle would move too. Two minutes later Alon returns and without introduction, reviews the same set of questions, word for word, registering the needle's reaction and on to the next question without moving a muscle, except for the wrinkling of his nose. When the set is complete, he rises from his chair and exits the room quietly once more, leaving Weiss to stew in his sweat, then again returns, going back over the same questions. By now Weiss is reciting them in his head along with Alon, no longer waiting for the end of the question, no longer hoping that his lips will stop trembling. Finally, after two hours of sitting and thirteen rounds of questioning, Alon comes back in and slams the door.

"Okay, how much longer are we going to do this?" Alon spits.

Weiss shrinks: "You're asking me?"

"You see anyone else wasting my time?" Alon's eyes are wide.

The corner of Weiss' mouth twitches involuntarily. "I don't know what you want." He tries to keep calm.

"I want you to quit lying!" Alon raises his voice and Weiss jumps slightly in his seat. His father would shout like that, using those very words when he found out that Weiss had forged a letter to his teacher or not reported a failing grade.

At first, he would cry, "like a girl," as his father described it, but later he learned that by biting his tongue hard enough, not the cheek, that can break the skin, he could stop the tears, and in time the tears stopped coming altogether. He can't remember the last time he cried. Actually there was that time about six months ago, when he realized what he'd done.

He can't think about that now, it's the worst possible time to think about that. "Bro, relax, I don't understand what you want from me," he says.

"Bro," Alon annunciates the word mockingly, "I am cool, calm and collected and *because* I'm this relaxed, I'm giving you one last chance to tell me everything, without reporting that you lied on your polygraph, which would be a shame: You actually have pretty good evaluations," he says, and Weiss wonders if he really saw his employee evaluations. Alon opens a notebook and selects a pen from a metal case. "Would you like to share anything that you are hiding from your superiors?"

"Dude, are you serious?" Weiss exclaims, feeling his blood boiling, "I'm not hiding and I'm not lying, I'm telling you."

"Fine," Alon says calmly and closes the notebook, "If that's how you want it. They will arrange a follow-up." He stands and releases him from the device.

His legs fail him a little as he stands, maybe because of how long he hasn't moved them, or maybe out of fear. He shakes the whole way home, driving in the dark of night, and the blackness outside mixes and swirls with his thoughts until they're that much darker. No way is this the thing that'll take him down, that'll make him lose it all just like that. He can't let that happen.

He enters his apartment, which smells of cleaning products and the pear-scented air freshener that Zoe buys at those soap stores. He sits down heavily on the living room sofa which groans with him, and doesn't turn on the light. The darkness masks the red in his cheeks and eyes and he feels less exposed.

He holds his head in his hands, trying to catch his breath and get a hold of himself.

"Why're you sitting in the dark?" Zoe comes into the living room wearing jean short shorts and an oversized sweatshirt of Weiss's and turns on all of the living room lights at once; a ceiling light over the metal living room table, three small lamps above the three black and white portrait photographs, and an industrial lamp in the corner of the room. Weiss turns away from the light and from Zoe's searching eyes, but she does not seem to notice that anything is wrong.

"I missed you," she sits beside him and presses close to him, nuzzling her cheek against his rough one.

Her skin is smooth and her hair smells like honey and gently tickles his arm. Weiss pulls back his arm, kisses her quickly on the mouth and mutters, "Me too."

"I called a few times and you didn't answer so I came to wait here," she spreads her tanned legs, laying them across his and turns on the TV, "Where were you?"

"Yeah, sorry, busy day."

"So busy you couldn't answer the phone for a second?" Zoe asks without looking at him.

"Lay off, would you?" Weiss moves Zoe's legs and sits up straight, "I said it was busy."

Zoe turns her head in surprise and looks at him wide-eyed. "Sorry, baby," she says. "I didn't mean to bug you."

"No, I'm sorry I lost it," he pulls her arm towards him, "I'm just a little edgy from this whole day. Want to get in with me?" He nods toward the shower and forces a smile.

"I showered already," Zoe replies, and Weiss wonders if she is avoiding him, if she notices something different about him, but actually, if she hasn't noticed until now, why would she notice today? That feeling that he is not exposed, that he is not really seen, comforts but also weighs on him. Sometimes he feels it is actually when he goes unseen that he most manages

23

to be himself. But there must be a contradiction in there some-where.

"No such thing as too clean," he takes off his shirt and throws it at her. "Come on."

Zoe smiles, folds the shirt, places it on the couch armrest and stands up to follow him.

4

The sunrise casts an orange glow over the sky as our plane descends towards Leonardo da Vinci-Fiumicino Airport. Weiss wakes beside me with a start, grumbling about how he hates falling asleep on planes. In another four hours our objects will land at this airport. We will wait for them at Arrivals to make the initial identification, while two additional squads will be at the exit, awaiting our instructions.

After collecting our bags, we survey the terminal and settle on a secluded bench. A man in red overalls on a ride-on floor scrubber examines us closely and I avoid eye contact. Two security guards pass and I wonder if the overalls guy sent them. I wear an aloof expression and look at Weiss, who pulls me in tight for a hug, then takes out a tablet and we watch "Mission Impossible 7" with our heads resting on one another.

At 7:20 a.m. the objects' flight appears on the arrivals flight board. Forty minutes later the hall fills with dark-haired, bearded men, all fitting our targets' description. Everyone is in constant movement, dashing around the baggage carousel, their beards blending into one another. Suitcases start spilling out of the maw of the conveyor belt and passengers start to leave. We report to the squads waiting outside that we have not yet identified the targets. If they leave without us noticing, it'll be difficult to find them later. We relocate to get a better view, still keeping a safe distance, when suddenly I feel Weiss' elbow in my hip.

"Your two o'clock, across the carousel. Confirm identification," he says quietly.

I look slowly and for a moment all I see is the jumble of beards, but then among the crowd I spot them, perfectly matching the photos we memorized.

Mustapha Aziz is a big guy. His broad face features a long, combed beard which frames a small, pursed mouth. He's wearing a plaid shirt and too-tight pants in a brownish mustard color which accentuate his round thighs and make his midsection bulge. He's holding a green rain jacket and black briefcase and has sunglasses perched on the front of his head. In other circumstances he could totally pass for a Tel Aviv hipster.

Ali Mansour is a little shorter and thinner. He's wearing a tight-fitting sweater in shades of red, green and black, and black pants. He has a meticulously trimmed beard, a small nose, narrow eyes and an earring sparkling in one ear. Ali Mansour is sexy. In my bachelorette days I'd have totally gone out with him, but it was a short, if not short enough era, in which I said yes to just about everyone who asked me out.

"I'm just giving it a chance," I claimed at the time, but Maya, my best friend since high school, dismissed my words, as she has been doing since high school.

"You don't know what you want," she declared. As if every girl knows what she wants to do with her life at age thirteen. Maya knew, of course. From age thirteen she knew that she would be an interior designer, and she was right, both about herself and about me. I really didn't know what I wanted, not just romantically, but professionally. To get my mother off my back, I did a noncommittal degree in political science and communications, and when I completed my studies I did not, as expected, find work in my field. So when, by chance, Pinto ran into me at the coffee shop where I was waitressing and suggested that I try to get in at the Agency, I had no good reason to wave him off. Not that anyone can wave Pinto off.

"You want me to be a spy?" I asked, amused, "Are you nuts? I'd be terrible! I can't lie!"

"I actually think you'd be good at it," he didn't laugh, just looked me over with those mocha eyes of his and his long eyelashes fluttering.

"At lying?" I asked, trying to wring a smile from him.

"At thwarting terrorism," he replied with profound gravity. If I had heard someone else talking like this, I would have asked him for a map to the dream world he lives in. Only Pinto can talk about his patriotism and values and sound believable and not like he's two hundred. "Besides," he went on, "what do you have to lose?"

What did I have to lose indeed? A coveted position at "Cafe Reines" and a pouch for tips that wasn't cool even in the eighties? I could give up both of those easily enough and was already beginning to imagine myself surrounded by numerous sturdy Pintos, all of us dressed in black, climbing the wall of some arch-terrorist's house with impressive acrobatics, or dressed in a James Bond outfit and ordering apple schnapps shaken, not stirred. I had no idea what they did at the Agency. In reality, I sit at the airport, freezing from the air conditioning, with an itchy wig on my head, next to Weiss who is tearing into his energy bar.

In retrospect, I can see why Pinto said I'd be good at it. I was good at tracking ever since training. Something in my face inspires trust, and I can blend in almost anywhere without arousing suspicion. Once, in Budapest, I was dressed as a cop and our target approached me, pointed at my mission partner, and said he suspected he was following him and had a weapon. We staged an arrest and got the hell out of there. We were both burned and couldn't continue on that mission, but it could've ended much worse if the object had approached a real cop.

Besides, I have a head that's perfect for wigs. I didn't know that there was such a thing until the Agency hair stylist, who does all of our wig-fittings, complimented me on it—something to do with the shape of my skull and the direction of hair growth.

Maya thought it would be great for me to work someplace where most of the personnel is male, especially to work with Pinto, who had not yet advanced to management.

"What are you crazy? He's like a brother to me," I scolded Maya.

"Brother my ass," she said with her usual grace. "He's not your brother and he's crazy hot."

He really is hot. Not in an inflated beefcake way like Weiss, who puts more into his appearance than even his sexist jokes, but sexier—with stubble on his chin and mud on his boots and ropes for rock-climbing always in the trunk of his car. But he was also married then, and a year later I met Jonathan and Pinto was promoted.

Weiss speaks into the two-way radio, updating that the targets have been identified, and we get in line for the taxis behind them but are buffered by an elderly British couple who make it hard to listen in on the targets' conversation. When we get to our taxi, Weiss swings the suitcases into the trunk and takes the time to complain about my heavy bag—what did I pack in it and how many lotions does a woman need? I'd bet that he has more lotions than I do, but I keep quiet. We ask the driver to follow the targets' taxi and he looks surprised.

"That's my wife there in the taxi," Weiss says to him in English. "*My* wife and *her* husband," he points at me, "together. Get it? We're gonna put an end to this."

The driver looks at Weiss through the rearview mirror, then looks at me. I return a sad look and he smiles, "The truth is better than the best lie. As they say in my family." It probably sounds better in Italian.

"Don't lose them," says Weiss, and the driver nods vigorously. "Trust me," he says, but within a few zigzagging minutes, the targets' taxi disappears among the dozens of other cars on the highway. Weiss curses under his breath.

"I'm sorry, they drive like psychos," says the driver who has not slowed below 130 km/h the whole ride, "what do we do now?"

"We head to the city center," I say.

We inform the two other squads that we lost contact, but they're still tailing them, heading toward Rome's center. Within half an hour, Sharon updates that they are in the Trastevere neighborhood. We direct the driver to the new address. "This is my husband's favorite part of town," I tell the driver, "so we'll start here."

We drive slowly, matching the traffic, circling roundabouts dotted with small lamps, like diamonds on the wrist of a wealthy lady. Finally we arrive at the side street of the targets' hotel. Sharon has charmed the reception clerk to get her and Hadad a room on the targets' floor.

We find another hotel at the edge of the street and direct the driver toward it. Ours is smaller, red brick with colorful flowers cascading from hanging pots. "Romantic," Weiss mutters and pays the driver. It's cold outside. Weiss tightens the scarf around my neck, I straighten the collar of his coat, and we enter, embracing, through the heavy wooden doors.

The lobby is all wood and the floor creaks under our feet as we enter, announcing our arrival too loudly. The whole hotel is a love song to Rome, as if out of a Woody Allen movie. I miss Woody Allen's movies. I wish perverts could just make bad art. In some other reality I would be happy to stay in such a hotel with Jonathan, but we had planned our honeymoon at a hotel in Israel, which we anyway had to cancel because of an urgent operation.

I give the front desk reception clerk a toothy smile and he

29

welcomes us, inquiring amicably where in Israel we're from, if we're married, and how we got to this particular hotel. Weiss chats calmly, chummy but not revealing unnecessary information. He looks relaxed and gives off the ease and comfort of someone on vacation. My wide smile starts to hurt my jaw. The clerk unhurriedly types in our passport details and points out recommended restaurants on a paper map, and we survey the lobby, plotting the spread of the security cameras. The clerk spins around to his key cubby and produces a key. "Our very best room," he declares with a heavy Italian accent. "Excellent view," he adds with pride.

We thank him, Weiss wraps his arm around my shoulder and we walk, smiling, to the old elevator, which barely holds the two of us. Weiss lets me out before him, then resumes hugging me around the waist. He opens the room door for me, gesturing courteously with his hand, then grabs my ass a moment before the door closes.

"Watch it," I push him away and drop the smile and the wig.

"Quit being such a drag," he grumbles, closing the curtains, then looking out through a narrow gap. "So," he turns to me, "what about a quickie before we get to work?" He winks and nods at our shared bed.

I take a deep breath and abstain from kicking him in the head. This would not be professional, and besides, Dalit the couples' therapist says that God does not test us beyond our strength. I plug in my work phone and text Pinto our location. He wishes us luck and I wait a moment, but there's no further message from him, the exchange is over and I'm alone. With Weiss.

Weiss makes himself at home, scattering his things all around the room, then takes his shirt off and farts. This guy is as disgusting as he is handsome.

"Weiss! We can't open the windows here, remember?" I wave the front desk map under my nose.

"Sorry, Sweetie, I promise to hold back," he says and lets out a little burp. "What? I swallowed it!" He protests in response to my eye roll.

Within an hour we hear a knock on our door. "Room service." A middle-aged man in a waiter uniform rolls in a metal cart bearing a tray, then bows and retreats into the corridor. I lift the cloche from the plate and there, beside the omelet, the bacon and the sausages, is a Fiat key. The rental car. Weiss goes outside to install a surveillance camera on it that will transmit the goings-on in the street.

When he gets back we eat a little breakfast and go explore Rome, taking pictures by the fountain in Piazza di Santa Maria and the Basilica and its Madonna statue, to back up our vacation cover story. We stop for a short meal and ice cream at a touristy restaurant in the piazza and when the streets get dark and grow cold, we catch a taxi back to the hotel.

"My back still hurts from the flight," Weiss mutters as he sets down a plate with an egg white omelet and sits across from me at the breakfast table. "When I replace Pinto, we'll fly business."

When I replace Pinto. Unbelievable. I don't know if he's saying that just to annoy me or because he really believes he's better, or because I'm a woman, or because he hasn't taken his head out of his ass for years and is unable to see anyone else, least of all me?

I think I wouldn't be half bad as a manager, I'm a people person, good at strategic planning and big picture perspective, and I'm also pretty good in stressful situations, as long as they're not related to my personal life. I also know that Weiss sees me as a threat, because any time Pinto asks for my opinion in a meeting, he bites his lips.

I take a deep breath: The worst thing would be to let him see that he's getting to me. "Let's wait and see, you may have lots of coach flights ahead of you."

Weiss smiles as if talking to a slow child and says, "You're right, we should wait, it really isn't finalized yet. Just going by Kiki's unofficial hints. You know we work out together, right?" Kiki is the department head, and I know they work out together. Weiss makes sure to mention it weekly.

"No kidding," I try to convince myself that he's just saying that to shake me and I can't let him see that I'm shaken. But I am. I've lost my appetite and push my plate away. The last thing I need is for Weiss to be my manager; not only would I miss the next round of promotions but he would also delay other advancement possibilities for me for as long as I depend on his recommendation.

We eat in silence in front of the window which gives us a comfortable view of the street lazily waking up. It's a shady side street, inlaid with small, crooked stone pavers. The church bell sounds every hour on the hour to remind us that time here does not stand still.

Towards 10 a.m., Sharon indicates that the targets left their room, and a few minutes later we see them heading to the bus stop down the street. We hurry out and stage a romantic selfie, covertly photographing our targets on our way to the Fiat. At the end of the street, I locate Hadad on a parked motorcycle. Sharon stays behind to keep an eye on the targets' room, and Yardeni and Harari are in another car around the corner.

"So, Fishman," Weiss turns to me in the car, "You put on a little weight, ah?" I look down at my belly then jerk my head up, but Weiss noticed. "You're not offended, right? Don't be so sensitive, I'm just concerned. I wouldn't want you to become one of those women who neglects themselves once she's married. You know what happens to them, right?" He doesn't wait for a response before continuing, "They wake up one morning to an empty bed. That's what happens when you love carbs more than you love your husband."

It isn't the carbs it's the hormones, I want to say, but keep

32

quiet. A competitor who is doing fertility treatments is even better than a female one.

After a year of marriage, when we decided that we were ready for a child, I assumed it would happen very quickly. I'd had two unwanted pregnancies in my early twenties, at unwanted times, with unwanted men. Everything in my life was random, and I felt that I had no control over it and I felt pretty sorry for myself, and Maya comforted me that at least I know I'm fertile. At that time this did not amuse me at all, but when Jonathan and I got together, I'd joked that he should be careful because just touching my armpit could be enough to get me pregnant. I was certain that all I had to do was decide that I wanted a child and it would come. But a month passed and then two and three, and I was less and less convinced. I spent hours lying on my back with my legs up, because god forbid one little sperm that was destined to be our child might drip out. We calculated ovulation days, reduced our consumption of alcohol and simple carbs, ate dates, blueberries and nuts, drank pomegranate juice and had a hot bath with apple cider vinegar before bed to cleanse the body of toxins. Frustrated, Jonathan suggested that maybe we really should try my armpit, since we'd already tried everything else.

Our sex life became scheduled, timed and well-scripted so that it more closely resembled an Agency mission than an act of love. Desire and spontaneity were irrelevant to our strict schedule, built around my ovulation. More than the sex between us, I started to miss the old Jonathan, who saw me as his best friend, his partner, and not just the manager of our most important project, who repeatedly failed to reach his goal.

"Remind me when you became such a relationship expert?" I hurl at Weiss.

"It doesn't take an expert to notice a bulge around the waist."

"Maybe if you focused less on the waist and a little more on, I don't know, a woman's personality, your advice might be valid."

"Fishman, I don't know how to tell you this, but I'm not seeking your permission to speak my mind." I recognize a hint of anger in his voice and remind myself that I too am capable of shaking him, but then he smiles. "I'm basically a philanthropist, offering my wisdom to the world. Everyone can take from it what they wish."

I open my mouth to answer, but the targets' bus arrives at the station and Weiss starts the car.

When the targets get off the bus near the Villa Borghese gardens, we park the car and follow them on foot. They take nonstop pictures, at every fountain, statue or duck they see, eat snacks and throw the wrappers right beside the trash, never inside it. They eat in restaurants, buy souvenirs and take more photos. We trail them rigorously, but nothing actually happens.

For three days, we track their cultural and culinary preferences and their waste disposal habits, while in Israel there are reports of something big about to be implemented in Italy.

On the evening of the third day, we're sitting in the hotel room. I'm looking at the screen of my work phone which shows the quiet street, while Weiss is leaning over the hotel desk covered in maps, gripping a pencil and a compass and drawing circles.

"What're you doing?" I ask without much interest.

"I think I've identified a pattern in their itinerary," he replies without looking up.

"Do you mean the pattern of eating pasta, making duck faces and going to sleep?"

He does not reply, just audibly chews the pencil and frowns. "Look," he finally turns the scribbled-on map towards me, "Every restaurant where they've been to this past week is less than a mile away from a Jewish site."

"Ah?" I mutter with disinterest. When the facts don't support our suspicions, Agency people have a tendency to find "evidence" of their suspicions.

"Here," he points at the map, "Yesterday they ate at Flor Farina," a thousand feet from the 'Beth El' synagogue," he draws a thin line between the two points, "'Angelo de Napoli,' 400 feet from the 'Agudat Ha'ashkenazim' synagogue. 'Bistro Linda' is 650 feet from the Chabad house. Remember 'Piperno,' that romantic restaurant by the Tiber? 750 feet from the Great Synagogue. And remember when we didn't understand why they took the bus all the way to Fortuna Street just to buy a coke at the corner store? Eight-hundred feet away is 'Beth Shalom' synagogue, not to mention that the area around Villa Borghese where they've been walking is right by the Israeli embassy." He hands me the map and points at its markings.

This could impress me a great deal, and when people use a compass and scale, I really could be blown away, but I know that all Weiss sees is his promotion, and he can be very creative with inventing theories.

"Ohmygod! Look!" I point at the map with fake excitement, "There's a bank here, and here and here! Maybe they're planning a robbery!" Weiss takes a breath in to say something, but I go on, "There's a pizzeria here, and here and here and here and here! Maybe they're doing corporate espionage for Dominos!"

"Fishman..."

"Look!" I interrupt him, "Public toilets! I don't know what it means, but it must be serious!"

"You done?" He asks me like a grownup patiently handling a mischievous child.

"No but you get my point," I say matter-of-factly and hand back the map.

"I didn't say that they were necessarily going to blow up a synagogue tomorrow," he sighs, "But I have a feeling that we're onto something big here. Remember what I'm saying. I have a nose for these things," he taps his nose with a finger. "Plus their whole trash can thing takes on a different meaning. Maybe they're checking the vigilance of security guards in the area.

We have to inform Pinto." He straightens the map gently, takes a photo and sends it to Pinto along with calculations, explanations and hypotheses, then folds it carefully, places it gingerly in his backpack and turns to do some exercises on the rug.

Within a few minutes we get a response from Pinto. *Interesting direction. Will continue to investigate this. Good work.* Weiss looks pleased, and I note a point for him. If Pinto takes him seriously, I probably should too.

"Sorry, I shouldn't have blown off your theory. Well done," I say to Weiss who's doing plank exercises, noticing a tiny smile of satisfaction rounding his lips and a blush flashes across his cheeks.

For a moment he appears vulnerable, and I smile at him. He leans on his forearms and smiles back at me, and I think that maybe he isn't so terrible after all. But then he purses his lips and sends me a loud kiss and I shake my head in despair and stare back at my phone screen.

5

It's our fourth day in Rome and we're in Sharon and Hadad's hotel room, which is identical to our targets' room. We study the layout and the safe, and when the hallway is empty, we examine the lock on the door. We also receive updates on the "students"—those suspected of operating the targets. The teams surveilling them report that they left campus today with an unidentified young man. His photograph was sent to Israel immediately, and within an hour we received information about him. Antonio Roccelli is a twenty-year-old electronic engineering student from Naples, with an academic scholarship and a living stipend. No criminal background or contact with hostile forces, so far.

"Interesting," says Hadad, "until today, there hasn't been any information or contact person linked to the students, apart from the email we sent from the targets' computer. They're probably changing devices and keeping a low profile."

I rack my brain. Apart from the targets, this Roccelli is the only connection we have to the "students." How is he related? And if he isn't, how can we leverage him? I've got to come up with something here. I have to gain some advantage on this mission, I can't let Weiss always take the lead.

"Hey," I ask, "what if we make him an asset?"

"Who?" Asks Weiss.

"This Roccelli."

"Sure," Weiss nods at me, "go ahead, make him an asset." He opens the door and gestures towards the hallway.

"Shh," I check the hallway and close the door. "What's up with you?"

"What do you mean, make him an asset? Don't you know how it works? You have to identify a weakness, you have to..."

"You have to be proactive, make contact, be creative," I cut him off. "They said he has an academic scholarship, right? So he's probably a good student and can help the targets somehow. And if he's on a stipend, he could probably use some extra cash."

"Cynicism doesn't suit you."

"And it's not like you to be slow. I'm telling you, we can recruit him, we can't be so picky about sources."

"It's not a bad idea," Hadad frowns.

"I'm messaging Pinto," I say.

Weiss bites his upper lip, which is a sign that I'm onto something. Not that I need Weiss' endorsement. When Pinto, on the other hand, promptly writes me back, *Interesting idea, will check feasibility*, my heart leaps. *We'll catch up after you visit your uncles,* he adds, referring to our plan to infiltrate the targets' room.

The following day we're in our hotel room waiting for Harari and Yardeni to confirm that the targets are out. I'm in a bob cut wig with bangs, and Weiss is in round glasses and a short mustache. He doesn't mention the asset idea, but seems tenser than usual.

"I don't get Pinto," he complains. "What's he doing sending Sharon and her butterface on this kind of mission? The only thing she had going for her is her body, but she lost that when she had a baby."

Sharon is my friend and she has a perfectly nice face. But while I'm trying to string together a moderate response, Weiss goes on, "and why is she even here and not at home. This is no job for a mom. Poor kid."

"The kid has a father too," I manage to mutter through pursed lips.

"A normal man doesn't spend his days with children. A normal man goes to work and comes home in the evening, when the kids are fed and bathed."

That description suits my father perfectly. Only my father isn't entirely normal. A year after Shahar was killed he was diagnosed with depression, and I suspect he has a few other undiagnosed issues. He didn't want any psychological evaluations and was angry at my mother for labeling his legitimate grief as depression, but she told him that it wasn't normal to stay in bed all day, not bathe, and put on 25 pounds. She showed him studies and grim statistics about divorce after a loss in the family and told him that if he didn't want to be a statistic himself, he should get out of his boxers, brush his teeth, and go to a psychologist. From there it was a straight shot to antidepressants. My father's condition improved, he went back to work, but he never really recovered. He struggles with sleep problems, outbursts of rage, and sexual dysfunction, as my mother shared with me when I was fourteen. So between a dead brother and a father who's not really there, I remain my mom's only hope.

I want to respond to Weiss, but am distracted by a stabbing pain in the chest and stomach. I know these are side effects of the hormones, but that doesn't help. I breathe into the pain like Jonathan's naturopath suggested, which helps a little, but the heaviness in my chest still threatens to drag me to the ground. Could I be producing milk? I know that's only supposed to happen during pregnancy, but who knows what all these hormones that I'm putting into my body might do? Apart from the many disadvantages of being a woman at the Agency, I'm also faced with physical challenges. My body is a burden, demanding special attention and diverting focus from the mission.

I move with discomfort and Weiss gives me an inquisitive look.

"All good?" He asks.

If it were anybody else, I might believe his concern, but I'm wary of Weiss. I nod quickly, not wanting to give him further ammunition. It was precisely because of such moments that I postponed the treatments for as long as I possibly could.

It was only after a year and a half of failed attempts to get pregnant and considerable pressure from Jonathan which I could no longer resist, that I went to my gynecologist, not sure what answers I was hoping for. The doctor referred me to a fertility clinic, and following blood tests, an ultrasound, an X-ray and pelvic inflammation from an unsuccessful catheter insertion, Jonathan and I sat before Dr. Plotkin at the fertility clinic. The wall was full of pictures of smiling pregnant women, evidently meant to convey optimism, but I felt like they were taunting me. The doctor didn't look at us, just stared at the test results on her computer screen with her little blue eyes. She nodded to herself for a few long moments, until her thin eyebrows rose, then dropped, and she turned to face us, her thick gold hoops swinging.

"Well, alright, everything's fine with you," she said, removing her glasses. "Time to check the husband."

Out of the corner of my eye I saw Jonathan shrink in his chair and straighten back up so fast that I wondered if I had imagined it.

On the way to the semen analysis, he sat beside me in the car looking aloof, cupping the warm container of sperm, wrapped in a sock for insulation, in both hands as if cradling a baby chick that had fallen from its nest. He shrugged his shoulders sporadically and muttered, as if to himself, that he did not understand why this was necessary. I was torn between wanting to figure out why I wasn't getting pregnant and move past the uncertainty and the dreams of fetuses hovering in the air, and the seemingly incidental questions from our respective mothers and the looks of criticism and compassion—and my fear of Jonathan's response if they found something, if they determined him to be defective. I promised him that everything would be okay, that even if they find a problem we'd get through this. He narrowed his eyes and said in a cold voice that he really didn't think there was a problem.

"Okay, there's a problem," said Dr. Plotkin two days after the semen analysis, again without raising her eyes from the computer screen, "low sperm count. We'll need to do intracytoplasmic sperm injection—ICSI." She printed the referral and handed it to us, gesturing towards the exit with her outstretched arm. I looked at Jonathan, who did not look back. He sat ramrod straight in his chair, his eyes fixed on the pinkish uterus model sitting on the doctor's table. I took the referral and she went back to her computer screen.

"Just a sec," I said. "Can you explain what a low sperm count means?"

She looked up at me, surprised by the question, and then spoke slowly, "It means that there is not a lot of sperm in the semen and insemination will be required. Take the referral to the front desk," she pointed at the form in my hand, "You get Form 17 and you do a blood test and ultrasound to know when you're ovulating."

Jonathan continued to silently scan the silicon uterus, his face opaque, but I saw his Adam's apple rise and fall and his jaw tighten. I placed a hand on his thigh but he didn't respond, so I pulled it away. Dr. Plotkin looked at the pile of documents on her desk.

"Jonny, everything okay?" I asked in the car.

"Yes. No. I don't know." He sat slumped in the driver's seat, empty of air and of words, like the time he lost nearly $200,000 to his biggest client because of a technical error.

41

"What do you want us to do?" I asked.

"What do you mean?" He looked at me in surprise, "do we have a choice?"

"There's always a choice. If you want to wait a bit, we can wait," I said and was proud of not showing my relief in light of this news.

"Why would we wait?" Jonathan sat up in his seat. "We've already wasted a year and a half, we can't afford to waste any more time," he said angrily, adding after a short pause, "you're thirty-two, you know."

A throat-clearing in my earpiece draws me back to the hotel room, as Harari updates us that the coast is clear.

Exiting the elevator on the targets' floor, we spot Gideon, dressed in the uniform and badge of the hotel staff and we exchange indifferent glances. Further down the hall Burstein, disguised as a room attendant, wheels a cart piled with towels. We enter Sharon and Hadad's room, put on our hotel uniforms and proceed with a big cleaning cart to conceal Weiss jiggling the lock to the targets' room.

"In a way, covert infiltration is the exact opposite of sex," Eitan, our training course commander had instructed, "it should be imperceptible and over quickly."

"For some of us that is the definition of sex," laughed Ashkenazi, clapping Matias on the back. Matias was tall, gawky, and embarrassed any time sex was brought up, which was all the time. I once told him that he should tell them to stop talking to him like that, but he got annoyed and told me to mind my own business.

"Quiet, Ashkenazi," Eitan wore his serious face. "This is a delicate art." He looked directly into my eyes, "You must be strong but restrained, attentive to your surroundings and to your partners, and save your explosive force for the end." I am not proud of the fact that this turned me on.

Eitan, being the committed and decent manager that he was, waited until the end of the course to do me in the briefing room. And indeed he saved his explosive force until the end. I don't know how, but Weiss found out about us. I was really young then, at the beginning of my traineeship, and he, who had three years of experience and the pretension of the Mossad director, advised me ("as a friend, yeah?") that people talk and that's not the way I want to get ahead nor the reputation that I want to make for myself.

"I appreciate your concern," I said. "But I can make my own decisions."

"Suit yourself." He lifted his hands as if in submission. "I'm saying this for your sake." He put a hand on my shoulder and went back to the operations room to flirt with Nofar, the command post operator.

Now he's gently moving the lock up and down. When he's focused, he narrows his eyes and sticks out the tip of his tongue. He's likeable like this, serious, quiet, concentrated on the task, and I can understand what girls see in him. His handsome face is lit by the wall light above him, emphasizing his high cheekbones, his sandy blond hair which is starting to gray at the temples, but for men that just adds sex appeal. Men get unfair advantages in everything, even pigmentation.

A middle-aged man is approaching. His hair is gray, he's wearing thin-framed glasses, jeans and a button-down shirt. We straighten up quickly, I tense and involuntarily glance down the length of the corridor. Gideon peeks over from the end of the hall, to see if there's a problem. The man asks for a roll of toilet paper, and we apologize that we don't have any with us and assure him we will assist him once we finish our current task. This does not put him at ease, and he also requests a refill of the soaps and wants help operating the safe. "No problem," Weiss replies with a broad smile, "we will be with you shortly."

Finally the man relents and leaves, and Weiss goes back to the lock which finally opens with a click. We hang a 'Do Not Disturb' sign, enter and begin scanning the room.

The room is identical to Sharon and Hadad's, only much messier. The bed is unmade, with empty packages and rumpled clothes on the floor and unwashed cups piled in the sink. I head directly for the safe in the closet, while Weiss checks the contents of the backpack perched on the armchair. I pull out a racket-like device from the cleaning cart, attach it to the bottom of the safe, which quickly resets and opens. I fumble around and take out two passports, neatly bundled euros and a thumb drive, all of which I take photos of. Weiss retrieves several cables from the bleach bottle in our cart, connecting the thumb drive to his phone to transfer the data. Within seconds he disconnects the cable, returns it to the bottle and the thumb drive to the safe along with the rest of the items. We continue our survey, checking the suitcase in the corner of the room, rummaging through the pockets of the pants on the floor, under the mattress and inside the toiletry bag in the bathroom. Finally, we replace the room's lightbulbs and pens with new ones, equipped for surveillance. With the listening and video devices installed, we conduct a final scan before we leave.

Back in our room, Weiss backs up the files from my phone and we sit on the bed to examine their contents. Among the many photos, all captured during a walk by the Tiber, the targets' faces are notably absent, yet the Great Synagogue features prominently in each shot. I look at Weiss, and he looks at me and nods.

6

We send the information to Israel, then sit, pleased with ourselves, while Pinto praises us over the phone. Sometimes I ask myself what motivates me more—thwarting terrorism, getting promoted, or gaining Pinto's respect. But as I float on a cloud of praise, Pinto goes on, saying that our return to Israel will be delayed because we need to tighten tracking on our targets. *Fuck.* My smile disappears and my forehead contracts. If our return is delayed, I won't make it to the blood tests or insemination. Jonathan will be pissed.

Jonathan is pissed.

I leave Weiss in the hotel room to enjoy our moment of triumph by himself and go out. I buy a local sim card and an espresso, then station myself on a bench opposite a florist. Taking a deep breath, I exhale vapor, and call Jonathan to inform him of the change of plans.

I can't remind him how important my work is, that'll only infuriate him more, so I just provide the dry details and a general apology for my existence. The other end of the line is silent.

"You there?" I ask.

"For now." I liked his silence better.

"What's that supposed to mean?" I ask with zero desire to hear the response.

"It means I don't know how much longer I can stand this," he says matter-of-factly.

"Are you threatening me?" I hear my voice rise involuntarily. "Is that an ultimatum? What am I supposed to take from that?"

"Take what you want."

"Jonathan, do you understand that I can't just up and leave?" I stand up, then sit back down, not to draw attention to myself.

"I understand all of it: Your priorities, and that I can't expect anything else from you."

"I'm sorry," I remain sitting, holding the phone, even after the call is over.

Again I'm apologizing; again he blames me. Sometimes, I feel like this whole whirlwind of treatments is his chance to punish my fertility, flaunting itself in his face.

"What a lovely uterus you have," came the voice of the ultrasound technician from between my legs. "Look at this follicle," with her free hand she pointed at a blotch on the little screen, "And here's another, isn't that pretty?" She turned to Jonathan.

"What? Yeah," he muttered weakly, shifting uncomfortably in his creaky chair. It wouldn't hurt him to show a little more support. At least one of us is fertile.

"Great," the technician removed the condom-clad wand from between my legs, "You're ready for insemination. Now it's your turn." She handed him a plastic cup, which he took between two fingers as if it were contaminated.

He and his cup were sent to the sperm lab, where the cells underwent 'sperm washing' and were placed in artificial fluid, then injected into me. We waited for two weeks, stressed and optimistic ahead of the beta test results, but it came out negative. Dr. Plotkin told us to start taking Clomifene, to increase follicle production, and continue monitoring the follicles and the mucus viscosity.

"Ummm... I can monitor that myself, right?" I asked casually, "I can't commit to tests with my travel schedule."

"You can time it alone, but it's not recommended," she replied, her thin eyebrows rising and falling with emphasis.

"And what if it doesn't work?" Asked Jonathan.

"After a few treatments, if the insemination alone doesn't work, we recommend FSH shots."

"After how many treatments?" He wrinkled his forehead.

"Between three and six," replied Dr. Plotkin.

"We've done three already," Jonathan looked at me.

"Then we can get started," Dr. Plotkin replied, "if that doesn't work either, we can start the IVF procedure."

"No, no, we are *not* there yet," I said quickly.

"If we need to, we will be," said Jonathan.

"But, Baby," I tried to sound calm, "how can I do fertility treatments when I'm out of the country half the month?"

"What's more important, your job or the pregnancy?" That was the first time this question was asked aloud and not through clenched teeth.

"The pregnancy, obviously," said Dr. Plotkin.

"It's not a competition," I ignored her. "Both are important."

"They're not supposed to be equally important. At the end of the day it's just a job, Avishag," said Jonathan.

It is *not* just a job and he knows that.

"Give me a chance," I asked him in a conciliatory tone, not forgetting for a moment that he is forcing me to beg thanks to a problem that he is responsible for, "I have a good feeling about this Clomi shit."

"Clomifene," the doctor corrected, as if someone asked her.

Jonathan hissed at me, "Three months."

I started treatments with a Chinese Medicine practitioner recommended by Jonathan's naturopath. She pricked me with needles, made me a "fertility-enhancing" menu, and advised me to avoid intensive physical activity so as not to rock the uterus, so I wonder if my bloating is due to the hormones or the decrease in aerobic activity. For three months I ate pineapple, beets and pomegranate as if my life depended on it, munched peppers and added legumes and cruciferous vegetables to my diet.

Those three months of grace that Jonathan granted me ended a week and a half ago, with the arrival of my period.

I doze off on the hotel bed and Weiss is watching the phone display broadcasting the quiet street, when Hadad signals that the targets have left their room.

"Get up, they're heading out," Weiss jumps to his feet, grabs his big jacket and wallet and heads for the door. Outside the hotel we slow down, so as not to stand out in the sleepy street. The targets hail a cab a moment before we get into the Fiat, and we trace their route past the train station into Esquilino, past Chinese signs and a cluster of shoe stores, turning right twice after the taxi until it stops beside a closed corner store. The targets slam the door with a bang, and we park under a dark street lamp. I take off my jacket and tights and remain in a tunic, to which I add fishnet tights from the glove compartment. I apply pink lipstick, while Weiss dons a wool hat, and we get out of the car, proceeding on foot. The air is cold and the streets are dark, but there are a surprising number of people walking around. Maybe 'walking' is imprecise. They are trudging, dragging, stooped and staggering. Apart from a few small narrow-eyed figures darting and swallowed into entryways, most seem drunk, drugged, or both. Their eyes are empty, some mutter to themselves, some shout, and a rowdy group of drunks laugh out loud, while two of them urinate on a shop window.

The targets stop on a relatively well-lit street corner, and we sit down on the curb, huddled together, peering at the sidewalk but keeping them in our peripheral vision. Aziz leans against an electric pole, and Mansour is chatting with a foreign guy stopped beside them. Their faces are so close they are almost touching. After a short conversation, Mansour turns to Aziz and nods. Aziz holds out a note or a bill, and the guy hands them a swollen paper bag in exchange.

Are they buying drugs? I look at Weiss, who raises his eyebrows at me without changing expression, then refocuses, watching the targets. The guy who sold them the bag settles on the street corner, drawing more than a few bleary-eyed passersby. Weiss and I wait for our moment. When one of the guy's customers, young, thin and clumsy, hardly carrying his own weight on unsteady, noodle-y legs, passes by us, I signal to Weiss, rise and follow after him.

"Hey sweetie, got anything good for me?" I match his steps and wiggle my butt in a sashaying walk.

He stops and studies me, examines my legs, then my face, his expression less glazed than it appeared at a distance. He eyes me for a long moment, and I wonder if I'm not attractive enough for him. I suck in my belly, push out my chest and wait. He finishes examining me and smiles a slightly frightening smile, exposing his teeth without changing his facial expression.

"Depends," he replies in a sharper tone than I expected, "Do you have anything for me?"

As we stand face to face, he approaches me quickly, and with no warning, crushes my right breast in his hand. I smile and he presses close to me, but I put a finger on his chest and say to him, "No, no, no, first you give me something, then I give you something." I hold out my hand and open it to him.

I'm afraid he'll be annoyed by the teasing, but he smiles his scary smile and takes a white pill from his bag. "Open your mouth," he instructs and holds the pill to my lips.

I smile and shake my head, but he grips both my arms with surprising force, presses his forehead to mine, looks me in the eyes, his eyes are red and narrowed, and pushes the pill into my mouth. I try to spit it out but the guy seals my lips shut with his steaming mouth, and I feel my gastric juices rise. He grips my shoulders and presses me against a dirty brick wall, dirtying my tunic. The pill dissolving beneath my tongue both frightens and intrigues me. I wish I could escape reality a bit. The main mind-altering substances I consume these days are hormones, which send me into bouts of frustration and anger and anxiety and confusion and sadness. So you could understand my desire to escape every now and then. But not from work. I never escape work, even when the drunk's sticky tongue is stroking my collarbone and giving me chills of panic and disgust.

I am waiting for the right moment to kick him between the legs, when I hear the sound of breaking glass, and a strong hand grabbing and tearing me from the noodle-y man. Weiss stands between us, gripping a broken beer bottle and holding it close to the noodle's neck.

"Next time you touch my woman, I cut you, *comprendo*?"

That last word was Spanish, but I think that he made his point because the noodle gapes at him, wide-eyed, then nods and limps away as soon as Weiss releases his neck. Weiss grips my wrist and tries to pull away, but two big drunks block his way. They call out unclearly, and one of them pushes Weiss backward. Weiss pulls me behind him. He let go of the broken bottle already, and now faces them with bare hands. The pill keeps melting in my mouth and I feel dizzy. I hesitate before removing it from my mouth, clenching it in my fist and joining Weiss. The drunk in front of me is two times my size, but I don't back down. Weiss nods at me, and we kick, with imperfect timing, at the pair. As they collapse in pain, Weiss lands an elbow between the neck and shoulder of one while I deliver a kick to the stomach of the other. Around us, people begin to gather and call out, whether to encourage or admonish us is unclear. We don't wait around to find out, we've drawn far too much attention as it is, the targets aren't far enough away, and the whole situation screams danger. Weiss grabs my wrist, and we run to the Fiat. He starts the car and we leave the neighborhood. I take the pill from my sweating fist and put it in a bag.

"Are you okay? Did I hurt you?" His voice is surprisingly gentle.

"I'm fine, thanks," I say, wary of Weiss' gentleness more than his prickliness.

"Good work," he points to the white pill in the bag.

The road is smooth as we speed. The city is a whirlwind of colors and darkness, and I whirl in it, crash at its feet, up and down in circles, like an amusement park carousel that has spun off its axis and lost control. The smell suits an amusement park too: Cotton candy and corn, evoking feelings of home and of vacation at the same time. I stick my head out the window to feel the wind. A police siren plays an old Coldplay song, while a dalmatian walks the street with his owner and wags his tail to the beat of the music. I blink, and when I open my eyes, the city is a blurry streak, lights mixing with the sounds of traffic, blending with the music. My cheeks and forehead flush. I blink again, and the city is bright lights like disco balls, blink, and its thousands of neon eyes blink, and its blinding rays of sun blink, and it's painted in pastel colors of the rainbow stretching after the car like a unicorn's tail.

Fuck.

I realize that the pill has started to kick in, and am impressed with myself that, despite the drugs, my mind is surprisingly sharp. I look at Weiss and he's so handsome in the sparkling city light. I reach out to run my fingers through his lush, sandy-blond hair. It's smooth like classical music, and I hum to myself, enjoying the tickling touch, sending currents through my whole body until Weiss grabs my hand.

"Fishman, don't tell me you're high."

After considering it, I say calmly, "Maybe," and resume stroking his hair. He doesn't stop me, just keeps driving, his face impassive. Impossible. Impostor. I have a feeling that I'm onto something important here, something that could destabilize me. Agonize me, dazzle me, hassle me, blind me, define me. Unleash me. Release me. But then the words diverge and scatter in two separate directions, drifting away like clouds, then dissipate like a wave crashing. The carousel slows down.

My hand is still in Weiss' hair. It's so nice of him to let me. He was so brave to protect me from that Italian man in the alley, and I'm filled with love for him, like filling your lungs with air before diving into a pool. Full to the brim. My gaze drifts from Weiss' tanned, muscular, just-the-right-amount-of-hair-y arm to his hand's network of veins. How sexy are bulging veins? They practically burst out of his hand. I see them pulsing and hear the blood gushing. *Gushhh*, what a word. Also Weiss' neck. Would he be mad if I stroke it? Would that be considered sexual harassment?

The carousel stops. We're parked.

A woman crosses the street wearing a T-shirt that says 'Your life is a lie.' I frown after her. Does she really mean that? Then I shake the thought from my head. She doesn't mean it. I love my life. I love being here.

"Let's go dancing!" I cry to Weiss, and he turns his handsome face toward me and says in a low, sexy voice, "Fishman, you have to drink a ton of water to dilute high. And you know we can't go dancing. We're on duty."

"Fine," I lean my head against his for ten minutes, or a moment, "So dance with me in the hotel."

"Fine," he's probably just saying that so I'll get out of the car, but I'll convince him. Anyone can be convinced to dance—everyone has the one trick that works on them. Like recruiting for the Agency. Some people, in order to dance, need to see other people dancing, or need to practice, or learn choreographed steps, or start by simply moving in their chair to the rhythm. For Weiss, I sense that the challenge of losing control is so great that you have to coax him to lose control before he even starts dancing. So once back in our room, I consider using a bra from my luggage as a blindfold, hoping it won't be considered sexual harassment either. It might be, because Weiss blushes intensely, takes off the bra and tells me gently, "Fishman, I have to keep monitoring the targets."

I put my bra down, grab his hands instead and jump. Weiss cooperates with me, swaying to the rhythm, but his gaze remains fixed to the monitoring screen. I know that he loves me. We're soul mates and our energies are finally lining up. Warm currents stream all through my body. The screen shows the targets' room and casts a shadow on Weiss' face. He's so handsome. Like a Disney prince. And I am Snow White, talking to birds and squirrels, having already eaten the poisoned apple, now waiting for the prince to save me. No. I'm Ariel, the Little Mermaid, rebelling against my father and selling my voice for true love. \No. I'm Pocahontas. No. Moana.

Feeling warm I start removing my shirt but Weiss stops me.

"It's hot!" I cry and try to push his hands away, but he holds me firmly and it's nice, his touch, and I sense something special is happening between us. Weiss is panting from the jumping and I'm panting too, and we look one another in the eyes, and there are golden dots around his pupil and he is even more beautiful now, and so close, and I'm still panting, and Weiss is quiet and looks me deep in the eyes, but then looks away. I try to draw him back but he points at the screen, where the targets are emptying the contents of the paper bag onto the desk. The image quality prevents us from seeing exactly what is being poured onto the table, but it's pretty clear that those aren't drugs.

7

The following day they go back to the targets' room to verify the contents of the paper bag. This time the infiltration must be more concentrated and finished before the targets return from breakfast. Fishman, still muddled from the night before, is taking her time resetting the safe. Weiss is losing patience. The targets could come back at any moment. Finally the safe door opens and Fishman probes deep inside it. Her face is frozen for a moment before she pulls out a gun. She puts her hand back in and extracts another one. This is happening. Weiss feels a small flutter in his stomach and recognizes the familiar mix of excitement, urgency and nerves.

Fishman gives Weiss a piercing look, and he feigns indifference: She shouldn't think he's too easily excited. From the safe she pulls out six local sim cards, the bundle of bills and the drive that were there on their previous visit. Weiss quickly copies the contents of the drive again in case new data was added. He has not yet finished when Hadad's quiet, clear voice in the earpiece states, "they're on their way up."

Fishman hurries to photograph the contents of the safe spread across the double bed and returns everything to its place. Hadad hisses into the earpiece, "They're in the elevator," and they cast a final glance at the room, waiting for the right moment to exit. When Gideon signals that the coast is clear, they quietly close the door behind them and hurry towards the stairs. They're almost at the end of the corridor when the bespectacled guest from last time appears.

"You still haven't fixed my safe," he stands in their way. Fishman casts a quick glance at Weiss, and he can sense that in her current state it's hard to respond sharply. These are his favorite moments, when she depends on him.

He straightens up and envisions himself expanding, like concrete. "Sir, I apologize for the delay." He places a hand on his chest, "I assure you, someone will come assist you in the next ten minutes," he says, trying to sidestep the man.

"Ten minutes won't do. I'm heading out. I need someone now," says the man.

Gideon approaches, "Is there some kind of problem, sir?"

"My safe doesn't work," the man says, shifting slightly towards Gideon as the elevator bell rings.

Seizing the opportunity, Weiss and Fishman dart away. Behind them, Weiss hears Gideon say, "come, sir, I'd be happy to help," and the elevator door opening just before the stairwell door slams behind them.

Once on the stairs, they cast off their housekeeping uniforms and remain in sportswear. Fishman lets her hair down and Weiss removes the glasses and puts on a baseball cap. They emerge, hugging, into the lobby and hurry out the front door. Fishman looks pale, and Weiss feels his heartbeat slow down as he inhales the cold air deep into his lungs. They made it.

If his father could see him now, he would be proud. That's the downside of this job. You can't tell anyone and Weiss loves telling. He makes do with a mysterious smile when asked if he's involved in the cases that come out in the paper. He usually doesn't but does it hurt him to smile? It works on Zoe which is a double win, granting him both admiration and space. It's much easier to manage a relationship when there aren't constant inquiries about location and activity. Maybe that's also related to Zoe's age, that she allows him that freedom. She hasn't even suggested moving in together. In addition to all of her merits, there's also Zoe's dad—Dan Shelmon. Dan, a titan of earthworks contracting, rubs elbows with mayors and city council members. But he remains a working man, with rough hands, oversized footwear, and a mud-splattered jeep. He once invited Weiss to come off-roading, just the two of them. Dan let him drive most of the way and praised his driving and coffee-making. Weiss once even signed a guarantee for him, securing a huge loan for a major development project.

Back in their room, Weiss checks the copied files but there's nothing new. He sends an encrypted transmission of the pictures they took to Israel and Pinto answers at once, *Good work. Await further updates.* Weiss smiles. Fishman is puking in the bathroom. It's not her fault that the whole pill scenario turned out like this but Weiss can't help but feel a little bit pleased that she also trips up sometimes, she isn't always perfect, not always composed. When she emerges, pallid, he asks, "Are you okay?" Because what's it to him to show her a little mercy when she's down.

She nods unconvincingly and lies on the bed. Weiss debates whether to say anything else but doesn't. He places a glass of water beside the bed and she doesn't thank him, just closes her eyes.

8

We return to our hotel where Weiss sends updates to Israel while I feel that the morning's troubles have sapped my strength. I lay my heavy head on the pillow and fall asleep. When Weiss sits down beside me, I wake up from the sensation of his weight tilting the mattress and his eyes examining my face.

"How do you feel?" He asks.

I take a deep breath, close my eyes and reopen them; my head feels lighter and reality a little sharper than in the morning but still a little blurry, as is Weiss.

"Let me know if you need some time to get it together, because I have some operation updates," Weiss says less decisively than usual. He looks bothered and maybe even... guilty? Is it possible that he looks guilty?

"Go ahead, I'm fine," I say, refusing to show weakness around him and forcing myself to sit up slowly, but it's still too fast.

Weiss looks at me skeptically, as if uncertain that I could grasp the situation at the moment. "I spoke to Pinto. I'm staying here, we got the green light to recruit Roccelli. You're heading back to Israel to recover and they might want to send you for testing, you know how the Agency is."

I narrow my eyes, the hammers in my head are pounding, and I realize that he simply sold me off to Pinto to continue this mission solo. I shouldn't be surprised. He'd sell his own mother for peanuts. But what did he tell Pinto? Obviously I didn't get high on purpose, it was a work accident!

I urgently need to talk to Pinto, he has to hear my side too, I can't let them drop me from my own mission. Sure asset recruitment is Weiss' domain, but it was my idea! How can Weiss get the credit for that?

"Wow," I say with relative calm, "I wish I could say that I wouldn't believe you had it in you, but I totally do."

"What are you talking about?" Weiss looks up at me, his eyes wide. He's a master at charming recruits, but I'm not falling for this.

"You're seizing the first opportunity that comes along to kick me off the mission."

"Who's kicking you off, you weirdo," he says, "You took drugs—God knows what kind of rat poison was in them. You need a checkup and rest, or whatever Pinto decides... nobody's taking you off the operation."

"They're just sending me back to Israel immediately."

"Jeez, Fishman, you're delusional. They're looking out for you and you manage to twist it." I'm impressed with how offended he manages to look.

"Yeah right, looking out for me."

"Uh, people in glass houses..." He looks pleased with himself. The only person to talk to about this is Pinto. I have to speak to Pinto.

I land in Israel at 7:15 PM with a headache that has not let up since morning. The arrivals hall is buzzing with people, helium balloons, overpriced flowers and colorful hand-drawn signs. Two little kids run towards a woman roughly my age who hugs them with a tired smile, while a couple in their fifties embrace a girl with dreadlocks and an oversized backpack. No one's here to greet me.

I shake off the childish thought. I'm on duty and I love my job, but I do sometimes wish for a simpler, more ordinary life. Dalit says that life *is* simple, it's people who complicate it. I start thinking maybe her phrases aren't that helpful to me.

Israel is no less cold than Rome.

"It's not the cold, it's the humidity," remarks the taxi driver, just before I put in headphones to insulate me from his two cents. When we arrive, I trudge up the stairs, panting, to our front door with our names written on a simple sticky note. The first year we lived here I planned to replace it with a real sign, but I stopped looking for one a long time ago.

Jonathan isn't home and the apartment is dark. Dropping the keys on the kitchen table, I switch on the living room lights, crack open a window, turn on the TV and set down the M&M's I pick up for Jonathan on every trip. Then I head to the kitchen to make myself something to eat. I open the fridge decorated with magnets from other people's celebrations. In them Jonathan and I are smiling, happy, optimistic, stupid. The earlier pictures are from friends' weddings. We were younger and happier. Over the years the weddings dwindled and the *bris* ceremonies multiplied, along with the white hair at Jonathan's temples and the dark circles under my eyes. The last bris I didn't attend. It was four days after my miscarriage.

I miscarried after a year of attempts. A year in which everywhere I looked I saw women defiantly stroking their baby bumps. A year of constantly dodging questions about when we'd have children, repeating mantras like "It'll happen in its own time," and "We're not in a hurry," until I practically convinced myself. A year of consuming folic acid and avoiding alcohol, shellfish, liver and feta and thoroughly cooking eggs, because maybe this month would be the month.

Then suddenly I had two lines on the stick, and Jonathan hugged me, his heart beating through his shirt, whirling me around the room until we fell, intertwined on the double bed and were as happy as in those old magnets.

I did a blood test that came back positive, and together we went to my gynecologist who squirted cold gel on my belly and pointed at a gray blob, called it the gestational sac and found a pulse. I smiled until my mouth hurt, and Jonathan smiled back at me, eyes sparkling, blinking away tears. He gently wiped the gel off my belly and helped me up from the doctor's chair. We walked home, following the aroma of chocolate and berries to a bakery where we bought huge muffins, watching the cafe dwellers crowding the street and laughing for no reason. He was supposed to be born in the spring, so we envisioned hosting a celebration of his arrival in my parents' garden, preparing all the food ourselves – Jonathan on the appetizers and mains and me on the desserts and sangria. We argued over names and at home Jonathan put his head on my belly and sang lullabies as we dozed off like that on the sofa with renewed tranquility.

Two months later I dreamed about the birth. It was effortless. A few aches in my abdomen in a brightly lit room, surrounded by lots of doctors and nurses stroking my head and saying, "Push, honey." I woke up with the light cramps that I had felt in the dream. I waddled, half-asleep, to the bathroom to discover that I was bleeding. I winced in pain, as if I'd been shot in the chest, blood flowing from between my legs. I closed the door, sat on the floor in my skull-patterned pajama pants that Jonathan had bought me, now soaked in blood, and cried quietly so as not to wake him. I cried over the *bris* that wouldn't happen in the spring, over our birthdays which wouldn't line up as anticipated—Jonathan in March, the baby in April and me in May—over celebrating my thirtieth birthday without a baby. I cried because I was stupid enough to believe in this pregnancy.

It was early morning when I slowly got up off the floor, undressed and showered. I put on clean pajama pants and washed my face, forcing myself to calm down with slow, deep breaths, and only when I was no longer gasping, I went back to bed to wait for Jonathan to wake up to tell him before he noticed the stained sheets. When he woke up, I looked him in the eyes and took his hand.

"I lost him," I whispered in a measured voice.

"What'd you lose...?" He asked, still half-asleep.

I wasn't sure if he really didn't understand or insisted on not understanding; either way, I couldn't answer.

"Shagi, what did you lose?" He asked again, but then I saw his face, twisted in pain, "The baby? You lost the baby? How did that happen?" He bolted upright.

The pain pierced my chest again, but I breathed deeply and said in an only slightly trembling voice, "I got up and I was covered in blood, I'm sorry." Jonathan wrapped his arms around me. "It's not your fault," he whispered, but looked past my shoulder. "It'll be okay," he said slightly louder, as if to himself. "At least we know that you can get pregnant, it'll be okay," he said, but I heard the doubt creep in.

I make grilled cheese, adding a hard-boiled egg and corn, the way he likes it, and text him, *I'm home. When will you be back?*

The cheese starts bubbling and fills the room with a pleasant, salty aroma. While it's cooking I unpack my suitcase, arranging everything just how Jonathan likes it when he gets home. I tidy up the bathroom, sort the laundry, and return the unworn clothes to the closet. The closet is half-empty. His half is empty. I look around. Nothing in the bedroom has changed. The bed is made, my shoes are in place in a row against the wall and the curtain is partially drawn.

I wander back to the living room and check the closets and drawers. Apart from his jacket and wallet, everything is in its place. I close the doors quietly and head back to the bedroom to check Jonathan's bedside table drawer. His passport is missing, perhaps misplaced. Where would he even go? I leave the drawers open and make for the bathroom, opening and closing cupboards and drawers, rifling through piles of things, mixing makeup implements in the medicine basket. Here I don't need to worry about keeping a sterile area. I shuffle around, objects falling on the floor but I don't pick them up, just keep searching, I don't know for what. My eyes wander until I notice that my toothbrush is hanging alone from the mirror in its panda case. Jonathan's matching crocodile case hanging beside it is empty. I slowly close the cupboard above the sink and my reflection stares at me from the mirror. I examine the dark spots under my eyes that the morning's concealer struggles to conceal, the pimples on the forehead, the fatigue and sense of abandonment.

Is he really gone?

I call Jonathan, but he doesn't answer and I send him a voice message.

"Babe?" I start, hesitantly, "We need to talk, I am really, really sorry that it went like this, just come back and we'll talk, okay?"

From the kitchen I smell a burning smell.

I eat them anyway, the burnt grilled cheese, shoving them into my mouth with big bites, almost without chewing, burning my palate and tongue, not tasting the bitterness and on to the next bite. Jonathan would tell me to use a plate, but Jonathan is not here. The grilled cheese doesn't fill the void in my belly. How could he leave me like this? Just because I was late for treatments one time? Or maybe he was planning this for a while, waiting for the right excuse? Maybe he's had enough of everything, the treatments, the fights, the disappointments, I'm always disappointing him, it's a wonder he stayed this long with a woman who's hardly home, who's hardly with him, who doesn't want what he wants, doesn't get excited by the things that excite him, who looks for excitement outside, who's looking for herself outside, for whom home isn't enough, being with him isn't enough, who gives him the feeling that he's not enough, and maybe he isn't. I am alarmed by this thought and quickly banish it from my mind before it takes root. It's not that someone else would be enough, I'm just that kind of person, who isn't satisfied, always have been. There's a hole in me that will never be filled. I want to jump over it and leave the hole behind, but every step I take digs it deeper, as the ground crumbles beneath my feet.

The sound of my chewing pounds in my temples and I'm afraid of the silence between bites. I eat until nothing remains, only to be met with this defiant silence that echoes in my ears. My breaths are short and shallow. I pour myself a glass of water and drink it in panicked gulps over the sink, but it doesn't wash away the lump that has formed in my throat. I grab the keys and flee into the street, almost running; the faster I move, the less my body trembles. The street reeks of urine and the cold wind blows dust into my eyes and dishevels my hair. My jacket is too thin. Shivering, I keep walking. Cars whip past, their headlights blinding as the pain in my eyes climbs the front of my head and stays. A sudden burst of light at the end of the street sharpens the pain. I look up and see the all-hours kiosk sign. Inside, the shrieking music repels me and the neon lights of the refrigerators are blinding. I grab a Carlsberg and head to the cashier.

"No smile for me?" Says the cashier as he opens the bottle. I stare through him without interacting, taking the beer bottle and drinking it beside the shop, like medicine. It's for the best, I tell myself. Perhaps Jonathan will get some perspective from friends who could scold him for taking me for granted and complaining, and abandoning me the first time I screw up. I can't believe he left, that idiot. Where does he even have to go? And what if he doesn't come back? Is that a possibility? That this is how it'll end? So casual it doesn't deserve so much as a text? Could he just disappear from my life without so much as a note? Then again, I'm wordless too.

After finishing my drink, I go back inside to buy another bottle. I drink it slower, panting less, and call Jonathan again. Again he does not answer and again I record a message.

"I just can't believe you left," I cry. "I simply cannot believe that's how you'd handle this." My voice cracks and I clear my throat and say in a more restrained voice, "Jonathan, come back."

The cashier comes out with a bottle of beer, takes a noisy sip, then hands it to me and says, "So not even a little smile for me, Princess?"

Without saying a word I take the bottle from his hand and smash it on the wall. The sound of the glass shattering momentarily clears the fog from my mind and I look at the cashier in surprise.

"You psycho!" He cries. "No wonder you look so miserable!"

I stare at him for a moment, then blink and walk away, trembling, and send Jonathan another message.

"What's this juvenile bullshit, not answering? Are you a child? Why don't you face a reality that doesn't fit your excel spreadsheets for once? Why don't you face me for once?"

I send the message and stop at the entrance to our building. I don't want to go in.

I get in the car, but I don't have anywhere to go. Sharon is in Rome, Maya lives up north and I don't want to find out how much further this evening could deteriorate, so I don't go to my mother's.

I look at our old building. We moved here four years ago, and in my mind's eye I can see Jonathan carrying boxes to the entrance. He insisted that movers are a waste of money and that we can handle it all ourselves. I made it clear to him that I have no intention of carrying anything, and he didn't flinch, just carried all the boxes himself, including eight boxes of books that weighed more than the two of us combined. Watching over our things from beside the borrowed van, I found myself smiling at the sight of his muscles working.

"What are you smiling about?" He pressed against me between trips, sweaty and sexy.

"Nothing. I just like watching you work," I muttered, pressing my lips to his.

"Wait 'til you see me hang curtains," he whispered in my ear and turned to lift the microwave.

"Wait 'til you see you ditch your wife in the middle of fertility treatments," I hiss at that Jonathan, the naive Jonathan, but he isn't listening, just flexes his biceps at the old me, blows a kiss and disappears into the stairwell to get more boxes.

I turn from the empty entrance path, start the car and drive aimlessly. Two traffic lights and ten cars flashing their lights at me later I realize that my headlights are off. I keep driving, feeling the effect of the beer I slow down, focusing on the road and the traffic lights, holding the steering wheel with both hands, leaning forward and squinting with concentration. For lack of any other destination, I decide to drive to the Agency, but miss the turn. "Shit," I curse in a whisper, consider reversing and driving up onto the sidewalk. There's a friction sound and a hubcap goes flying. My pulse quickens. Cars go around me honking, and I stop, frightened and breathing heavily on the side of the road. I force myself to regain my composure, inhaling and exhaling slowly to regulate my pulse and drive on the shoulder of the road until the gas station where I leave the car and take a taxi to the office. No matter what time I get there, the office lights are always on and there are always people around. Nobody raises an eyebrow as I walk, a little wobbly, down the hall to Pinto's office, hoping to rest a little there. There are comfortable couches there and a TV. And Pinto. I did not expect to find him there at this hour. With hair damp from a post-workout shower, he's wearing light jeans and a dark blue sweatshirt. While reading something on his computer screen, he's muttering to himself, as always. His office is reminiscent of a bachelor pad, with the wilted plant, the ivory chess pieces and three bottles of whiskey in the glass cabinet, only instead of a Marlboro model poster there's a picture of paratroopers at the Western Wall. My throat-clearing catches his attention and his broad smile makes my heart swell.

"What's up, Fishman? Did you come straight from the airport?"

"Kind of, but I didn't think you'd still be here," I feel the 600 mL of Carlsberg slowing my speech. I'm not used to drinking much, certainly not since trying to get pregnant.

"You've given me lots of work to do, you and Weiss," he smiles, "I didn't know you were into MDMA," he laughs, then sees me recoil. "It'll be fine, Fishman, you did what seemed right in the moment, you demonstrated courage and resourcefulness, Weiss mentioned that you performed excellently."

Is that what Weiss said? I frown.

"Don't underestimate yourself," Pinto continues. "What do I always tell you? You need to learn to accept compliments." He reaches out and touches my hand, and I feel chills through my arm and get confused. I take a deep breath to ground myself when I get a call from Jonathan. I pause for a moment, then answer.

"You probably figured out that I left," he's using his radio announcer voice which at another time used to turn me on.

"Yep," I reply, my voice choking again.

"I need time to think. You do too. Think about what you really want, Avishag," he speaks to me as if I'm a client deliberating between different levels of risk in her investment portfolio.

"Fine," I barely manage to get out the words through the lump that's back in my throat.

"Can I ask something of you in the meantime?" He sounds hesitant.

"What?" I ask; the lump dislodges a little.

"That you water my plants," Jonathan treats the plants on the balcony like the pets we don't have.

I freeze for a moment, then hang up and throw my phone forcefully at the floor. It comes apart. Without saying a word, Pinto bends down, picks up the pieces and puts them back together. I snatch it from him and throw it back on the floor. Pinto looks at me and then at the cracked screen.

"All good?" He asks.

"Golden," I say and my voice trembles.

"Come," he guides me toward the door.

"Where are we going?" I ask although I don't really care, I want to let him guide me.

"To get chocolate," he sounds as authoritative as when he's teaching about establishing contact with a foreign agent.

We stand facing a row of vending machines, and I choose a chocolate-covered biscuit that falls with a thud to the bottom of the machine. Pinto nods seriously and buys nougat-stuffed peanut snacks and Coke Zero. We take our loot out to the balcony and settle there. It's cold outside and Pinto disappears for a moment and comes back with a blanket from the break room. Wrapping it around me, he sits down and waves his can in a kind of 'cheers' gesture. I attempt a smile but can't.

Pinto pauses briefly before setting his can down, drawing his chair closer to mine and putting his heavy arm around my shoulders in a hug that I am afraid to interpret as other than paternal. Leaning my head on his shoulder I inhale the scent of black coffee mixed with apple hookah that he smokes with Weiss and Yardeni on the balcony. A stark contrast to Jonathan's clean smell of milk and honey shower gel.

The feeling of being hugged is pleasant, and I realize that I haven't hugged someone in a long time. Realizing that I'm enjoying this a little too much, I shake off and extract myself from his arms.

"Sorry," I sniff, "didn't mean to collapse on you."

"Feel free, what else am I here for?" He smiles and I wonder how I appear to him, with my red nose and concealer which conceals nothing.

"Wanna tell me what's wrong?" His gentle voice turns my stomach.

"It seems that Jonathan has left," I choke, hurrying to get the words out before I run out of air.

"Just like that?" He asks.

"I missed insemination treatments because of Rome," I look down at the floor. "Ah," he is quiet, thinking. I blow my nose, grabbing a handful of his snacks from the package. "You want me to talk to him?" He says finally.

"No, Pinto, I don't want you to talk to him," I say.

"Why not?" He's either playing dumb or really doesn't understand.

"First of all, because I'm not ten years old," I say, "and I'm also not sure that a call from you wouldn't do more harm than good."

"I just don't want you to make the same mistake that I made," he says.

"What mistake?"

"Thinking the Agency was the most important thing in the world."

I turn to him sharply, which makes me dizzy. I've never heard him talk like this.

"If you quote me I'll deny it," he smiles and pats my shoulder. "Come, I'll drop you off at home, you need to rest a little."

We get into Pinto's car where I notice two booster seats and an empty bag of snacks strewn on the floor. Pinto sees my gaze and nods, "A person needs kids." He reaches out and puts the snack bag into the little trash receptacle between the seats. "And one also needs a partner. Don't push him away," he says and looks back at the road.

"Do you and Orli ever speak?" I ask.

"Just about coordinating schedules and paying for capoeira," he looks at me and I must look even sadder because he adds, "It doesn't need to be like that, it depends on you," and I don't understand if he's trying to get me to give up the promotion or convince me that I really could manage both.

We stop at my place. "You'll be okay?" He touches my shoulder and I get chills again.

"Of course," I sniff. "I'm always okay."

He gives me a long look, which I search for hidden meanings. He pulls me close for an embrace, planting a warm kiss on my forehead. The heat of his lips lingers even after he pulls away. I look for his eyes, but he's already reaching into the back seat to hand me my coat.

As my heart pounds, I force myself to breathe deep and get out of the car. Before entering the building, I can't help but turn back and I see him watching me. Smiling, I push the front door and only when I am in the lobby do I hear the growl of the engine as he drives away.

9

He's sitting, waiting in the car. Yardeni gets in first and surveys the place. He's thorough, Yardeni, and Weiss trusts him implicitly. It's not that Fishman isn't professional or something, and it's not that he has anything against women, it's just that some jobs are better suited to a man. Fishman is totally fine at tracking, for example, even under stress. But he doesn't feel comfortable working with her like he does with Yardeni. Her presence is threatening. No, not threatening—irritating. Yes, that's it. Wherever he turns, there she is, walking around with her too-straight posture, and her too-smug smile, as if she knows something he doesn't, as if she knows something about him, as if she's on to him. He actually tried to connect with her in the early days, tried to bring her up to speed, advise her, direct her so she wouldn't make rookie mistakes, but she pushed him away, insisted that she knew better than him, as she insists to this day. Sometimes he's almost convinced and has to stand firm and remind himself that he knows too.

She nearly convinced him that there was nothing going on with this op., and now look. Where would it be without him? And now that she's back in Israel by surprise, he can take advantage of the situation and gain momentum, but for that, the asset recruitment has to work.

Yardeni comes out with an espresso and signals that the

coast is clear, and Weiss strolls into the coffee shop to which Roccelli was invited the day before. He is wearing a wig with a ponytail, glasses with round frames, and sporting an itchy, ginger beard.

"You look gay," Yardeni whispers in his earpiece, his words echoing unpleasantly in Weiss' ears; he feels a need to shake his head, shake them off. His heart is beating hard, anxiety burning his chest up to his windpipe. He can't start the meeting like this and he forces himself to stop, take a deep breath and breathe out slowly from his nose, then again, before he wipes his sweaty hands on his pants, straightens his back and shoulders, pushes the glass front door and enters with his chest out. He locates Roccelli at once, sitting at a corner table, perched in his chair, scanning the other customers. Weiss approaches him with broad steps, sets down his slim, brown briefcase on a chair, then pulls out another chair and sits facing Roccelli with legs spread. In moments like these it is important to convey confidence, to make the other side understand from the get-go that you are the one running the show, you're in control, and he wants to work for you.

Roccelli looks at Weiss with wide eyes and asks, "Are you David?"

When Nofar called Roccelli for a meeting, she went by Carla, secretary to David Walker, director of software development at a large British business espionage company, which had opened a Rome branch and was scouting top-tier students. Roccelli asked how they heard of him, and she replied that they had their ways. Which was true.

"Yes, I'm David. And you are Antonio Roccelli," Weiss isn't asking.

"Yes," Roccelli replies at once.

Weiss holds out his hand for a strong handshake, "And you're here about the student position. Did they tell you what's involved?" Weiss asks although he knows the answer is no. The only things Roccelli was told on the phone were the name of the company—so that he could check the website designed especially for him—and the salary, which was high enough to crush any resistance.

Roccelli shakes his head no. Without a word, Weiss reaches for his leather briefcase, pulls out a form and fountain pen and gets him to sign. Anything you say will sound more impressive after a confidentiality agreement.

He scans Roccelli's face while he reads the contract details. An elongated, youthful, almost childlike face, a few bristles on smooth, flushed cheeks. He wears a tricot shirt under a jean jacket and looks cold, even indoors. In his awkwardness, his lost expression looking for an anchor, looking for someone to take him under his wing and provide security, there's something about him that inspires compassion. Maybe even reminds Weiss of something, someone. He catches himself staring for too long, straightens up and calls over the busty waitress standing by the cash register, looking her in the eyes until she blushes, letting his eyes scan downward and orders coffee for both of them.

"O-kay," after Roccelli handed him back the signed form, he brings his hands together. "So as you've probably gathered, if you were clever enough to have a look at our website..." He pauses to wink at the waitress as she returns with the espresso, she smiles back and serves them cookies on the house. "We're a business espionage company, the biggest in Britain, third biggest in Europe," he speaks in a thick British accent. "I manage the software division, and we are setting up a Rome branch and looking for a student for a position that'll require both office and fieldwork. I can see from your resumé that you chose to specialize in information systems." He looks at Roccelli, not waiting for a response. "The experience you will gain will give you a leg up in the job market. Most students opt to keep working for us. Of course we only keep the cream of the crop." He laughs and goes on. "We don't believe in job interviews. Instead, we'll send you for a short field test. You pass? You're in. You'll work with the best of the best. You don't pass? You can carry on sleeping through your present job. You work in IT at the moment, yeah?"

Roccelli appears to be struggling to keep up with Weiss' speech, but he nods and asks about the test. Weiss smiles and explains. Roccelli is asked to infiltrate the salary report at the bank where he has a student job and extract all of the salary data of all of the employees.

Weiss senses Roccelli's hesitation. This is to be expected, but Weiss feels himself tense. He has to make this happen. He must prove that they cannot do without him, that he is irreplaceable, no matter what they find out about him.

"They will fire me if they find out I did something like that," says Roccelli.

"True," Weiss confirms, calmly. "If you think there's a decent chance they'll catch you, don't do it. You won't be accepted anyway."

Roccelli still appears hesitant, but Weiss must transmit control of the situation. He starts to pack his things with ease. "Look," he says, "I assume you checked out our company before coming here. You'll work with the best, you'll get professional experience you'd never get anywhere else. And compensation that you definitely won't find anywhere else."

He looks at Roccelli with a piercing look, knowing where to apply pressure, "But we'd never force anybody, of course, believe me, plenty of quality people want in, and not just because of our outrageous compensation." He lets out a big laugh.

"So just get the salary data?" Roccelli asks hesitantly. He might just take the bait and Weiss tells himself to relax, reduce some pressure and create a closer, more pleasant atmosphere.

"Yep," Weiss confirms, "names and salaries. Don't worry," he leans toward Roccelli, lowering his voice, "you strike me as a guy who gets it, it's just a matter of finding the right loophole, then there's no risk."

"Okay, I'll think about it," Roccelli says, still resistant. "Who do I send it to?"

"Carla, who invited you here. You have a week."

If Roccelli can't do it in the next few days, the Agency tech department will covertly help him find loopholes. The aim is for Roccelli to succeed.

They part with a handshake. Weiss's is strong, certain and a little painful; Roccelli's is hesitant and gentle.

According to protocol, Weiss is supposed to stay close to the source, to keep an eye on him and be available in case of unforeseen problems, but Weiss has a follow-up polygraph scheduled for tomorrow, so he'll be flying back to Israel tonight.

He sits in first class in a business suit, eying the flight attendant distributing miniature drinks and does not bother to smile at the passengers, as if this were not the one thing that her job requires of her. Weiss wonders if they would fire her if they found out that she does not smile, if it would threaten her professional future. He examines her. Her name tag reads, "Luna." Tanned and slim, she has a long, thin nose that gives her character. She's busy with cans and carafes in the cart she's pushing, her face is serious and impassive. When she looks up at Weiss, he shoots her a smile. She does not respond and lowers her eyes, but he notices the corner of her mouth curling up a little and relaxes. Everything's fine. Luna offers him whiskey but Weiss declines. Since that incident, he makes sure not to drink. Bad things happen to him when he loses control.

Weiss's eyes close and his head hits the window. He startles and sits up straight, resisting sleep, as always. Sleep is also a loss of control. Luna, holding two glasses of champagne, offers him one and, with his permission, sits in the empty seat beside him. Up close, her nose is even longer and thinner, with a light plume of hair gracing her upper lip. This does not put him off. On the contrary. There is something poignant about it. He smiles and clinks champagne glasses with her. A drop hangs over Luna's lip, and she reaches out her tongue to lick it away without taking her eyes off him. He knows she's game. And he is. And he isn't bothered by the mustache shadowing her little mouth, and without a word, he pulls her gently by the hand, they get up, and head to the bathroom stall. On the way, they pass Weiss's father and his two brothers who are sitting in the cheap seats by the toilets. They wave to him, whistle and call out crude remarks, like that time Tali, a girl from his class, came over to study for a test with him, but he doesn't respond, his eyes are fixed on Luna's back. She is taller than him and sturdy, with broad shoulders, emphasized by the tight flight attendant uniform, and in the bathroom, she holds him with her big hands. They are pressed closely together now, and Weiss can smell a thin smell of sweat rising from her. Squished between the plastic walls, he lays his head on her flat chest and closes his eyes.

He jerks awake as the plane hits an air pocket, his heart beating. Luna is pouring tea for the passengers a few rows ahead of him. This lie detector test is screwing with his head. He has to pass it and be done with it already. He reminds himself that he isn't hiding anything relevant to work, or that affects it, or national security. Unlike some employees—and he's got names if anyone asks—he doesn't submit receipts for the restaurants where he ate during his free time, doesn't print assignments for school on the office printers, and doesn't use his diplomatic passport to skip lines. He's straight as an arrow—like his impeccable posture. He repeats this to himself every day in the mirror and on solo car rides. He practices breathing and relaxation every evening. He is an outstanding employee. He is a leading candidate for the promotion. He can pass it. He can pass.

He fails.

The exam is shorter this time. At the end, Alon the examiner comes back into the room and says in his deep voice, "I see you've decided to waste our time."

Weiss's face drops, and he wants to drop with it, but continues to look at Alon with a frozen expression. He's still sitting, bound to the device, his hands gripping the arms of the chair so tight that his knuckles are white. He tries to think where he went wrong. How could it be that despite the practice and the meditation and the breathing and the self-talk—he failed again. It cannot be. What will he do now? He goes through the questions and his answers over and over, once again feels his pulse race with every question he whispers in his head and realizes that he did not really stand a chance.

"The test does not take pity on liars," notes Alon.

This ticks Weiss off: Who is Alon to call him a liar?

When Weiss was a child, he lied a lot. Not to glorify himself or get out of trouble. Just to feel like everyone else. What he wanted most was to be like everyone else. To look like them, dress like them, hit on girls like them, play soccer like them. These things came easily to his brothers. So easily that Peleg, the middle one, spent two years with a green mohawk and safety pins holding his torn clothes together. So easily that he seemed to despise this privilege of appearing normal.

Weiss did not seem normal. He could not lie about his weight, but he could invent a girlfriend from a different town and American uncles that sent jeans with a label that nobody recognized, not admitting that he couldn't find "Diesel" jeans in his size. He lied about his results in the 2000-meter race and claimed he would join the armored corps, despite his low profile due to his weight, landing him in the Ordnance Corps. It isn't lying, he thought, he would improve his profile and get to armored corps. It's not like he was aiming for Special Forces like his father wanted, or the Golani infantry brigade like half of his class, just the armored corps.

And he got there. But it took him four months. Four months in which each time he went home from the base he changed into civilian clothes, skipping the free rides for soldiers on public transport, so that the lack of a weapon would not be obvious. It was the first time in his life that he had no appetite and hardly lied. It was complicated to invent stories of basic training for the armored corps, so he cut off contact with his friends from high school. He blamed fatigue, busyness, a new girlfriend, getting a ride... He would turn his phone off, go into his room and not come out, apart from going running. His father was pleased. Every evening he hit the running track that encircled the base. At first he walked, later he jogged a bit, and three and a half months later, just before his transfer to the armored corps was approved, he conquered the whole track at a slow, panting run.

When he got to the armored corps, he was 15 pounds thinner. At first he didn't even notice, he was so consumed by keeping up, not falling behind. Eventually, he advanced in the swarm of running soldiers, no longer the slowest, not the one who had to be dragged or pushed, to his great shame, up the hill. His fitness level rose and the pounds dropped, but the flair for the dramatic and the need to become someone else, remained.

He chose his sergeant, who was a revered figure in the troop, imitated his body language, the way he sat with his legs crossed, not pressed together, spread out, one foot resting on a knee, and sometimes both feet planted on the ground and body leaning forward, elbows on the knees, chin resting on his hands in a listening posture. But the legs were always apart, he noted to himself. Legs always apart. He was the actor of the group. Not the clown, there's an important difference. He wouldn't let them mock him, but very much enjoyed being the center of attention, and for that he was sometimes willing to laugh at others. They weren't like him: They were strong. They'd survive.

After the army, he dreamed of studying acting. He was already registered and passed the first auditions at two top acting institutes when he got the call from the Agency. They wrote letters like this to his entire cohort, but his felt personal. He did not know what the position entailed, but as becoming part of the organization was a real possibility, it was hard to ignore. This was an amazing opportunity to be everything his father wanted him to be.

And now everything that he had accomplished, everything he'd fought for, everything he lived for—was about to fall apart because of some polygraph examiner who doesn't have a clue. He has no idea what he's on to, no idea that it isn't remotely relevant to work. He has no idea that if they find out, Weiss's life would crumble, leaving him with nothing. He has no idea.

"Out! Get out of here! They'll be in touch with you," Alon mutters angrily, and Weiss is jolted from his standstill, hurrying to loosen the straps and get out of the too-bright room. He passes quickly by the candidates waiting in the corner, avoiding eye contact and makes it to the guards at the entrance. "Open up," he barks at them as they hand him back his phone. But one of them is on a phone call, and the other is eying the ID card of a young man in glasses. Weiss feels like he's out of breath, his heart is racing and his mouth is dry. He needs water. There's a kitchenette in the corner of the waiting room, but he won't go back there. He needs to get out of here. Now.

There's a candidate on the other side of the door, and until the guard identifies him, he can't open the door. The security guard instructs him to hold up his ID card in front of the security camera, but he's struggling to find it. Weiss tries to take slow, measured breaths, like he has practiced dozens of times. In—three, four, five, out—three four five six seven eight.

It didn't help with the polygraph. He wipes the sweat from under his nose and on the back of his neck and grinds his teeth. Come *on*.

Finally the security guard IDs the guy. Weiss pushes the heavy steel door, hears the tongue of the lock release as the door opens. He's outside, trying to breathe the air into his lungs, but still does not manage. A shrill ring cries out from his pants pocket and he jumps in alarm. The caller ID flashes, "DO NOT ANSWER." Weiss stares at it for a moment, then curses and presses hard on the screen, answering the call.

"How many times do I have to tell you not to call me anymore!" He shouts in a trembling voice and hits the phone again to hang up.

"Everything okay?" The security guard's voice comes out of the intercom. "Yes, yes," Weiss mutters and hurries away.

He takes the elevator down and gets quickly into his car, his blood burning his body. He balls up his fists and hits the steering wheel, imagining himself punching Alon the polygraph examiner right in his smug face. This image makes Weiss feel better. Alon has blood running from his nose. Not a lot, just a red drop pooling above his lip. Weiss punches him again in the exact same spot, hearing the crack of broken bone. Gaining momentum, he swings again and blows out the broken bone, thinks that he sees part of it come out, stabbing the skin, and Alon screaming in pain. This is nice but not enough for Weiss. He kicks him in the stomach, holding both shoulders as Alon crumples in pain, and Weiss brings him in closer and then knees him in the face. Alon falls to the floor and Weiss is panting and kicking him again and again, mostly in the face, now an unrecognizable pulp of parts and blood.

A knock on the window makes him jump. A young woman bends down, peering at him. He opens the window.

"Are you okay?" Her eyes are gray, her wavy hair rests on her shoulders.

"Yes," he clears his throat, "why?"

"Sorry. You were shaking. You looked like you were going through something, sorry to bother you," she apologizes and scurries away.

Weiss touches his forehead. It's cold and wet. He breathes deeply, he has to calm down. He has to speak to Pinto. Better he hear it from him.

On the way to the Agency, his head is spinning with thoughts. He'll talk to Pinto about the mission, about Roccelli, remind him how good he is, how much he can be trusted, how he has never disappointed or screwed up, and only then, once he's sure he's on his side, as always, he'll tell him calmly about the polygraph and clarify that of course he'll pass the next one for sure, no question, he's on it. He is in control. His life is not going to be ruined. He isn't going to lose the only stable thing in his life. His father was wrong.

But in Pinto's office he forgets everything. All the examples that he prepared are getting mixed up in his mind and the words are confused when he tries to explain what he does not understand himself, he's getting dizzy again and he has no air and he has to catch his breath.

"Hang on, hold your horses," Pinto interrupts him, "I can't understand anything, mumble more clearly."

Weiss stops and takes a deep breath like they teach in meditation, damn meditation. "I did a polygraph today. And failed. For the second time," he says, looking at Pinto, checking his response. Pinto is not his father, he won't reject him because he isn't like him, just because he's weak sometimes.

"O-kay," says Pinto, nodding like it isn't the end of the world. "Over what?"

"I can't say."

Pinto raises one eyebrow, looking much more alert. "You know that I can't help you if you don't tell me."

"You don't have to help me, it's a technical issue, I just wanted to let you know. I'll sort it out, I swear," says Weiss, praying that this is true.

"Should I be worried?" Pinto gives him a serious look.

"No," says Weiss.

But he should.

10

"Avishagi, sweetie, how are you?"

"Hey Rina, is he here?" I dart past Jonathan's mother, standing in the doorway wearing a broad, floral house dress, into his parents' little apartment. I scan the apartment for hints of him, skirting the big dining table that takes up half the kitchen and half the living room. I hate dining tables. When I lived at home, my mom insisted on family dinners every evening. She would drag my dad out of bed—he hated getting out of bed only a little less than he hated fighting with my mom—and he would shuffle around in his ragged slippers and worn out burgundy pajamas, and the three of us would sit silently around the oversized dining table and eat pasta or shakshuka or meatballs, all made with Shahar's favorite tomato sauce.

At Jonathan's parents' place, the TV is on and there's noise coming from the balcony. Through the window I can see a blurred Jonathan in a cloud of dust. He is bent over a small table holding his father's electric saw, bare-chested; even through the glass I can see his muscles flexing as he confidently works the saw.

Jonathan's father has a small woodworking shop and Jonathan spent a lot of time there as a kid, playing among the wooden planks. As he got older, his father gave him bigger and bigger tasks. During his army service, when he'd come home for weekends, he built and assembled furniture on his own. To this day his tough hands are one of my favorite things about him.

When we first moved in together, we slept on a double mattress on the living room floor. Jonathan built us a bed. He handpicked each piece of wood from his father's shop, and day by day, for a month, he would come home from university or from his shift at the direct insurance company, measure, saw, screw, hammer and sand. I would come home, grab a folding chair from the kitchen and watch him work. Oh man, he looked good with his bare chest, glistening with sweat, wood chips and sawdust in his wavy hair which he had not yet cut short. He wouldn't use a sander, said it had no soul, and sanded the whole bed manually, with sandpaper. I loved the sawdust smell of Jonathan and our bed and us. When he finished, we'd roll into bed. We had a lot of sex in those days, which feel like another lifetime.

I open the sliding door wide and inhale the scent of sawdust. A shiver of longing and intimacy shakes me and makes me forget what I'm here for. Jonathan still doesn't notice, over the sound of the saw, and I restrain myself from reaching out to brush the wood chips from his hair.

"Jonathan," I say, but he still doesn't hear me.

I reach out and touch his shoulder and he jumps. He turns to me, and the expression of surprise gives way to an expression that I don't know how to decipher. He sets down the saw, slowly pulling the shirt hanging from a plastic chair over his muscles and looks at me for a long moment, eyes like a laser beam, pupil to pupil. For a moment all I want is for him to embrace me, take me home and press me against his chest until I fall asleep. I lift my hands to reach for him, to close the distance between us, but then something in his body stiffens. He looks away and asks, "Did you water the plants?" I pull my hand back.

"Seriously?" I ask him, "That's what you have to say to me?"

My voice rises, and without the noise of the saw it carries through the whole house.

"Avishagi, please, come have a seat," Rina pops up at my side, placing a perfumed hand on my shoulder, and her hand is soft and warm like well-kneaded plasticine. "Why don't you talk like civilized adults."

"Civilized adults don't just bail when things get hard," I cry, forgetting the chills and the sawdust.

"Stop yelling," Jonathan says in a tired voice.

"I will stop yelling when you start talking," I shout in an attempt to jostle him, to shake him up. The quieter he remains, the louder I get. But Jonathan just grimaces, looks defeated, rises heavily and heads to the living room. I follow him as he passes his mother and goes into his parents' bedroom.

"Quit running away like a child, I'm not going anywhere until we talk." I sit down cross-legged on the pink bedspread.

He stands there, blinking, shoulders hunched, then takes a breath, and slowly his figure grows into its usual size, and he looks at me and says, "Suddenly it's urgent to solve things? Suddenly you can't take your time?"

Before I manage to reply, I hear his mom's voice.

"Jonny, come on, talk to her, she came all the way here," Rina stands in the doorway, "And you know that doesn't happen every day." She doesn't hold back.

Jonathan sighs, "Mom, please, give us a moment alone."

"Don't mind me, I'm just grabbing something and leaving," she goes and rifles through her makeup drawer, which rattles until she finally chooses a hand cream, waves it over her head and leaves the room.

I smile at Jonathan who tries to stifle a smile.

"Okay, maybe you could at least sit next to me, or you'd rather stand there like an idiot?" I pat the large lacy flower on the bedspread, and he sits down heavily.

"I really need some time to think, Vishi," he says in a softer voice.

"And you can't think at home? I'm not there most of the time anyway," I smile at him but he turns serious again.

"Okay, not funny," I nod.

"Not funny," he repeats like a faint echo. "Why do you even want me to come home?" He looks up at me, and am I imagining it or is he pleading?

"I'm just..." I get stuck. Why *do* I want him home? I'm asking myself if I really miss him when he isn't around, if I feel his absence. I know that I miss who he used to be, that Jonathan who peeped out from his eyes a moment before but quickly receded, yielding to the heavy sense of alienation that settles between us.

"I just want everything to be okay," I say finally, and his expression reveals that this answer is far from satisfying, that he expected something else and once again, I did not meet his expectations.

"But everything isn't okay, Avishag," he sits up straight and his voice hardens. "You're always pushing me away and disappearing to your things. You think I'll just stick around no matter what while you do whatever you want."

"I don't think that," I say. "Maybe we need to replace Dalit."

"And then what? You'll share more about what's going on with you? You'll work less? You'll be more committed to the treatments? You'll want this child more?"

"Sometimes I feel like you love this child more than you love me."

"Don't talk nonsense, there isn't even a child yet."

"Exactly," I say, staring at the wall plastered with framed family photos. Wedding photos of Jonathan's parents, childhood photos of Jonathan and his sisters, sticking their tongues out at the camera, rolling with laughter in a pile of children in Purim Care Bear costumes with angry faces. There are also photos of his sisters' families in photography studios with light blue backgrounds and matching shirts, a photo from our wedding, and one free space, on the left side of the bottom row. When I was pregnant, Rina was quick to make space on the wall, and even though it felt premature, I didn't say anything. Since then that space remains vacant.

"We still don't have a child, but we have a family, we have a home," I say.

"It's hard to call it our home when you're not there most of the time." I take a breath before responding, but he continues, "And even when you are there, you're always hormonal and tired and irritable and it's not entirely pleasant to be around you."

"Are you serious?" I explode. "Why am I tired all the time? Why am I irritable? Why am I hormonal? Why am I doing these fucking treatments? Maybe because your fucking sperm aren't doing their fucking job?" My heart is beating hard and I already regret it as the words spill out.

Jonathan reels. "Bitch," he says, the curse coming from his mouth like a groan of pain.

"Sorry," I mumble, "I really am hormonal."

"That's no excuse to be an asshole," he stands up.

"And what *is* an excuse?" I ask him, and he looks at me, confused. "I'm genuinely asking. Is there a reason that would excuse my acting *not* like a woman from a catalog? Are there circumstances in which I am permitted to lose it a little? Not to be so careful around you all the time? And not be afraid to tell you what I really want or feel?"

He turns to me slowly, "Is that how you feel? That you're afraid to talk to me?"

"Sometimes," I say in a softer tone, "just sometimes."

He sits beside me. "I don't want you to be afraid to talk to me," he says in a tired voice, "but I also don't want to be afraid to talk to you, and I feel like every time I mention my desires you feel like it's a criticism of you. It isn't criticism. I just want us to be parents, to be a family, and you want to run around the globe, protecting the security and liberty of the homeland. I'm not belittling it: It's just a bit insulting that it always comes at my expense."

"The liberty of the homeland," I repeat after him.

"If we have a daughter, we'll call her Liberty," he reminds me of our old joke.

"Wow, your mother would freak out," I smile and inch closer to him.

"Come on, Shagi, what kind of name is that? They'll think she's an antivaxxer," his impression of her isn't bad and I laugh.

"Come home," I reach out my hand, but he doesn't take it.

"I need a little time alone, Vish," he says and goes back to being serious.

I sit there a few more moments, waiting for something that isn't happening, and the space between us grows again.

"Fine," I finally mutter. "So I'll go." I get up, lingering, to give him the chance to stop me, but he keeps on staring at the pictures on the wall and says nothing. "I'll call you tomorrow," I say.

He looks up at me. "Better if you don't," he says. "I'll call you in a few days, when I've done some thinking."

He continues to pull away from me, and I feel like I've been stripped of all of the invitations to get closer. He doesn't suggest anything or meet me in the middle or give up his innate prerogative to always be right, and I'm tired. I quietly get up from his parents' bed and leave the room, passing Rina on my way out, rubbing hand cream into her elbows and trying to convince me it'll be okay, he'll come to his senses, we're a great couple destined to have lovely children and we can't give up.

I drag myself out to the car, get in, slowly key in the code, start the ignition but don't start driving. My body is tired and heavy, and I lean my head on the steering wheel and close my eyes.

My ringing phone makes me jump.

"Ah, great, are you in town?" Dalit cheers on the other end, "I've never met a marketing manager who flies abroad this much, don't you have employees for that?"

My cover story for acquaintances is that I'm a marketing manager at a software company, most of whose clients are in the US. It's meant to explain my long absences, but does not always satisfy everyone.

"So when are we scheduling for?" Dalit goes on, "we haven't met for two weeks already, and you know how crucial therapeutic continuity is."

"Yeah..." I hesitate. "It's a little tricky for us to book right now."

"Are you flying again? Avishagi, if you keep traveling so much you won't have any partnership to work on in our meetings," she laughs, and I start sniffling.

"Avishag?" Dalit cries, "is everything okay? Oy, sweetie, I was joking, it was super unprofessional of me, I'm sorry." Dalit was never great at maintaining professional boundaries, and most of the time she talks as if she's my friend and not my couples' therapist. Most of the time it doesn't bother me.

"No, no," I try to explain and my throat tightens. "It's not you, it's Jonathan. He left the house, he left me." Saying these words out loud makes them even more painful.

"Ohh my love, it sounds to me like you need a big hug right now," she stops and her voice gets practical and urgent, and I hear the rustling of papers. "What are you doing tomorrow?" She asks. "I've got an opening. You come to me tomorrow at 2 PM and we'll talk." She doesn't ask, she schedules our appointment and I find myself sniffing in consent.

The next afternoon I go to Dalit's clinic. I've never been here alone before, and I look at the place as if for the first time. There are lots of empowerment and inspiration posters hanging on the wall, some of which I suspect Dalit wrote herself. In the middle of the room is a round turquoise carpet with long tassels, and on it a beige two-seater Ikea sofa. In the center of the carpet is a small, round table, on which sit two ugly enamel mugs that look like they were handmade, badly, filled with herbal tea, and a box of tissue.

Dalit, with meticulous makeup, hair probably straightened the Japanese way, and high lights in it, pounces on me with a hug, the thin gold bracelets on her wrist jangle, and I'm buried in her huge, soft chest, smelling the perfume that she sprays in her cleavage. She's right, I really do need a hug and am in no hurry to be released from it. I feel good here, protected and enfolded.

But after a few moments Dalit loosens her arms, holds my shoulders and examines my face. "Not great, but not terrible," she concludes, sitting me down in one of the armchairs and settling across from me, squeezing her wide hips between the wooden armrests.

"So tell me," she leans in, "what happened?"

"I got stuck abroad because of work and didn't make it to the insemination this month. When I got home, he was gone."

She gives a long nod with an emotionless expression. I feel like she's criticizing me. That she thinks I deserve for Jonathan to leave, and that she's surprised he waited until now. I'm also kind of surprised.

"You expected this," she says finally. "You're thinking—how did this not happen until now. You don't really think you deserve to be happy, Avishagi."

I straighten up to resist this statement, but then sink back into the armchair and consider it. I assume I deserve to be happy, doesn't everyone? So what makes me different? I just don't know what would make me happy, and who. Once, I thought a child would help. And it might, but the journey towards that made me miserable. Once, being with Jonathan made me happy, but it has been over a year that things between us are so fraught with so many sensitive spots that it's grown into one huge spot of sensitivity. But I still need him in my life. He needs to be there for me to feel that I can count on at least part of my life not to fall apart. That he'll be there tomorrow. That we're okay.

"I don't think I need him to be happy," I say finally and hesitantly, partly to Dalit, partly to myself.

"Of course you don't need him!" Dalit cheers me on, and all the empowering phrases around her flicker, "Of course not. You only need yourself. The question is if you *want* him," she points a long red fingernail at me. "Let's try an exercise," Dalit suggests, "Let's do a guided meditation. Close your eyes," she gets up to dim the light and turns on calm music accompanied by the sound of trickling water. "Come on, close them!" She urges, seeing that my eyes are still open.

I give in and close my eyes, struggling to give in to the situation, and she begins to speak in a quiet voice. "Take a deep breath through your nose, and let the air out through your mouth. And again. Take a deep breath, and let it out. Again." I frown but obey, and she continues, "now relax your body, limb by limb...feel the heaviness. Head, chin down...release the shoulders... your pelvis sinks into the chair...legs are heavy, pulling you down...back is relaxed...belly out... nobody is looking, nobody is examining, nobody is judging. Now. Imagine yourself in a nice, calm place. You can choose any place you want that makes you feel good, that you feel free and natural to be yourself there, to love yourself."

I imagine myself on the balcony at the Agency. It's high up and rises above the surrounding low buildings, setting me apart from them. The whole Tel Aviv metropolitan area spreads out before me, the whole world spreads before me, and I am tall, strong and far from the daily worries and I have peace there, hear my thoughts clearly and am free to say and do whatever

I want.

I feel the warm wind on my face and hear Dalit. "Now a familiar and beloved figure approaches, someone you want in your life and you know will be there to overcome all the obstacles with you, who will help you and protect you."

I'm not a child, guided meditation is cute, but I know how to control my imagination and decide who I envision at any given moment. So I imagine Jonathan approaching me, with his big, confident steps, smiling the smile with the eyes that I haven't seen in ages. He holds out both of his hands to me, indicating to me to enter into them, and holds me close. His chest is broad and solid underneath his starched shirt, his arms hold me tight and it isn't clear if he's protecting me or clinging to me.

"Okay, you can open your eyes. Who did you imagine?" Dalit asks, and I tell her I saw Jonathan, and she's pleased with herself and the exercise. She praises the guided meditation method and says how it helped her to decide what she wanted to study when she nearly chose account management. I half-listen to her but am not really focused, because I can't stop thinking about Pinto's broad, solid chest, and his arms around me last night at the office, a hug that just enveloped me and did not ask anything in return, and I can't stop thinking how I want to go back to that embrace.

11

The moment I leave Dalit's clinic, tears streaming and head hurting, I get a call, as if on cue, from Gidi, Pinto's assistant, summoning me to an urgent one-on-one.

"And he wants it today. How soon can you get here?"

It's important to Pinto to meet me one-on-one today. I feel my eyes drying up, my back straightening, the conversation with Dalit retreating, and I tell Gidi I'm on my way. In my car, I fish around in my bag for my lipstick among the keys, tampons, bag of cranberries, wallet and passport. I apply it to my upper lip which I press to the bottom one, comb, then muss my hair a little. It is a thin but critical line between looking natural and effortful. A glance in the mirror reassures me.

I start the car and merge into traffic. Luckily, the streets are pretty empty and I zigzag between lanes, racing against Waze, trying to take minutes off the ETA, accelerating at green lights and cursing the reds slowing me down.

I shaved off a minute. Back in training I excelled at operational driving. I'm curious and a little nervous to hear what Pinto has to say. Maybe it's just in my head and he won't even mention what happened between us yesterday, maybe it was nothing, just my need for warmth making me overanalyze innocent, everyday situations. But then why the sudden urgency to see me? And what was the meaning of the hug and the glances and the long kiss on the forehead? Was that just fatherly? Maybe he sees me as a kid, a little sister, like that summer break a hundred years ago when he took me to the amusement park? Maybe I'm the only one on the roller coaster right now and he's on the teacup carousel...

Sixteen minutes later I'm at the office but can't find parking. That's what happens when you turn up in the middle of the day. I drum irritably on the steering wheel and make another round of the farther parking lot, maybe some space will suddenly open up. In the end I leave the car on the side of the road beside another car whose driver gave up on legitimate parking, fold in the mirrors and walk, taking big steps. When I get to the office, my shirt is sweat-stained: I can't let Pinto see me like this. I head to the dressing room and rifle through the hangers until I find an airy, white shirt with a low neckline. I replace my shirt with the clean one and fix my hair again, puffing it up a little so it isn't stuck to my scalp, closely examining myself in the mirror and then again from a distance, sniff my armpits and head towards Pinto's office.

Liat from human resources catches me exiting the elevator. She wants to discuss something about my pay stub, but I don't slow down, just say I'm in a hurry and I'll catch up with her later. I cross the hall toward Pinto's office, but his door is closed and Gidi doesn't look up from his screen as he says, "Another half hour."

Now I have time to go back for Liat's updates on per diem payments. I half listen to her lecture on the importance of dental insurance, but am mainly looking over her shoulder at the clock hanging on the wall, counting the minutes until my meeting with Pinto.

Gidi's desk is at the entrance to Pinto's office, and this time when I show up he nods and points to the chair across from him, muttering to me to wait. I feel like he's enjoying this. As if he can see the panic in my eyes and is mocking me, like he's saying, "what do you think is going to happen in there? Pinto will confess his burning love? Maybe instead of deluding yourself you should put that energy into your crumbling relationship?"

"Do you mind?" Gidi points at the pen I'm vigorously tapping and I apologize and quietly put it down.

I sit on my hands, stare at Gidi's watch, and after seven minutes and twenty-six seconds, a long beep startles me and Gidi answers the phone in a low voice. A moment later he says, "Fine," and hangs up. "You can go in," he nods towards the door and I grab my bag, straighten my shirt, run my fingers through my hair one last time and open the door.

My heart starts pounding as I enter the room. Pinto is sitting at his desk, playing with paper clips, a paper cup on a piece of printer paper beside him, stained with a coffee ring. He's wearing a short-sleeved shirt, though it's cold out, and now I notice that he's deep in conversation with Shabtai, our department head, and the two of them look up at me as I enter.

"Fishman, join us," Pinto calls and gestures at the chair beside Shabtai; I sit down and wait for them to finish their conversation.

But they stop talking and Shabtai turns his chair toward me and asks how I'm doing, averting his eyes from my face to my cleavage meant for Pinto, still stuffing handfuls of cracker jacks into his mouth. I say that everything is totally fine, because at this moment, in Pinto's office, everything really is fine as far as I'm concerned. Shabtai grills me about the effects of the pill, if I did blood tests yet and if I want sick leave. I refuse, and he praises my idea to recruit Roccelli. I thank him politely, struggling to hide my impatience, which must be working because Shabtai is entirely at ease, reclining and smiling in his chair, scratching his big belly, cleaning crumbs off it and then asks if I'm pleased with my position, at work in general, how things are at home and how's Jonathan ? I give the usual answers – no one really wants to hear about follicle tracking or the husband leaving, certainly not one's boss. He prefers operational quiet, and this is what I deliver. Finally his questions end and he smiles, rises and pulls his pants over his huge paunch, so that his belt squeezes and divides it into two. I smile back at him, expecting him to leave, but instead of turning toward the door, he lifts his chair and moves it over beside Pinto.

"My office is being renovated, so we preferred to meet here," he says, maybe sensing my confusion.

"So, Ms. Avishag Fishman," he begins with an official tone as if we did not just engage in ten minutes of tedious small talk. "You must be wondering why we summoned you," he keeps smiling his satisfied smile at me, and the mole at the corner of his eye disappears. He leans back, his arms bent and his hands at the back of his neck, as if preparing to do sit-ups. His underarms are sweaty, but it doesn't seem to bother him. He doesn't pull down his shirt so it won't cling to his belly or arrange his thin hair when a sudden wind blows and ruffles it. He's relaxed. I'm not.

"Listen, girl." I am listening, even though he's calling me a girl, and he goes on, "We've been following your work for some time now, and you've managed to impress us," he says, looking at Pinto who nods in approval.

I look at Pinto's matter-of-fact expression and wrinkle my forehead. The compliments are nice, but I anticipate a letdown. I didn't rush over here for these kinds of compliments.

"In fact you're so impressive, sometimes we almost forget you're a woman," he laughs and chokes on a phlegmy cough. "Just joking," he coughs again. "You should know I'm a feminist and you women are much better than us. At the end of the day, we're real animals, right Pinto?" Pinto hums noncommittally and Shabtai goes on, "And you probably know that the next round of branch head nominations is approaching."

I nod, no longer disappointed: He's got my attention and I'm alert, trying to calm myself, to regulate the excitement and anticipation. Of course I know those nominations are coming up.

"And we'd like," Shabtai continues slowly, stroking one of his three chins, "for you to apply to Pinto's position."

"Oh wow," an involuntary smile comes to my face. It's one thing to aspire to a promotion, and another for my superiors to encourage me. The effect of his words spread through my belly like hot chocolate, calming me and flushing my cheeks.

I immediately think of my mother, as I do with every accomplishment or landmark in my life, and wonder if she'll be pleased, even though I already know—she won't. My accomplishments seem to bother her, depriving her of the only real pleasure in her life—complaining. Not that I'm criticizing her. My mother has plenty of reasons to complain, and when I was a kid, I made a real effort to make her happy. Sure my father was the one diagnosed with depression, but while his depression made him shrink and fade, my mother's suffering only continued to grow, filling the house. Even when I tried to give her reasons to be happy, she would push me away and fiercely defend her right to suffer.

When I was accepted to the Girl Scouts' international summer camp, the only one in my grade from my town, I was determined not to let her take my accomplishment from me, not this time. I told her about the phone call I'd received, insisting on being excited about it even in the face of her raised eyebrows and pinched mouth.

"Don't think I'm not proud," she began. "Good for you for getting accepted, really, but what business do you have going to California?" She asked and without waiting for an answer, "And what about your final exams? What about me and your father?" And also, "Fine, go ahead, you always do whatever you want anyway," which infuriated me most of all because it failed to acknowledge all of the concessions and accommodations that I'd made in the past. I decided that this time I would go no matter what. No matter how many faces she makes, how much she sighs, and how ungrateful I'll feel for leaving her on her own: I want to go and I will. And that's that.

In the end I didn't go. I told everyone I was going, made packing lists, did my pre-matriculation exams early, I signed up early for winter graduation, and received the blessing of my teachers and the envy of my friends. And then, three weeks before the departure date, my father's depression got worse and he was hospitalized at the Geha Mental Health Center.

My mother told me that it wasn't a good idea for me to go anyway, and I told my friends that I'd realized I didn't want to be so far from home for such a long time and I'd have lots of other opportunities to go to San Diego. I couldn't tell them why I really stayed. My mother didn't want anyone to know about my father's depression. So I said he had gallstones. From a young age I learned to apply concealer, to cover up fatigue, and the truth.

I would draw my lips up into a broad smile, squint—because I once read an article about body language in a teen magazine which taught me that a smile without the eyes is not a real smile—and go out to battle.

My father's roommate at the hospital didn't speak at all. The sticker on his bed said his name was Mr. Bloom; I thought of him as Mr. Gloom. He would sit in bed for hours staring at the blank television hanging in the corner of the room, saliva leaking and gathering around the gray stubble on his chin and the folds of his neck.

At 9 p.m. a nurse would come to make sure that every patient took his sleeping pills, and Dad would fall asleep at once, escaping wakefulness like a bad dream. But Mr. Gloom would shout in his sleep, screaming like a wounded cat. I would faithfully take the night shifts at my father's side, but could not sleep and got 71 in my English matriculation exam. Mom was not pleased.

Now I know that she won't be pleased about the possible

promotion, which diminishes the butterflies I'm feeling. "That's great, Shagi, but why right now?" I can hear her say, "Can't you wait a few more years? Give me a couple grandkids and then...?"

"No, Mom," I answer in my head, "I can't wait. Opportunities like this don't happen every day and I want the job and even think I'd be good at it, which I can't say of motherhood. Anyway, I don't know what'll happen with the treatments, if we'll even proceed now, with Jonathan out of the house..."

Jonathan. He creeps back into my thoughts and for a moment I want to call and tell him, I wish he'd be happy for me, but understand that won't happen, that he too won't be able to see my desires amidst his own needs and wants. So I try with all my might to push him out of my mind and not think about what he'll say, but I see his bitter wrinkle deepen before I expel him from my thoughts. I look from Shabtai to Pinto, and my pulse increases as they wait for my response. "Are you sure?" I finally ask, and at once regret the question.

"Why, don't you think you'd be good?" Shabtai laughs and his belly dances. "Don't get too excited. There are other strong candidates and there's the tender and all that shit. But it's important that we make sure that the *relevant* candidates," he emphasizes the word "relevant," "apply."

"Thank you so much, I really appreciate it."

"If you decide to apply, there will be a standard tender," Pinto clarifies, "we just think you're one of the top candidates."

"What do you mean if?" Shabtai gives a dismissive wave, "of course she'll apply."

"You don't have to decide right away, think about it," Pinto says and smiles.

"Of course not right away," booms Shabtai, "you can give us your answer tomorrow." He laughs aloud, then pulls himself up by the chair's armrests into standing. "Okay, I'm running late for a meeting. If you have any questions, talk to Pinto," and he pulls his pants up over his belly again and exits the room and leaving us alone.

"You don't have to apply, just so you know," Pinto says. "It was important for us to offer it to you, but if it doesn't suit you... does it?" He asks, which stresses me out.

"Of course," I say quickly, then add, "I think."

"Of course or you think," Pinto insists, "because Shabtai is inclined toward Weiss."

"Oh, really?" I can't hide my disappointment. So what was this whole song and dance about if he's going to give the job to Weiss?

"Hey, Shagi," Pinto gets my attention back, "competition is healthy. And you have Rome to prove exactly what you're worth. But no stress, yeah?"

"Of course no stress. That suppresses ovulation."

"What?"

"Nothing, it'll be fine."

"Will it?" He insists, "and what about the baby?"

"What about him? I'm sick of my whole world and desires revolving around a baby. I don't know when I'll have a baby, but I know I want this job."

Pinto lifts his hands in surrender, "Okay, okay, no need to convince me," he smiles, "I'm happy we can keep working together."

I look him over, seeking hidden intentions. "Yes, we are good together," I look deep into the brown of his eyes, and he returns a penetrating glance of his own and I think, *There's something more, I'm not just imagining it*, and I keep staring even after we pass the point when you look away out of embarrassment or lack of interest, and for a moment I forget about Shabtai's suggestion, and Jonathan, and my mother, and just look for clues in Pinto's eyes, but then the shrill beep of the intercom interrupts and Pinto looks away and answers.

"Yes, Gidi."

"Your stand up with Kiki," Gidi's voice says from the speaker.

"Shit," says Pinto. "Coming."

12

For the past couple of days, he's got the feeling that someone's tailing him, breathing down his neck, hiding in the
shadows. But who? Who's after him? He can think of one person, the person he least wants to think about, even though,
to be honest, it's not working so well, the not-thinking, especially at night when he closes his eyes and there's no work, no
meetings, no jokes with the guys to distract him. But it's day-
time now and it's not in his head, he isn't paranoid, he knows
what a tail feels like. He could lose him if he wanted but it's
more important to figure out who's following him to the gym.

Every half minute he peeks at the rearview mirror to see the
Toyota Corolla still there, following him, nonchalant, to the entrance of the gym, parking four spaces behind him. He gets out
of the car, doesn't turn or look at the driver's face. Instead he
takes the stairs three at a time but doesn't enter the gym. He
takes the elevator down to the old, underground parking lot.
He comes back out into the street, some thirty meters behind
the white Toyota, whose driver appears not to have noticed
Weiss slipping away. Amateur. As Weiss jots down the license
plate number, it hits him and he's infuriated. He storms up to
the car from behind and bangs on the windshield with an open
hand. The driver jumps in alarm, collects himself, smiles and
rolls down the window.

"What's up, Weiss?"

"Pitussi, you loser," he rages. "Are you seriously tailing me?" Pitussi shrugs, looking uncomfortable. He did combat training with Weiss but they lost touch.

"You failed two polygraphs, Bro. People are concerned."

Weiss feels his cheeks redden, he balls his fists and forces himself to take deep breaths but his legs shake beneath him. This has gotten totally out of control. It can't be this bad. How did he become an Agency target? How can his career be in jeopardy? If he doesn't do something soon it'll all fall apart. His career will be ruined, Zoe will leave him, his father will die of shame. He'll die of shame.

He leaves Pitussi to watch over him and proceeds to lifting weights as if everything's fine. He nods to Yossi, the gym owner sitting, eating edamame in the entrance, and heads for the ab machine. Drake is singing over the speakers, it's still early and there are only three other people at the gym. The one closest to Weiss is working on his biceps. He's tall and thin, with very broad shoulders, and at certain angles, his pecs are visible through his tank top. He has a deep dimple in his chin and narrow eyes. He swings a large barbell and grunts every time he lifts it, disrupting Weiss' concentration. He tries to ignore him, but his gaze keeps wandering back to the revealing tank top and the muscles and the groans.

"Bro, keep it down, will you?" Weiss calls to him.

The guy looks at Weiss and keeps lifting. He grits his teeth but continues to grunt steadily from deep in his throat.

Weiss tries but is unable to calm the storm brewing in him. His blood is burning, his body piqued. *Why is it so hard for people to shut up?*

"That's enough," he calls to the guy, who turns to him.

"What's your problem?"

"You're my problem," says Weiss, knowing he should take a step back. That would be the responsible thing to do, but he's getting closer until he's facing him.

"Dude, it's a big place, go find some other corner if you don't like it here," the man tries.

"I like it here fine. This is exactly my spot right here," Weiss points at the floor. "But you are getting on my nerves." He pokes his finger into the guy's chest and comes a little closer rather than backing off, nearly touching him.

"Okay, what's wrong with you? Back off!" The guy reaches out and pushes him back, and that's all it takes for Weiss, especially now when everything is bubbling up and his grip is loose. In one quick motion he grabs the guy's hand, bends it backwards, pinning him against the mirror behind him, steaming up from his damp shirt.

"Hey, stop it!" Yossi shouts.

Weiss is breathing heavily, his face up close to the guy's, still bending the man's arm back. He feels the heavy breathing on his cheek and the sweat wetting his shirt. He presses even more, feeling the guy's body heat, twisting his arm further and hears him groan. He lingers for a moment, then another, and there is silence between them and sweat and a pulse and Weiss feels he's in dangerous territory and a disaster could happen any moment and in another moment it'll be too late. He releases his grip, pushes the guy aside, kicks the bench in his way and heads for the door.

"Come on," Yossi grips Weiss' shoulder and steers him away. "Sit down, rest, cool off, what's got you so edgy today?" Weiss doesn't respond, he's panting, wiping his forehead with his rough towel and gathers his things.

His heart pounding, he heads to his car with heavy steps, until he opens the door and sits down, drained. His phone flickers: four missed calls from Nofar. What does she want from him? As if he doesn't have enough problems. He doesn't have the energy to call her back, but now she's sending texts: *Call me back, now.* What's her problem? He's tired and ignores her messages but his phone rings again and again; it's her.

"What, Nofar?" He answers, exhausted.

"Where are you? I've spent the last hour trying to reach you."

"I was at the gym. What's with the hysterics?"

"Shabtai is looking for you. He asked me to locate you urgently."

He straightens up, starts the car, floors the gas and within fifteen minutes he's at the office.

Shabtai welcomes him with open arms and vigorous pats on the back, "Here's our champ, come, how was Rome? Spill the deets, want some cracker jacks?"

"He's on a diet," Pinto smiles and winks at him.

"Diets are for girls," Shabtai cries, gesturing for him to sit down.

Weiss gives Pinto a penetrating look, was he trying to humiliate or diminish him in front of Shabtai? He wants to give Pinto credit, but you can never tell, one should always be on alert. He smiles at Shabtai, takes a demonstrative handful of snacks from the bag and describes the meeting with Roccelli and the photos they found in the safe.

"We still don't know the timeline. That's the key thing to figure out right now."

"Yes," nods Shabtai, "it's crucial we don't fuck this up. We can't afford another snafu like in Brussels," he raises his eyebrows, "And you especially cannot afford it." Weiss looks at him, wondering if he knows, if this is a hint or threat or warning in case, in addition to the polygraph, he screws up. Is he the one who sent Pitussi after him? Is this how it'll be from now on, that no one'll ever believe or trust him again.

"Do you get why it's crucial that you look out for yourself in this op?" Shabtai asks.

Weiss nods feebly.

Shabtai smiles, not noticing how pale he got. "Because I want you to replace Pinto."

Weiss is speechless, his heart skips a beat, and a few seconds pass before the words translate into real meaning and his mouth widens into a big, involuntary smile. He was not expecting this. That is, sure he expected, hoped and even thought he deserved it, truly deserved it, but the pressure of the polygraph messed up his thinking, made him doubt himself and his future at the Agency, not just the promotion, but all of it.

When he had just joined the Agency, his brother Peleg asked him, "are you crazy, what do you want with them? Didn't you want to be an actor?"

"This is better than acting," Weiss replied. "This is real life."

"Leave it," his father interjected. "He won't last two days."

And during the long year of training, whenever he considered quitting, when he broke his nose in Krav Maga, sprained his ankle twice and tore a ligament, his father's words echoed in his head. He won't break. He'll prove it to his father. He'll prove it to everyone.

He tries to temper the smile as he tells Shabtai, "I'd love that, you know that."

"Yes, I do," Shabtai sighed, "But you're giving us trouble. What's this I'm hearing about the polygraph?"

"I'm taking care of it," Weiss replies quickly.

"Weiss," Pinto stops him, "you already promised me you'd take care of it."

"Yes," Weiss nods, "I did."

"So, what's the latest?"

"I'm taking care of it," Weiss mutters. "By the way, you know that I'm being followed?"

"What do you mean?"

"I mean I caught Pitussi tailing me today on the way to the gym. Is that it? You've run out of things to do?"

"I didn't know about that," Pinto grows serious, "That's not right, I'll check how that got past me. But Weiss, listen, sort it out. I can only cover for you for so long and keep up business as usual. I trust you, but I need to put this behind us."

"Yeah," mumbles Weiss.

"The promotion isn't in your pocket," Pinto insists. "Fishman's in the running too."

Weiss bites his lip. Fishman. Always a step behind him, like gum on your shoe, like a leech, lurking, waiting for him to slip so she can step on him on her way to the promotion.

Shabtai rises and concludes, "I trust Weiss'll do what he's gotta do, right, my man?"

"Of course," Weiss replies immediately, but doesn't meet his eye.

13

I'm sitting alone on the balcony, breathing with the wind, in and out, trying to calm my tingling nerves and repeating to myself, "I'm gonna get that job;" then firmer, "I am going to get that job!" When my phone rings, I almost shout into it, but it's Jonathan and I hold myself back, answering in a livelier voice than usual.

"You sound pleased," he sounds suspicious.

"Yes, I am," I try to convey restraint. I know I have to break the news to him gently.

"I heard you met with Dalit," he says.

"Ah, yeah," I reply. Shit. I don't want him thinking that's why I'm pleased.

"She called. She told me your heart's in the right place," he goes on.

I don't know what that means, I think. "I don't know what that means," I say and feel my excitement give way to the more familiar feelings of anger and disappointment.

"She told me I should come home," he updates me matter-of-factly.

"*Dalit* said that you should come home. *Really*," I emphasize, "Good thing *Dalit* said it. Maybe you'll listen to her. What's she doing calling you anyway? Is that part of therapy?"

"Don't get upset. She's on your side," he tells me gently, as if it's the relationship between me and Dalit that matters. As if he has nothing to do with it.

"And you?" I shoot at him.

"What about me?" He sounds surprised.

"Are you on my side?" I ask him.

"I am on *our* side," he replies. Why can't he just say yes? 'Yes, I'm on your side,' is that so hard?

"So, you're only on my side if it serves you too?"

"Did I say that? Why do you do this, Vishi? What's with you?" Jonathan tries to keep calm, but I can hear in his voice that he's no longer his reserved self which is kind of gratifying. I don't want him feeling like the mature, reasonable one all the time. I don't want him and Dalit discussing whether my heart is in the right place or deciding what the right place is for me.

"They want me to apply for Pinto's position," I say, disregarding my plan to break it to him sensitively. I kind of want to shock him.

"What do you mean?" Jonathan has a tendency to deny news that he does not want to receive. No wonder my mother likes him. They have a lot in common. Both act like their wishes are the only ones that count and are disappointed and hurt when reality proves otherwise, as if an unsigned contract was violated.

"What do you think it means?" I answer with a question.

"I didn't even know that Pinto's leaving: Didn't you think to tell me?" His tone is no longer restrained, but it's not as satisfying as I'd hoped.

"I was waiting for the right moment," I reply.

"And *this* is the right moment?" He asks angrily, "I thought we said that you'd slow down at work."

"We agreed that I would slow down for the treatments, not forever. Anyway, a promotion doesn't just happen overnight," I reply.

"And what did you think? That you'd get pregnant and then gear up? How does that work exactly?"

"If you want something enough, you make it work," I tell him, refusing to listen to the small voice inside wondering if he's right and I'm deluding us both.

"We'll figure it out," I say decisively, both to Jonathan and the little voice.

On the other end of the line, Jonathan says nothing. I can hear his quiet, measured breaths. "That's not good enough," he says, and after a short pause adds, "I need to go."

"Good for you, Vishi, I'm proud of you," I mumble to myself, the phone still in my hand. Not that I really expected him to be pleased. It's unrealistic to expect him to be happy about it. After all, he doesn't want me to advance, I know that. He wants me to quit and find "normal" work with "normal" hours and be a "normal" wife, and makes me feel abnormal because I don't want any of that.

The excitement of moments ago is gone and in its place, the abyss of Jonathan's disappointment gapes before me again.

For so many years I've lived for others, placating them and meeting their needs. I always did what was expected of me, and all that I expected in return was love. But I've had enough. I don't want love that demands such a high price, I need to know that I'm loved because of my ambition and not in spite of it. And this new need to be seen has ignited in me a great, insatiable hunger, that I shouldn't have to compromise, and despite attempts to suppress it, it will multiply and spread, like a black hole that cannot be filled. And although I know who I am, not only what others want me to be, dismissing my needs deepens the hole, and because its foundation is so brittle, the slightest touch can shatter it and let all the doubts rush back in.

"You can't do things just to please others all your life, what kind of life would that be?" Maya once reprimanded me in 11th grade when I consulted with her about whether to sleep with Itamar Bergman. We were going out for four months and I was smitten like only a 17-year-old girl who is going out with the volleyball team captain can be. I had already gotten naked with him, but I did not feel ready to go all the way; on the other hand, I knew that he had done it with two girls before me. Not that he pressured me, but I knew exactly what he wanted and I could see it in the faces he made, which I wanted to avoid. I was always afraid people would be unhappy with me.

Ultimately, I didn't sleep with him, maybe partly to please Maya. He didn't say anything about it, but broke up with me after five months, and two weeks later started going out with Osnat Gavrielov who had a nipple piercing, and I don't know what happened between them, but he looked very pleased, and I spent the next six months wondering what would have happened if I had slept with him and how painful a nipple piercing was.

"What would have happened? Nothing would've happened," spat Maya, who even back then had a kind of conviction that I lack to this day. "You think if you'd slept with him you wouldn't have broken up? It might have taken longer, but in the end it would have happened anyway. Ultimately, everything comes to an end."

"You're still here?" Pinto pokes his head out on the balcony where I've been sitting and staring ever since the conversation with Jonathan. I shrug. "What're you doing here alone? ... Up for a run?" Pinto asks.

I am. I want to escape my thoughts and release some endorphins and get back some of that vitality that filled my belly just now. I put on my running clothes in the changing room and try to recreate the excitement, declaring in my head, "I'm going to get the promotion," but now it embarrasses me. I sound pathetic and am unable to understand how an hour ago this childish self-talk worked on me.

I join Pinto, both in black lycra, and we head out through the compound gate. Pinto's pace is usually much faster than mine, but not today. As we run, our feet hitting the ground, I'm filled with adrenaline, galloping ahead, startling birds, kicking aside pebbles and feelings of guilt. After forty minutes I'm a bit tired. Pinto notices and adjusts his pace to mine. *Breathe*, he motions to me with motions. Or *take it easy*, or something like that which says, *I care about you, I'm with you*. But I must have been running too fast because I start to get dizzy and my head is pounding and my mouth is dry and I slow down more and more, and don't feel relief but the opposite. Something in my head blurs until I have to stop entirely. Pinto looks concerned, which is kind of nice but also kind of embarrassing. I don't want him to see me as weak, or to keep taking care of me. I want to be strong and worthy, but the dizziness almost knocks me over; he supports me back to the office and I lean on him, and between bouts of spinning I also enjoy this closeness and the gentleness with which he holds me and doesn't let go until we reach his office; he sets me down so he can pour me water and then everything goes black.

14

I open my eyes and am momentarily blinded by the bright fluorescent lights. I close them and turn my head. When I open them again, there's a blurry face close to mine. I blink until I see better and, like in an old movie, the face grows sharper until I recognize Pinto, and he's so close that I notice the faded freckles on his nose for the first time and the little scar at the corner of his mouth. I inhale his black coffee smell, and his breath warms my face like a cloud of cardamom and longing and my eyes fill with tears.

This proximity is unsettling and I have no idea how I got here. Pinto comes even closer, his lips now drawn in a half-smile and he brushes aside a strand of hair that fell across my forehead. He doesn't speak and I realize that in another second his lips will touch mine, and I wait for contact, not daring to move closer myself. How long has it been since I had a first kiss—I almost forgot that the body can be this thrilled by a kiss that hasn't even happened, by lips that have not yet touched.

For a moment, the image of Jonathan pops into my mind, and he fixes me with his critical expression, chin down and eyebrows up, shaking his head and clicking his tongue. And that's what decides it for me, that *tsk*. Because if it had been the Jonathan who bought me guinea pigs when he heard I'd never had a pet; or the Jonathan who then braved the smell of the guinea pigs and didn't insist we return them; or the Jonathan who carried me around the house for a whole month after I broke my leg, then maybe I would have stopped, let that cardamom scent waft past me, wiped the tear from the corner of my eye and got out of there. But those Jonathan s haven't been around for a long time now. And only the tongue-clicking Jonathan remains: Jonathan who brings his laptop to bed; who replaced the Edison bulbs that I bought for the living room with energy efficient LED bulbs; who thinks my promotion ambition is another passing craze; Jonathan who left the house without saying a word and is now on his mother's sofa eating date cookies. I won't stop this for him.

I look at Pinto's tanned skin and black stubble, and his mocha, almond-shaped eyes. My heart is beating the rhythm of an African drum and my breaths are short. I open my mouth to get some air and think maybe he'll take it as a hint, a kind of foreplay of lips and breaths, and I stop myself from licking my bottom lip. But why not actually? Why not hint to him to close the gap between us? Why shouldn't I do it myself? Whose feelings am I always considering? Why don't I do what *I* want for once?

I want Pinto. Yes. This is what I want. It's happening. My heart beats faster and my smile is hesitant and I rise slowly to bring my lips closer to his.

"Hang on, don't rush," his lips suddenly speak, and the voice coming from them is too loud, and still far away, and I feel a stabbing pain in the front of my head. My head—it's heavy and it's on the floor, and I notice that I am sprawled on the floor in an uncomfortable position and that my shirt is soaked.

Pinto's smile masks concern and I notice the wet towel in his hand, "Don't get up, Shagi, you just fainted."

I turn my head despite the piercing pain and see my feet propped up on Pinto's ugly mustard sofa and my pink sneakers soiling the seat cushions.

"I called an ambulance to be on the safe side," he adds.

An ambulance? Why? His words jolt me out of the fog and back to reality. I cross my legs and try to get up, but the room is blurry again and Pinto hurries to support me and lay me down gently on the sofa. He tells me that I fainted and that it took me a few seconds to wake up and I need to get checked. I look at him, looking for hints of the kiss that maybe almost happened a moment ago, but he's inscrutable, practical as ever. He takes my bag and coat, keys and phone, holds my arm and leads me out of the office on our way to his Mazda in the senior staff parking lot.

We are walking down the hallway, his arm around my waist, pulling me to him, and I know that he's just helping me walk and has no other intentions. Still, my skin is tingling from the closeness and I don't know if my legs are failing from dizziness or because of him, and I just hope that he doesn't notice, while holding me, that my waist has grown a bit thicker in recent months.

The ambulance can't come into the office park, so we're heading to the address that Pinto gave them. He keeps stealing glances at me, but every time I seek his eyes they're back on the road too quickly for me to detect anything more than concern.

When we arrive the medical team is already waiting. I stay in the passenger seat and watch a big, redheaded guy with wild, wavy hair and two good-looking high school girls with ripped jeans and expressions of self-importance burst out of the ambulance, all dressed in white with the red Star of David of the first responders.

"Well this is the first time the patient arrived after us. Where'd you guys come from?" He surveys Pinto, hiding behind the black jacket collar, zipped all the way up, and dark sunglasses, "Shhh, we don't mention that, ah?" He winks and gestures with his head in the general direction of the office. "So, how are we doing?" He raises his voice and crouches at my feet.

I hate when people talk to me in the royal we, as if we're on a kibbutz, and don't hurry to answer. He grabs my wrist to take my pulse, and on the inside of his arm I see a big, colorful tattoo of a heart with leaves curling around it, and in big red letters in the middle it reads "Mom," and it looks both beautiful and painful.

"She fainted," Pinto begins to speak and goes quiet when I give him a look. He gestures in my direction and says, "Go on, your honor."

"I fainted," I try to say in a respectable voice, despite the wet shirt and the trembling voice.

The two young women quickly open their big bag. The blonde one with the bob and the perky boobs wraps the blood pressure cuff around my arm, while the brunette with hair down to her butt and the piercing in her chin fills out a form.

"I see," the redhead nods, "Do you have a history of fainting? Low blood pressure? Anemia?"

"No," I shake my head.

"Eighty over fifty," the blonde announces and releases me from the cuff. She looks a bit like Taylor Swift and she annoys me.

He nods at her and continues, "Do you take any regular medications?"

"I am doing fertility treatments, I have the whole plan in my bag," and I rifle through my things and produce the test plan that they printed for me at the clinic, straighten it and hand it over to the redhead.

As the paramedic looks it over, I hear Pinto chatting with Taylor Swift with the perky tits and her giggling. How quickly we learn to giggle.

"Good," the redhead claps his hands together. "You're coming with us for further testing. Is there anything you need to take with you?"

"No, I don't need to go anywhere, I'm fine, really," I try to get out of the car to show that I'm fine, but get dizzy and sit back down.

"You're coming," he smiles kindly at me. "Let's make sure you're really fine, alright?" I reluctantly agree. Pinto sits in the front seat, and I insist on sitting on the bench with the volunteers rather than lie on the stretcher. Pinto turns around to continue talking to the blonde paramedic, asking about her studies and if she wants to be a doctor; out of politeness he asks her friend questions too and only once asks me how I'm doing.

When we arrive, the paramedic hands my forms to reception and calls to Pinto, "Look after her," which would annoy me, but I'm just relieved to be rid of Taylor, wave a friendly goodbye, and we sit and wait. There are no numbers here and no way to know if we'll wait twenty minutes or twenty-four hours.

Pinto doesn't sit. He takes off his jacket and goes to ask the receptionist how long we'll have to wait and is there any way to move my turn up, then disappears down the hall and returns with a bottle of mineral water and an energy snack for me. "You said you didn't eat all day," he says, sits down beside me and then gets back up to change the channel on the TV until he reaches a news flash.

With his arm raised like that, his running shirt rises to reveal a small handbreadth of the side of his stomach. This is the soft, exposed, hairless area by the pelvic bone, overlooked in abdominal exercises, the part that reveals weakness. He's tanned there, Pinto, but not like the parts of his body that are always exposed, more of an old, pale tan, a reminder that there was a time when he was free to go to the beach, open a bottle of beer and just be a guy at the beach and not the Agency's Pinto.

He notices that I'm staring and looks at me inquisitively, "Need anything? Give it to me, give me something to do, make me useful."

116

I disconnect from his exposed skin and say, "Just sit down, it's stressing me out, you constantly running back and forth."

He sits, but stands back up every time the receptionist lazily drags herself to her station, and every five minutes checks if I need something else. I tell him no, but he still gets up and goes to buy me a pastry and orange juice at the booth by the elevators.

I am called by a nurse who takes a urine and blood sample, interrogates me about the treatments, the hormones and medications, and sends me back to wait. Two paramedics burst into the waiting room, leading a stretcher bearing a young man, looks not yet eighteen, his head in a neck brace. "Motorcycle accident," they tell the receptionist in a panic, "Head and neck injury." The receptionist nods and the bed disappears quickly down the hall. Pinto, who arrives with the pastry and the glass of juice, watches the stretcher being wheeled away, looks around, takes a deep breath and opens the bottle of sparkling water that he bought for himself.

"What?" I ask.

He waits for a moment before replying, "I have a hard time with hospitals ever since..."

"Since Shahar?"

"Yes," he says, and I recognize the expression on his face.

Sometimes I forget that it wasn't just my family that lost Shahar, that he had a whole life and left a void in places outside our home, too.

I didn't visit Shahar at the hospital. My parents consulted with a psychologist who said it wasn't necessary, that it wouldn't give me anything, and it might even be better if I didn't. That's how she was. Groping her way through ambiguity until she said what she really wanted to say. I liked her a lot. Her name was Shelly and she had long, wavy, red hair that

117

she would gather at the back of her neck with a girlish bow, a round face and baggy, colorful clothing; I wanted her to be my mom. Not that I thought that was possible, I was too old and too realistic for that, but I knew if it was up to me, I wouldn't hesitate to turn my back on my actual mother who in those days was busy chain smoking and shouting at my father to get out of bed and do something with himself, and go with Shelly, if only she would offer. We would play Atlas at her clinic and she would bring embroidery thread and sometimes we made bracelets and when I wanted we talked a bit about my feelings, and when I didn't we kept making bracelets, and she never made me feel guilty that I wasn't talking about what I was going through, or that I was talking too much, and she never said, "Look what you're doing to your father," and I could just tell some trivial story from school, about how Shir sat beside Oron even though she knew I liked him, and how I didn't say anything even though I was hurt by it.

"Does that happen anywhere else?" Shelly asked, "that you don't say what you're feeling or what you want?"

"Yeah," I shrugged, "sometimes."

"When, for example?" She tilted her head in a listening gesture.

"For example when I want to listen to music but Dad's resting all day, or when I want someone to take me to a friend's house but Mom and Dad are in one of their moods where they act like everything's normal, even though obviously nothing's normal, or when I miss Shahar but I know that if I start talking about him then my Dad's face will fall and Mom will start crying."

"Can you say more about his face falling?"

That was how she talked. She wouldn't ask what expressions he made but if I could say anything else about it, and wouldn't say, 'Let's keep talking about it, ' but 'Let's stay with that for a moment. 'But I didn't want to say anything else and I didn't want to stay with it for a moment, so I kept tying knots on the bracelet without answering, and that was okay.

"Are you okay?" I switch off the memory of Shelly's red curls and come back to Pinto.

"Yes," he says although his face still hasn't resumed its usual shade of tan.

"Do you miss him? Shahar?" I ask when he finally sits down beside me.

"Less and less," he says with an apologetic smile. "I miss the idea of him more than *him*. The idea that I have a best friend that I can trust with my life. I haven't had that since he died."

I also miss the idea of having a brother. When I was younger, I got some strange pleasure from going to Shahar's memorials and hearing people talking about me as 'Shahar's sister.' I haven't been anyone's sister in years.

I let Pinto drink some of my juice, which he inhales big sips, then wipes his mouth with the back of his hand like a construction worker in an ad for milk. Then, after his shoulders sink some distance from his ears, and he leans back limply, he gives me updates about his kids. The eldest is already in third grade and the younger girl started first grade this year, and how they give little kids so much homework, and who remembers all the grammar rules anyway? He didn't understand it even when he was in school, so how can they expect him to help his child with homework? Are there tutoring sessions for dyslexic parents? And they need to build a model of the Western Wall for the national heritage lesson, and host a group of six girls who only want to do arts and crafts with glitter, and anyway, girls are tons of glitter and driving to swim class and capoeira and ballet.

"All that? How many extracurriculars do they do?" I stop him.

"Forget it, let's not get into that, Orli wanted more. She says I'm cheap and skimping on my kids. I tell her she spoils them.

She says she loves them. I say there are all kinds of different ways to show love. She says it's interesting that I'd say that because she never saw any kind of love from me."

I met Orli once, at a departmental meeting, when they were still married. Her name is pronounced Or-*li*, with emphasis on the second syllable. She's a lawyer, tall and upright. Not super beautiful but impressive in her narrow skirt with her narrow waist, perfect makeup and stilettos. I never understood her and Pinto's connection. She sat on the side with a polite smile, listening to all the fart and sex jokes of the department guys, but her smile disappeared when they started talking about Nofar's ass, and I thought how she must think I'm pathetic for letting them talk like that around me, that she'd have put them in their place in an instant. It's easy to judge from the sidelines. Let her try convincing an entire department that calls her a downer, and humorless, and "What's wrong, Fishman? You offended? Your ass is great too, turn around for a sec so we can see."

"What? Didn't you tell her you loved her?" I ask Pinto.

"I did. Sometimes. I'm not great at expressing things," he plays with his bottle of water. "I show it with actions," he says, then looks at me and I look at the orange juice in my hands.

"Avishag Fishman!" The receptionist's hoarse voice makes me jump. She is holding an old pink cardboard binder in her upraised hand and waiting.

Pinto and I stand up, I look at him and smile, and he hesitates for a moment, then sits back down. When I reach the counter, the receptionist holds out the binder and says with a blank expression, "You have to go to women's emergency."

"What? Why?" I refuse to take the binder from her outstretched hand, "Did you find something in the tests?"

"I don't know, it's what the doctor decided, ask there," she holds the binder out again.

"The doctor still hasn't even seen me," I insist.

She shrugs, places the binder down on the counter and calls the next patient.

I try to speak with restraint, "Could you please ask the doctor if he could come out for a moment and talk to me?"

"He can't. He's working," she says, still printing stickers for the patient before her.

"Yes," I speak slowly, "I am his work. I came to the ER and I am asking that you address me and not just pass me from one person to the next."

Without a word she leaves the counter and disappears into one of the rooms. Minutes pass and she doesn't come back. I'm tired standing and drag myself back over to Pinto.

"They want to send me to the women's ER."

"Why?"

"The nurse doesn't know and the doctor isn't interested in speaking to patients. He's working."

"What do you mean, not interested?" Pinto sits up straight, "I'll talk to him," he declares, but just then I hear a tired, monotone voice.

"Yes, please, which one's Fishman?" Calls a short, unshaven man in rumpled uniform, a stethoscope around his neck.

We jump up and I get dizzy again.

"Come," he turns and goes into one of the rooms.

He sits behind an empty table and looks at us, bleary-eyed. "Yes, what's the issue?"

"That's what I wanted to ask," I reply, sitting facing him, "They told me to go to women's but didn't say why."

"Pregnant women are treated in the women's ER," he replies.

"But I'm not..." I hurry to reply and then stop, "I'm pregnant?" I look at the doctor, then Pinto, then back at the doctor. Neither of them reply. "You're telling me I'm pregnant?"

"Yes, that's what I'm telling you," he replies in a tired voice. "Now, please, would you be willing to go to women's ER?"

I want to answer but can't because my stomach is flipping, my diaphragm contracts, a large lump rises and burns in my throat and in a moment I throw up the energy bar, the pastry and the orange juice that Pinto bought me on the floor.

The doctor's face does not move a muscle. "I'll call the janitor," he says in the same tone in which he told me I'm pregnant and stands.

I rise after him but the room goes black for a moment and I stumble back into the chair.

"I will also request a wheelchair," says the doctor and leaves the room.

15

"Vishi!" Jonathan bursts into the room, panting. His starched shirt has come partially untucked and his forehead is sweaty. "Pinto called and said I should come," he stops to catch his breath, "Are you okay?" He hesitates a moment, then hugs me.

I look at Pinto over Jonathan's shoulder and he nods. Jonathan pulls away to look at my face and I feel tears wet my cheeks. He's scared.

"Avishag—what happened?" he strokes my head carefully.

"I'm pregnant," I say in a choked voice.

It's been barely an hour since the less than celebratory announcement of my pregnancy and the lump in my throat finally loosens. But crying does not ease the sense of anguish. I shouldn't feel anguished, of course. I should feel butterflies and joy and new life sprouting inside me. But I don't.

Jonathan straightens, his eyes wide. "You're what?" A tentative smile creeps across his face.

"Pregnant," I whisper.

"You're pregnant?" He cries and hugs me again, tightly this time, and I worry he'll tear off my IV bag. "I can't believe it!" He leans back and holds my face in his hands, "I knew we'd do it, I knew it! I told you!" He lifts a hand for a high five and I hesitate, then raise mine and give him a passionless clap. I wonder if he can see the lack of desire. If he can see me.

I can see Pinto out of the corner of my eye. He looks at me with a small smile, and leaves the room without a word. I don't want him to go.

"Wait," cries Jonathan, and for a moment I'm confused, thinking he wants Pinto to stay, but of course he isn't and neither am I. "I don't get it," he says, "how are you pregnant if you got your period three weeks ago?"

"The doctor said that some spotting in early pregnancy can happen during implantation and doesn't necessarily indicate a failed pregnancy attempt," I recite.

Jonathan nods, takes the ultrasound picture in my hand and examines my gestational sac. Then he sits on the bed next to me, holding my hand and crushing it in his excitement.

"That hurts," I tell him, and he apologizes and releases his grip a bit but it still hurts.

He looks at me gently and says, "We still need to talk, but let's try to be happy about this for a moment. You'll see, from now on things will be on the up for us."

I nod. I really try to be happy and I really want to believe that things will be better, but I can't forget how he left the house not long ago, and also the fact that alongside the fetus, an ecstasy pill bubbles in my belly. The doctor reassured me that it happens to lots of mothers before they know they're pregnant, but they aren't me and they didn't wait such a long time for this pregnancy and they don't have so much to lose.

"You're pale. I bet you're exhausted," he says and puts his hand on my cheek like I once loved. "Do you want me to turn off the lights?" I nod again. The truth is obscured in the dark. Jonathan switches off the fluorescent lights and then sits back down on the bed beside me. "Sleep," he says.

There's no chance I'll fall asleep with him sitting so close to me on the narrow bed, all excited and happy. How long since I saw him happy. How long we waited for this. I feel like it's hard to breathe. As I close my eyes I can feel Jonathan's gaze boring into me. I open my eyes and he smiles, close them again and don't open them until he quietly rises and leaves the room. I hear him ask one of the nurses where he can buy something to eat and only then do I fall asleep.

"Come!" Scolding outside the door wakes me with a start. "Here, Room 4, I told you Room 4," I recognize my mother's voice from the hallway and look around for Jonathan. He's standing by the window looking guilty.

"Sorry," he whispers, "she called me when she couldn't reach you. What could I do? You know I can't lie."

He doesn't get through speaking when my mother bursts into the room, carrying a huge pineapple-printed canvas bag, as usual, with a scarf and umbrella sticking out, bags from the bakery, and my father, who she dragged after her with his head down. "This is Room 5," he mumbles.

"Fine, Room 5, are you going to hold that against me all day?" My mom says, dumping her stuff on the floor.

"Hey, Shagi, good to see you," my dad approaches my bed and kisses me on the forehead. He gently lifts my chin, as if to check that I'm okay, and then sits down in the armchair in the corner of the room.

"Shagileh, Baby, congratulations! Let me look at you, how are you feeling?" My mother rushes towards me.

"I'm fine," I say quietly and she interrupts.

"How I worried, my heart nearly dropped when Jonathan told me what happened. Well, come on then, can we see the baby?" She points at the switched-off screen.

"It's not a television, you can't just turn it on," I say with restraint. "There's a picture, want to see?"

"Okay, a picture then," she sighs. I hand her the ultrasound picture and she snatches it from my hand, "Oy, how sweet, it looks like a diamond ring," she caresses the aura of my uterus in the picture, "Look, Avner, this is my grandson."

"Or granddaughter," my father mutters from where he's sitting deep in the armchair.

"Right," she agrees reluctantly. But she wants a grandson.

"Shagi," she sits down beside me on the bed and strokes my cheek. I yield to her caress, close my eyes and let my body relax from the whole day for a moment.

"Shagi," my mother says again softly, "I want you to call him Shahar."

My body stiffens, "Are you joking?"

"Why would I be joking?" She replies at once in the offended tone that she uses as if on cue, "I always knew that when I had a grandson, he'd be called Shahar."

"*You* always knew?" My voice comes out shrill and Jonathan puts a hand on my shoulder. I shake it off and continue. "Did you ever think to ask me what *I* want? Or you want to make this decision for me, like every other decision in my life?"

"Oh, come on, enough with the drama," says the Meryl Streep of Givatayim. "Who's making decisions for you? We're just chatting."

"And I am just telling you that there's no chance we'll call him Shahar. And anyway, what's that got to do with anything right now? I'm in the sixth week. We don't even know it's a boy."

"Shahar is a pretty name for a girl, too."

"We're not calling anyone Shahar!" I scream, and Jonathan puts his hand on my shoulder again.

"What are you giving me that look for?" I bark at him too, "You want to name your child after his dead uncle?"

"Vishi, let's not have this conversation right now," he gives one of his diplomatic responses which only annoys me more.

"Jonathan's right," my mother nods and exchanges looks with him as if the two of them are on the side of reason here. "We have plenty of time to talk about it."

"You've all gone crazy," I mutter and turn to lie on my side, "I want to rest now."

I think that I hear the word "hormones" said in a whisper, before the room door opens again.

"Jonny!" The high-pitched voice of Rina, Jonathan's mother, fills the room. "How are you? Avishagi, sweetheart, let me see you," she quickly circles the bed, bends down and kisses me on both cheeks, and the scent of her perfume burns in my nose. "Oy, sweetheart, you're so pale, have you eaten? Jonny, did she eat anything?" She looks at Jonathan who is quick to nod. "You have to look after her, look at her, she's all skin and bones! I brought you schnitzel and pasta."

"I brought pastries," my mother rustles the plastic bag that she brought with her.

"Nahama'leh," Rina turns to my mother and hugs her, "How are you? Well, how about Avishagi? Growing our next generation here," she pats me lightly on the belly.

"Touch wood," says Jonathan.

"Touch wood," my mother repeats after him.

"Of course touch wood, of course," Rina agrees, "Alright, you must want to sleep now," she strokes my head. "Let's give her some quiet, they opened an Aroma Cafe downstairs. Tea and pastries on me," she comes closer and covers me before gathering her things and leaving the room.

My mother hurries to me too, to straighten the blanket and pull it even tighter around me. She then grips my father's hand and they leave. Jonathan comes and bends over me.

"If you tuck in this blanket too, I'll suffocate," I whisper and he just smiles and gives me a kiss on the forehead and then on the lips and then on the belly through the blanket. He leans his head on my lower belly and I remain frozen while he hugs me around the waist with both hands, closes his eyes and remains there for a few moments. I deliberate if I'm meant to stroke his head now, it seems appropriate, but I don't really feel like it. Maybe I'll just put a hand on his shoulder, something to convey that I'm not totally ignoring him but also not totally drawn into this instant intimacy. But I can't bring myself to reach out and touch him and he's already pulling away and sitting quietly on the armchair in the corner of the room.

16

With each passing day his lungs contract, his airways constrict, and he's running out of air without a solution. It's like he's in tenth grade again, when his friends caught him in a lie. He doesn't know what he was thinking when he told them that he had kissed Sharona, the prettiest girl in their grade. Within three minutes his friends called Sharona over to the smoking corner where they sat and asked her if they'd kissed. He never forgot her expression of shock and rejection.

"What? No!" She cried, as if they could not have accused her of anything worse. "Why would I kiss him?" She pursed her lips in disgust. He ran home in the middle of the day and didn't come back to school for a week. Faked a fever and didn't answer calls from his friends. When he got back to school, nobody brought it up again.

But he's not in school anymore and problems no longer disappear when you ignore them long enough. On his way to the Agency, he sees people walking around or driving by him. Everyone looks mediocre to him, unexceptional, lacking essence, wandering the world aimlessly. He might soon be one of them.

At the office, he walks quickly down the corridor and nearly smacks into Fishman.

"Everything alright, Weiss?" She asks, searching him with her eyes.

"Sure, peachy," he replies, making himself relax his strained forehead. "Everything's cool," He repeats, "Congrats on the pregnancy, eh?" He says, so she'll stop looking so pleased with herself. He sees her face freeze, "What, did I say something I shouldn't have?" He plays dumb. A look of anger is always better than a look of pity.

"No, thanks, everything's fine," Fishman replies, still cold.

"You sure? Because I once said the wrong thing to my brother's pregnant wife and boy—if looks could castrate. Anyway she was crazy hormonal."

Fishman doesn't reply, and now he's clearly annoying her, which also makes him feel like he's in control, coming back to his usual self, and he goes on, "I really am happy for you. Now I can say that I didn't think it was a good idea for you to replace Pinto, just being super honest, yeah?" He put his hand on his left shirt pocket, "I really do respect you, you know, but what do you need that job for? Even if you hadn't gotten pregnant now, it would've happened in another year, two years tops? How long would your husband have been willing to wait? And then what? You'd come back from your mat leave and work 240 hours a month? Let's not even get into the question of whether women can lead an op. I'm just saying that it doesn't make sense expecting you to juggle this with a kid, no?"

"Thanks for the warm words," she says drily, "I'm still applying for the position." This takes him by surprise, and he doesn't manage to say anything before she disappears into Pinto's office, where Pinto greets her with a smile. He momentarily surrenders to the jealousy that spreads through his veins and weakens his body, then straightens up and goes out into the corridor.

By evening he's back at the airport on his way to Rome. Even though he's sitting in the middle of the departure hall, near the fountains, he can still smell the sweet-sour-spicy smell of hundreds of cheap perfumes sprayed into the air by the overly made-up flight attendants. He hates the Duty-Free.

When he'd just started working at the Agency, he would always buy his father a gift on his travels, and bring it as an offering at Friday night dinner instead of flowers. His father never thanked him, but Weiss knew he was impressed. Nobody else in the family was abroad as much as him and nobody else understood whiskey like he did. And he kept up with the gifts – aftershave, cigarettes, even whiskey. Until he made the mistake of bringing his father a box of fancy cigars. His father examined the box for a few moments before blurting out, "That's it, you've finally become a fag?"

A muscle in the corner of Weiss' mouth twitched involuntarily. His brother Peleg came to his defense, "Why are you being like that, Dad? Even Bibi smokes."

"Bibi? This guy?" His father pointed at him with an open palm. "He wishes. Going around the world, pretending he's James Bond, all condescending, as if he's better than us."

"He didn't say he's better than..."

"Forget it," Weiss interrupted his brother. "I get it. You don't want gifts, no more gifts then."

"You see? Thinks he's a big shot, handing out gifts. You always were a little upstart."

Weiss rose and left the house, slamming the door, and didn't go back for two months, caving in only to his mother's pleas. But he no longer brought gifts, not even for birthdays, and he hates the Duty-Free.

He meets Roccelli in a little cafe, not far from Piazza Navona. After Roccelli passed the job interview, Weiss began to engage him with small tasks against the "students." With his guidance, Roccelli began getting closer to the students, offering them help with their studies, sometimes even doing their homework, getting access to their cellular devices and apartment and installing surveillance and tracking devices in them. Everything went so smoothly that the Agency raised a suspicion that Roccelli was a double agent.

"It's unlikely but not *so* far-fetched," said Pinto, telling Weiss to be careful.

"Come on, I can smell that kind of thing from miles away, no way he's playing with us, I'd sign off on him."

"Careful, don't fall too hard for him," said Pinto.

"What's that supposed to mean?" Weiss puffed up.

"Listen, I trust you," Pinto replied, "but still, we can't be complacent, never trust them too much, sources can be very volatile."

Weiss didn't argue, but inside he was unconcerned: he trusted Roccelli. He didn't look like the type to flip. On the contrary, he struck Weiss as naive. To the point that Weiss was still a little surprised each time Roccelli managed a task undetected. Besides, he obtained valuable information.

The information from the wiretapping further substantiated the suspicion that the planned attack was imminent. They began to talk amongst themselves more and more about the "celebration" that the students were organizing, talking about the guests that the Agency believed were the targets and even referred to someone as 'the boy' as someone who might help them. The Agency believed the boy was Roccelli.

At the cafe, Weiss approaches Roccelli and pats him vigorously on the shoulder. "Good to see you, what'll you have?"

Roccelli's cheeks are flushed, his hair combed to the side, and one plume stands straight up, making him look like a baby chick and he gapes at Weiss. Weiss tries to repel the emotions that arise in him at the sight of the young, excited face. He's an expert at this. A significant part of his life he has been warding off emotions, and in this moment his operational work requires it of him. In the background, Adele sings through the speakers about love, because that's what she does best, and Weiss does what he does best. He orders a slice of rich chocolate cake for each of them and praises Roccelli for his hard work, "And because you've really helped us out with this project," Weiss keeps spinning his web, "Now I want to help you."

"Listen," Weiss leans over toward him, moving the cake aside, "I know that your sister is in poor health," he speaks quietly. "I can help you with that."

"What do you...?" Roccelli tries to ask.

"Terrible illness," Weiss interrupts, "it comes for every family, my mom, too." He stops in order to take a deep breath and overcome the discomfort. "But thank God we managed to get her the best specialists. Medicine cost a fortune, but she's still with us," he forces a sad smile with his mouth closed.

For the most part he doesn't mind lying, it's like a language he's fluent in. Just sometimes, occasionally, the lie sticks in his teeth and he needs to spit it out, and something about Roccelli makes it hard for Weiss to lie to him. Not that he won't, yeah? Just without the pleasure of spinning the lie.

He takes a white envelope from his bag and hands it to Roccelli. He's pleased he has something to sweeten the meeting, like giving a kid a candy after a doctor's visit. "Take this," he pats the envelope.

Roccelli opens the envelope and sees bills.

"There's five hundred in there," Weiss says casually at the sight of Roccelli's widening eyes. "I think that's fair, given the work you've put in. I told you, we take care of our employees, and their families too," he sighs and places a big hand on Roccelli's. The young man's skin is smooth like a child's.

In training they'd learned techniques for establishing close contact. They were taught that touching the other person's hand in conversation creates intimacy. They practiced on one another and everyone laughed when Danino fondled Weiss' hand as if they were on a date. Weiss made obscene gestures back at him with his tongue.

Roccelli, breathing heavily, finally takes the envelope and says, "Thank you very much."

"Thank *you*," Weiss wraps Roccelli's hand in his two before letting go, "Just keep it up."

17

I leave the women's ER with a progesterone prescription and six sick days that the doctor, Jonathan and my mother persuaded me to take. Jonathan is waiting for me in the car because "there's nowhere to wait." He helps put my bags in the trunk and I get into the car.

He says, "let's go."

I look at him curiously. We hardly spoke this whole time. We were constantly surrounded by visitors and doctors and beeping devices, and now, without the monitor strapped around my belly, I feel practically naked. Now that it's just the two of us I don't really want to talk. The thought of what might be said, what truths may emerge, makes my stomach turn. This is not the time for truth, this is a grace period and I want to take comfort in the pregnancy and the serenity that it brings even if only for a moment, even if it is just an illusion of serenity. A child is a blessing, as they say, every child brings luck, I remind myself.

"Where to?" I ask Jonathan and try not to look him in the eyes.

"Home," he says, "for now."

"For now?" My pulse starts racing and the calm fades.

"We'll talk about it at home," Jonathan smiles, but I'm uneasy.

When we get home, Jonathan unpacks the bags, whistling pleasantly to himself, either ignoring my restlessness or unaware of it. Some involuntary urge draws my hands to my belly, to protect it or seek movement that does not yet exist; maybe when I feel it I'll understand what's happening a little better, what's happening to me. In the meantime I feel normal, only a little more tired, ripe, fearful, and I'm looking for that excitement I'm supposed to have, that must be in me somewhere, but maybe it's hard to differentiate between excitement and panic.

When the bags are empty and the cupboards are organized, Jonathan makes me green tea in a big mug, but I'm too hot and stressed, and I shake my head no and just wait for him to speak already.

"So I talked to Dalit, I shared what happened and consulted with her about how we should proceed," he says, blowing lightly on his tea, then taking a sip.

"Okay," I mumble.

"She suggested we take advantage of the sick days you took and have a little timeout. Let's get out of here and go somewhere, just the two of us."

I look at him, still not understanding, and he pulls his laptop from his bag, opens his inbox and turns the screen towards me. My eyes flutter over the details of the document before me until I recognize the words 'Carmel Forest' and look at Jonathan. He smiles a big smile of satisfaction. We were supposed to honeymoon there. It was a small dream that I waited a long time for, but at the last minute I was needed at work and we had to cancel the vacation. He remembered.

We still haven't spoken about what happened, all the truths have not been told, but maybe we don't need to, certainly not immediately. I'm pregnant and maybe that's enough, maybe that's all we needed for things to work out, for me to start feeling. I take a sip of my tea.

Even though I informed Pinto by phone that I'd be away

from work for the coming week, I pop by his office before we leave for the trip. I want to show some presence following a few days of absence, and also to see him. On the way I run into Weiss who makes it clear that he knows about the pregnancy. I might have expected a little more discretion around the office but no, everyone's got their nose in everyone else's business.

"I'm really happy for you," Weiss says and smiles too broadly. "Now I can tell you that I didn't think it was a good idea for you to replace Pinto anyway." I tense and tell myself, ignore him, just don't engage, but he doesn't stop talking and says it was predictable that I'd get pregnant soon because how long would my husband be willing to wait and how could you work 240 hours in a month when you're a mom? "And I won't even get into the question of whether women can conduct an op. Really, let's leave that aside. I'm just saying that it doesn't make sense for you to juggle work *and* a kid, no?"

"Thanks for your warm words," I tell him, "I'm still applying for the position," and I don't wait for his response, just head straight to Pinto's office, wanting to see him already, knowing he will comfort me.

He stands with his back to me, talking on the phone. "Well what can I do, she's on bedrest, at least I have Weiss who works like a whole team. He's doing great work with Roccelli," he only notices me after hanging up.

"I'm not on bedrest," I say coldly. "Just taking a few sick days, which is what I came to say. And by the way, I'd appreciate it if you could not discuss my pregnancy with the whole world, especially not Weiss."

"Shit, Fishman..." I note to myself that he didn't call me Shagi, "don't take it like that, just the director is on my back with this op. You obviously have every right to be on bedrest."

"But I'm not on bedrest," I spit the words like a curse, "I'll be back before you know it, stop acting like Weiss is doing this mission by himself."

The last thing I need, for them to take me out of the picture, and for being pregnant, on top of everything else. If Weiss gets exclusive credit for this operation, the promotion will be in his pocket. Shabtai is on his side as it is. My pregnancy will be an excellent excuse for why a woman should never hold the position. Not that I'm here to fight the fight for all women. I just want the job, and don't want my uterus to thwart me on my way, not to mention confirming Weiss' nonsense about what is or is not suitable for women.

Pinto seems to read my mind and says, "Don't worry, Weiss has his issues too."

"Like what?" I try to ask indifferently.

"There's some kind of hiccup with the information security unit."

"Weiss lied on his lie detector?" I raise my eyebrows.

"Twice," Pinto sighs.

"Wow. So who's in contact with Roccelli now?"

"He is," Pinto sighs. "There isn't anyone else, he already made a connection with him and I really hope that he'll solve this soon."

I don't.

"Anyways," Pinto goes on, "you see why the situation here isn't optimal..."

"Good thing I'm not on bedrest," I smile bitterly.

"Sorry," he reaches his hand out, thinks better of it and retracts it before it touches mine, "You're not offended, right?"

"No," I lie.

He looks at me and his phone rings. He doesn't answer and I wait for him to say something else but he just says, "Use this time off to rest," and answers the call.

We listen to Bob Dylan the whole drive to the hotel. Jonathan sings in a low voice and I join him for the chorus. When we get to the hotel parking lot and cut the engine, it brings a silence that follows us to the reception desk, through the elevator and all the way to our room. I'm quick to find a music station on the TV, but just then the news comes on so I mute it. We check the room, check each drawer, unpack our suitcases and toiletries and take out white robes and slippers. I stand before the full length mirror by the bed and roll up my shirt to examine my belly. There's no visible difference and I try to inflate it, envision it for just a moment, and the sight reflected at me is strange and alien. I release my shirt and sprawl across the huge white bed in the center of the room. Jonathan, now finished organizing, lies down beside me. We're side by side, alert, like soldiers before battle, afraid but purposeful, knowing what is expected of us, determined not to fail in our mission. Jonathan turns on his side with his face to me, and I take a deep breath, eyes closed, feeling his hand stroke my cheek and neck to my shoulders and back. How long has it been since we touched each other like this, just for the hell of it, and not with the hope that maybe this time will be the time. I turn to him and he smiles at me and kisses my lips. He whispers about the softness of my skin and kisses my neck. I bury my face in his shoulder and think of Weiss. I wonder what could be so important to conceal that he's willing to fail the polygraph. Jonathan slowly lays me down on my back, gentler than ever, as if protecting me, and protecting an additional someone. He opens my robe, my chest is a bit sensitive and painful, I move Jonathan's head away and he continues towards my belly and below.

No way he fell for information security, he's not that stupid, and he doesn't smoke weed or take questionable meds. Maybe steroids? I freeze and Jonathan looks questioningly at me, attentive to my movements. I shake my head as if to say everything's fine, but he's still frozen.

"What?" I whisper.

"Are you sure it's safe?"

"Don't worry, we won't get pregnant again," I say and pull him to me.

"Come on," he raises his head. "Are you sure we won't do any, y'know, damage?"

"They didn't tell us not to. Would you rather be celibate for nine months?" I look at him and he's alarmed.

"No, of course not... I don't know, I just wanted to make sure," he thinks, then adds, "Let's just be careful. To be on the safe side."

"Let's be careful," I agree and smile at him, and he seems to relax and resumes kissing me and I resume thinking about Weiss.

How terrible it would be for him, I think, if this is his downfall. And for what? More muscles? That doesn't make sense to me, but what do I know about the inner workings of his mind. How insecure would he have to be to risk this much? I wonder and feel my heart contract, and Jonathan entering me slowly.

But then I remember that he's in Rome now, moving ahead on my operation, at my expense, and my heart contracts again for totally different reasons. And in order to shake off Weiss and the promotion and Pinto's distance, I straighten up and Jonathan stops and looks at me in surprise, and I get on top of him and increase the pace and he holds me around the waist and tries to slow me down, maybe to remind me of the gentleness that we agreed on, but I'm not slowing down. I look deep into his eyes, so deep that I don't see him and all my muscles are straining and contracting and I'm close and then Jonathan finishes with a loud groan and I sigh.

"Are you okay?" Jonathan asks and holds me carefully.

"Sure," I reply and get off of him,

He strokes me and turns toward the bedside table, hands me a tissue and smiles, his face lit up. I clean myself off and look back at him. He looks unfamiliar and good-looking, like when we met, even more. His youthful face has matured, and the fine wrinkles enhance his manliness.

"All of his female coworkers have crushes on him," Maya's friend who introduced us told me. She worked with him in a student job in direct insurance during her masters. Even now he draws looks, even the receptionist giggled at him before handing us the room key. Some of his charm is in his indifference and distance, which can drive me insane, his ability to look over and not at things—not noticing the situation right before his eyes evidently adds a lot to sex appeal in a first impression. But aloofness doesn't work on me, and on our first date, I spent most of the time deliberating between different versions of saying, "it's not you it's me." I had no problem with his looks, on the contrary. Back then he was still wearing his carpenter's uniform: ripped jeans from his days, a cutoff shirt from his military officers' course, and the smell of sawdust in his hair mixed with the scent of his shampoo. At first I thought he was a country boy. But his way of talking was the opposite of his appearance: Restrained, measured and serious; not a trace of flirtation. My mother always warned me about flirts. They're the most charming and the most dangerous, she said, and Jonathan did not know how to flirt, he never did. All through dinner he sat and spoke to me in a sexy, low voice, and a penetrating look, about solid investment leads. But I didn't want solid. I wanted wild.

At the end of the date, he walked me home and when we reached my door he bent to kiss me. I planned to allow it and then to break up with him by text to avoid the awkwardness. In the two seconds until his lips touched mine I mentally prepared myself for a dry peck on the lips, restrained and measured like his way of speaking. But Jonathan did not kiss like he spoke. He kissed me like he worked the wood at the workshop. Strong and rough. He pulled me against him forcefully, touching me only lightly at first, slowly increasing the pressure of his lips on mine, placing a big, rough hand on my cheek, and then down to my neck and shoulder. My skin shuddered under the gentle sanding touch of his hand, caressing and scratching. He continued to slide down my shoulder, dropping the strap of the tank top I was wearing, holding the upper part of my arm tightly, and then pushed me from him, panting.

"Wow, Avishag," he sighed into my ear in a whisper that was more intimate than the whole conversation we'd had at the pub. Then he held me a little farther and smiled. "I'll call you tomorrow," he said, placing a warm hand on my cheek, leaving me wallowing in the puddle that was myself.

We lie in bed in silence; Jonathan is flipping through TV channels and I'm feeling sad. I think that since Shahar, some kind of neural grief pathway was burned so deep into me that every time my mind is idle, when it's not busy solving something or worrying or excited about something, it slips back into the sadness groove. My eyes still fill with tears sometimes, without reason, but I've mastered blinking them away. I've been training for this since childhood and nobody ever noticed. Except for Pinto.

"Shuggy," he would play with my family's nickname for me, "You might be able to fool your parents but not me. You wanna tell me what happened?" He would sprawl on the carpet and take off his army boots, choking the room with the pungent sweat smell. And I didn't want to say but I didn't want him to leave, so I didn't say anything about the smell and I didn't blink away the tears, I just stayed in his presence, and he would sit and stroke my head and let me beat him at checkers, and tell me stories about his commander and the undercooked cafeteria chicken, and about his girlfriend, which were the stories I liked best. She peeled pastries apart while eating and drank hot chocolate instead of coffee and her name was Shoshana and once he got into a fight with someone who laughed at her name. That was the most romantic thing I had ever heard and I decided that when I would have a boyfriend, he would also fight for me, and I was a little sorry I didn't have a weirder name.

Pinto filled some of the void in my heart, and for a while my relationship with Jonathan did too, but maybe it isn't fair to expect that to last forever, and maybe I hold a grudge against Jonathan for that. There were times when I believed that a child would help fill the hole, but I don't think I believe that anymore.

Jonathan and I wait at the entrance to the dining room for the hostess to mark our names on the guest list and direct us to our table. I feel Jonathan examining me and look back at him.

"Your hair looks good off your face," he says, tucking a strand behind my ear, and I smile at him and for a moment want to drag him back to the room and sleep with him, with real intimacy this time, but the hostess turns her attention to us.

"What?" Jonathan asks. I must have been staring at him too long.

"Nothing," I shake my head and follow the hostess.

After we order our entrees from the waiter, Jonathan goes through every ingredient on my plate to make sure it's allowed during pregnancy. When he has doubts, he calls over our waiter who confirms that the eggplant dish does indeed contain raw egg and Jonathan beams with pride, as if he saved me and our future child from destruction.

At the buffet I recognize Nili, a round-cheeked and over-friendly woman who I knew during my BA, loading dolmas dripping with oil onto her plate. I avoid eye contact, but she recognizes me and cheerfully approaches our table, a guy who does not appear connected to her lazily advancing behind her and sits down beside her when she kisses my cheek enthusiastically and tells us that this is the first time they've gone away since their son was born.

"Until now he was breastfeeding so he wouldn't let anyone else put him to bed. Do you have kids?" She asks.

Jonathan and I exchange glances. "No," I reply, careful not to give anything away too soon.

"Do it. There's no greater happiness," she says.

"Remember that when he wakes up *again* at two in the morning and won't go back to sleep," the man beside her says without looking at her.

"I'll remember. I'm the one getting up anyway," she replies without letting the smile drop and turns to me, "don't listen to him, children are a gift, don't waste any time."

"We're on treatments," I say.

"Oh really," says Nili and her euphoria does not appear affected. "You don't look like someone doing treatment."

"Why, what does someone doing treatment look like?" I raise an eyebrow, even though I know her intentions are good. Maybe I don't look miserable or bloated or hopeless enough.

"Forget it," Nili is quick to say, "I don't know why I said that, everything in its own time, as they say. I'm sure you'll manage and will be excellent parents," she prattled.

"How are you so sure?" I ask. Nili just shrugs and says, "I can see it on you, don't worry, it'll happen," and she gives me a pitying look, and I hate her and her round cheeks and her breast-feeding child and her silent husband, but she doesn't seem to notice and goes on chattering.

Their son is named Omri, he's two, and he knows how to sing the entire opening song of Fireman Sam. After our communications degree, Nili worked as a TV producer for a few years and really enjoyed it, "but the hours didn't suit me anymore," and then after giving birth, she changed careers and now works as a mortgage advisor at the branch of the national bank close to her house, which also gave them a great deal on this holiday. It turns out that she and Jonathan have common acquaintances at the bank so they spend the next twenty minutes naming other finance people that they might both know.

Nili's husband's name is Tomer, he doesn't talk much, just

wipes the balsamic dressing from the artichoke onto thick slices of bread, pokes the pieces into his mouth and chews with his mouth open. "So what do you do?" He asks me when Nili and Jonathan are engrossed in a discussion of different interest rates.

"I'm a marketing manager at a software company."

"Interesting," he smiles an amused half-smile and doesn't try to pretend that what I said really interests him. Something in his expression and the way that he looks me in the eyes and then scans my whole body makes me uncomfortable. But when he looks away I want him to look back, because I kind of enjoy his glances and because smug Nili with her cute child and her convenient bank job and her sense of absolute truth deserves it.

When we go back to the room, I undress, Jonathan brushes his teeth, and I think about Pinto. I can't seem to stay mad at him even when I want to and I hope he isn't mad at me. I try to convince myself that there's no reason he should be. I think of sending him a message, but I don't have anything to say and it's late. I look for his name in my WhatsApp chats just to see if he's online. He was last seen over two hours ago and I feel lonely and turn on the TV. Jonathan joins me and we watch reruns of The Big Bang Theory until I fall asleep.

At breakfast I scan for Nili and Tomer among the tables, and spot them entering just when we've finished and are about to leave. Nili waves to me from a distance and Tomer just looks at me and smiles to himself. I look back and he turns too. He's no longer smiling, and his expression gives me chills. We don't run into them for the rest of the day, and pass the time between tea, almond cookies and binging on Game of Thrones.

"Are you having fun?" Jonathan asks. The pleading in his eyes makes my throat tighten.

"Of course," I answer him but break eye contact. We grab spots by the pool, Jonathan opens his laptop and I lose him to work emails. I try to read, but halfway through the page the words flicker before my eyes and eventually I give up and close the book.

"You coming to the hot tub?" I ask.

Jonathan looks up at me. I see that he doesn't want to and he's debating what to say, and that he's on the verge of standing up so I quickly say, "That's fine, I'll go alone," snatching my towel from the chair and scurrying across the wet floor.

I slowly immerse myself in the hot water, a vague thought about the risk to pregnant women crosses my mind; I'm not sure if I am making it up and I get in anyway. The bubbles are gentle, tickling, and I open my arms and lean my head back. The water is lapping at my hair and caressing my skin, and my ears are underwater so all I hear is bubbling, and I unwind.

I'm almost falling asleep when the water level rises suddenly, and Nili and Tomer join me, making big waves in the small pool. Tomer presses one of the buttons and big bubbles erupt in a volcano. The calm is gone. We're sitting in a circle, almost touching, Nili is short but her broad hips press against me, covered in a red swimsuit in a seventies cut. Tomer is man-spreading in Bermuda shorts, the hairs on his left leg touching-not-touching my legs. Nili doesn't stop talking about all the kinds of pillows the hotel offers. She chose the softest pillow on the menu, "How cool that there's a menu, right?" But she didn't manage to fall asleep all night, while Tomer, who went with a medium-soft pillow, both fell asleep and snored. That's how it is, she always had sleep problems and he always falls asleep before her and snores, and that only makes it that much harder for her. "Right, Tomer?" Tomer nods once, slowly, and doesn't stop looking at me and I feel something within me awakening.

After Nili finishes telling me about Omri's cute mispronunciations, she says the heat tired her out and gets out of the hot tub. Tomer stays.

We don't speak, what is there to say, he remains close to me, his leg touching not touching mine, his one hand resting on the lip of the hot tub and his other hand on his knee, and his pinky lightly touching my thigh, fluttering with almost impercepti- ble movements. I tense, wondering if he notices, if he's doing it on purpose, if I should move his hand or wait for something clearer, more unambiguous. If I move it without him noticing that he'd done something, it would be very embarrassing and he'll think I'm crazy and could make a scene. I hate scenes.

And there's another thing. The thing is that I kind of like it, his touch. I'm not sure it's because of him, he isn't my type at all, but this contact, this feeling, that a hand which is not supposed to touch me is touching, there's something arous- ing about it, not necessarily sexually, or, that too, but not only. Simply... arousing.

Now three of his fingers are fluttering on my skin and I think I'm probably not imagining anything and I think it's lucky I shaved. His hand is pressed against me, and I can stop him and make a fuss or just move my leg slightly, he'll understand and leave me alone. I don't move. I try to control my breathing, keep it slow and calm, while his hand, now it's his whole hand, advances up my inner thigh, still not high enough, but almost there. I don't look at him but keep staring ahead in the direction where Jonathan is typing away and Nili is dozing, a white towel over her eyes. Tomer squints slightly, his jaw is set. He doesn't look at me as his hand increases the pressure and rises further. His thumb pushes aside my bathing suit and I recoil. I didn't shave there, and God knows what he will encounter and what he'll think of me, not that it matters to me what he thinks. He notices, moves his hand a little and looks at me questioningly. This is the first time he looks at me since he started touching. I don't look back, just hold his hand and direct it back. It's hot and the bubbles around us are big and noisy. Tomer strokes me gently, but I hold his hand and press it to myself harder and harder, he penetrates with one finger, then another, and we're moving together with small, circular motions, invisible above the water. I feel tension in my muscles and waves of heat and electricity increasing, flowing up my belly and arms. I try to control my panting, close my eyes, then force myself to open them to ensure that Jonathan is still on the tanning bed, working. He doesn't look up, and the pressure between my legs increases. I move Tomer's hand faster and squeeze my muscles until a wave of heat burns my face and chest and I stop Tomer and hold his hand against me.

Jonathan's image blurs as I slowly catch my breath, one breath at a time.

18

Zoe's mother opens the door, smiling broadly. With one hand she takes the flowers from Zoe and embraces her daughter with the other. "Hey, honey, hey Gali," she hugs Weiss too, with the arm holding the flowers, and he gets a whiff of spicy perfume and slim cigarettes, very different from his own mother's cooking smells. "What's this, you working out?" She asks, groping his arm. Over her shoulder Zoe rolls her eyes at him, but Weiss is unbothered.

"Come in, come in," Zoe's mother says in a slightly hoarse voice, "we ordered in from Kidron's new Asian fusion restaurant."

Dan, Zoe's father, who's sitting in the living room, looks up at them brightly, "Ah good, you're here," he turns to an older couple sitting beside him and gets up to greet them. "Come in, I want you to meet," he sidesteps Zoe and addresses Weiss directly, "Gal-chuk, Dana'leh's boyfriend."

Weiss sees Zoe's face harden, "Dad, I go by Zoe," she tells him coolly.

"Dana'leh, your mother and I chose to name you Dana—that's your name," he smiles at the couple and opens his hands as if to say, "kids, am I right."

Weiss hears Zoe mutter, "If your name is Dan, why would you name your daughter Dana?" But either nobody else heard or else they didn't care.

Dan kneads Weiss's shoulder, who closes his eyes and deeply inhales the smell of cigars and expensive alcohol that wafts from his jacket.

"Come, sit with us," says Dan. "Well, what's new?"

A warmth spreads through Weiss's chest and he feels lighter, more important. Whenever he's in Dan's company, he's proud of the attention he receives and tries to quiet the voices in his head telling him to take Zoe's side and not let her father treat her like that. She's a strong woman, she knows how to stand up to him, he reassures himself, sinking into the soft sofa, holding his hand out for the glass of whiskey that Dan pours and asks, "How are you, Dan? How's business?"

Dan smiles broadly, "If it goes any better we'll go nuts," he clinks Weiss's glass. "When will you leave that engineering nonsense of yours and come manage projects for me?"

Weiss smiles: He's heard this question before. "Thanks, Dan, you know I actually really enjoy my work."

Dan makes a dismissive sound, "What does enjoyment have to do with work? Work is for money. For pleasure you have my daughter, no?" He winks, and Weiss feels Zoe shrink beside him.

Zoe had once told him she's afraid he loves her father more than he loves her. Then she threw her head back, shook her shiny hair and laughed too hard and he laughed with her.

"That reminds me," Weiss says to Dan, "I wanted to consult with you about my investment portfolio, if you have a few minutes."

Dan grows serious, lowering his chin and his voice, "You know the best financial advice I can give you?" He says in a stern voice.

"What?" Weiss comes closer, to hear better.

"Don't get married," Dan declares with a smile and smacks his own thigh with pleasure.

"Dad!" Zoe cries, her shapely eyebrows knitting together.

"We're just joking with you, Dana'leh," Dan says, and in a booming whisper to Weiss, "I'm not joking."

"Danny, that's enough," says Zoe's mom, who arrives with a tray full of dim sum, "Gal knows we're waiting for him to join the family," she lays a braceleted hand on his shoulder and squeezes it warmly.

Weiss smiles with his mouth closed and Zoe exclaims, "Mom, don't you see you're bugging him? Baby, ignore them, okay?" She hangs expectant eyes on him and he strokes her hand and wonders how long he can go on like this. She snuggles up next to him on the couch like a cat looking for body heat, purring every time he touches her and fixing her position every time he pulls away slightly.

In the army he'd had a girlfriend, Elinor. She was tall and a bit stooped, blonde with dark roots, and she would come with him to all of the nights out with his army buddies, and when they danced close, and he saw that everyone was looking, he'd put his hand up the back of her skirt, then wouldn't talk to her throughout the week. She didn't complain, and that feeling, that he was the one setting the terms, making the boundaries, that he could do whatever he wanted with her, filled him with power and emptied him of pleasure.

Zoe offers him to taste her stir-fry. He shakes his head no, but sees her face fall and takes the chopsticks from her and puts a few noodles in his mouth. She beams. The sauce in his mouth is tasteless.

For the six months of their relationship, he waited for Elinor to dump him, but it didn't happen, no matter how many days passed when he didn't talk to her or how deep he pushed his hand between her legs and how inappropriate the situations in which he did it. When his army service was over, he was surprised by the intensity of the freedom and loneliness that he felt without his team around, or the stressful routine. The quiet scared him, and the free time was more demanding than intensive training, but when he suggested hanging out with Elinor, he was surprised to find that she wasn't interested. After trying several times, she told him that maybe they were looking for different things from this relationship and it was over.

His phone flashes and "DO NOT ANSWER" appears and disappears, matching his heartbeat. Weiss clicks on the device and the screen goes dark, but blood is flushing his cheeks and ears and he stands up.

He holds his plate out to Zoe's mother and apologizes, "I have a few more things to take care of before my flight tomorrow."

Zoe rises after him, "I thought you had a free evening," her warm whisper in his ear gives him chills.

"Yeah, well, it's just a couple last minute things," he says, quickly putting on his coat.

"Dana'leh, don't be needy, that scares men off," Dan thunders from the far couch. "Good to see you Gali," he tells him in his fatherly voice, "come more often."

Weiss smiles and wonders if he'll see him again.

19

Tomer exits the hot tub, and I stay behind, alone, my heart still pounding against the bubbling water. I turn off the jet, and only small bubbles remain on the surface, caressing my body. It's quiet. My body is relaxed and calm. I feel alive. I tilt my head back and water covers my ears and silences the world around me.

Suddenly the water rises, entering my mouth and eyes. I swallow water, cough and quickly sit upright, trying to catch my breath. I open my eyes and see Jonathan across from me, close to me, too close, invading my space, looking unfamiliar. He looks at me expectantly, as if he's waiting for me to say something, which feels like too much pressure. What should I say? I look down and see my body, the goosebumps, the little hairs on my arms raised from cold or excitement. My whole body is still hot and throbbing, and I'm afraid Jonathan might sense it too, that he can hear my heartbeat, see my flushed skin. Or maybe he saw? He's still not talking and his eyes are looking me over, first my face and then travelling down my body like they haven't done in a long time. Maybe he really does notice something, maybe I'm different. My whole body tingles and my heart beats faster and faster, and I can't bear this closeness and rise to get out. When I stand up, my foot touches his and I recoil. He looks at me inquisitively.

"I'm tired," I manage to mumble finally in a hoarse voice, "I'm gonna try to rest."

"Wait, I'll come with you," Jonathan leans forward to straighten up.

"No!" The cry bursts involuntarily from my mouth and Jonathan winces and looks hurt. I force myself to smile, "You just got in," I say in a more subdued voice. "Stay, I'll just rest a little and come back."

"Are you sure? Everything good? Do you feel okay?" He asks in a warm voice and looks at me with concern, and his expression burns tears in my eyes.

"Yeah, of course," I turn my head so he won't see my eyes tear up, and get out of there.

I walk quickly, almost running through the lobby, and a voice in my head won't stop pounding. *What have you done? What have you done? Idiot.* I bite my tongue and lips so as not to cry and bow my head to the floor, facing the elevators and bump into someone.

"Sorry," I hurry to apologize, and again feel the tears bursting from my eyes.

I look up and see the clerk from reception. He points at my body and says, "I'm sorry, but you can't walk around the hotel in a bathing suit."

He brings me a robe, I grab it from him and mutter apologies. I hurry to cover my wet body, and only now do I notice the puddle beneath my feet. I apologize again and run away to the elevator which opens towards me, and I shake my head in disbelief again, mumbling, *Stupid. How could you be so stupid?*

I get into bed like that, with the robe and the chlorine and the nausea. I close my eyes hard so as to banish the thoughts and images, but Tomer's face appears clearly before me, and I feel his big hand on me, grabbing hard, and I cover myself with a blanket and cross my legs really tight, but he won't leave me alone. He is on me, and I can feel the weight of his body and I open my eyes to banish the image, but he is there before my open eyes, too, and I shake as if to shake him off me, but he's heavy and I feel him crushed against me, and I can't stop thinking about him and feeling him, and he keeps touching me on and on and doesn't stop until I'm moaning without wanting to, and I cringe all over again and let go and again wince, and then relax and the tears come.

"Vishi? You okay?" Shit. I hear Jonathan coming into the room.

I quickly pull the blanket over my head, still panting, forcing my breath to slow down. It's hard and I'm suffocating. The mattress dips as Jonathan gets in and lies down beside me. I have no air. The blanket is heavy on my face and I'm hot. I'm burning up. Fuck the goose feathers, I'm on fire. I remain still, trying to breathe slowly, although it's challenging. I try to pick up snatches of sound to figure out what Jonathan is doing. I feel his pillow being squashed and pray that he doesn't stay in the room. I reach out a finger to lift the blanket a little and let some air in. Jonathan moves from side to side in the bed, and it sounds like he's awake. I keep my breathing constant and don't move. What if he hears me? Or if he's testing me? Waiting to see when I will emerge, desperate for oxygen? What if he knows? My left hand falls asleep. I try to move gently but it doesn't help. I need to move around. I stretch out in what I hope could be interpreted as movement while sleeping and breathe a little air from the opening that formed. Jonathan moves again and coughs and sighs. He sounds tired or sad or both and I don't move, accepting suffocation, trapped under the heavy blanket and heavy thoughts.

When I wake up it's morning. The sound of rain rouses me and I open my eyes in alarm. Rain in December shouldn't surprise me, but the bright days and the vacation made me forget the seasons. And now I remember. I sit up in bed and look out the

155

window. It's gray outside. The rain beating down at a diagonal is obscuring the visibility and I can only dimly see the hotel staff running, hunched, across the lawns, hurrying to close the sun umbrellas and cover the tables and tanning beds with plastic sheeting. Too bad, I think, it's a waste of effort, everything will get wet anyway. The rain washes everything. The hotel, in its winter gloom, feels like a broken promise. The wind blows the trees outside, great thunder rolls in the gloomy sky, and the sleeping Jonathan lets out a tormented hum. I feel a kick in my belly. It doesn't make sense and doesn't match this stage of pregnancy, but I definitely feel something in my lower belly, like bubbles or dragonfly wings or a moth fluttering over my internal organs. Maybe it's just my brain trying to remind me of the pregnancy and what really matters, and maybe it's really the fetus feeling the need to give a sign of life right here and now. I stretch out in bed, trying to surrender to the bubbles and gently caress my belly, trying to imagine it growing round, stretching, growing, transforming me.. But I can't imagine myself different, and the bubbles don't stop bubbling, like ants tickling their way up my stomach. It's unpleasant and doesn't feel natural, and I also feel period pains; what does that mean? Maybe it's dangerous and I should get it checked, so I don't start bleeding again. Maybe I really shouldn't have gone into the hot tub yesterday and exposed myself to contaminants, not to mention Tomer. What do I know about him and his finger hygiene? That's something I always know about Jonathan. Jonathan is an island of hygiene and security and I threw all that away and now God knows what kind of bacteria and poison are swimming around in my body and I deserve it, I brought this upon myself, and I really hope it's nothing, but know that I ruined everything.

Jonathan moves again beside me and sighs, and I'm afraid he's starting to wake up. I still don't have the words and I don't know how to behave with him, but maybe I should tell him that something is happening in my belly, not that I want to stress him out and it's probably nothing, and everything's probably lost as it is. He'll probably blame me if I don't tell him in time and blame me that I got into the hot tub even though it's not allowed, and anyway he's right, what can I say, I really am to blame.

I should wake him up but I really don't want to. Don't want to talk to him, don't want to look him in the eyes and let him look after me as if nothing happened, and I don't know how we'll get through another day and a half here before heading home. Maybe I really should tell him I'm not feeling well, even though the bubbles have already calmed down, like a soda that ran out of gas. But then again, maybe it's best not to say anything. As he opens his eyes, I turn away, buying myself a few extra minutes, taking deep breaths to calm down, and over my shoulder, Jonathan asks, "Are you awake?"

I turn to him and make a tired face, and he asks me how I'm feeling and without going into detail I say that actually I don't feel so well and think maybe we should go home.

Jonathan sits up in bed and asks with a furrowed brow, "What are you feeling?"

"I think I'm getting a migraine," I say because once, before the wedding, there was a time when I got migraines and it was unpleasant, but less unpleasant than losing a baby or adultery.

"You want me to give you a massage?" He takes my hand and starts massaging the spot between the thumb and forefinger that is supposed to ease headaches. I pull my hand away.

"No, no," I say and sit upright too. "I feel like I need to get out of here."

"Too bad, we still have another night," he looks at me imploringly, "maybe we could try hiking a bit in the area? You could get some air, it'll probably clear up soon."

I give him an exhausted look. "I really want to go home, Jonathan," and barely get the 'Jonathan ' out of my mouth. "Don't be mad."

157

"Fine," his face hardens a little revealing his disappointment. "Too bad, I wanted us to have fun."

"We had fun," I'm quick to say, "but you know, this is how pregnancy is." At least I have this excuse for now.

We pack our clothes and toiletries quietly and after breakfast during which we also hardly speak, Jonathan loads our bags into the car and we are finally on our way home. I try to breathe deeply, but Jonathan is beside me and inside me and I can't escape.

"So apart from this morning, did you have a good time?" Jonathan asks interrogatively, still looking at the road, and again I wonder if and how much he knows.

"Great," I force myself to say and know that I should go out of my way to please him now, to make it up to him, to cleanse my conscience, but I can't bring myself to look at him.

I think of telling him. Maybe not all of it but something, maybe not about Tomer, just about me, so he'll know what I'm going through, if he doesn't yet. It's important that he know, important for him, but I don't know if it's important for me and I keep it to myself.

Ten minutes into the drive down the wooded mountain, as if punishment for my silence or perhaps some form of escape, I feel my stomach juices tingle their way up my esophagus, and I plead with Jonathan to stop.

He stops just a little before Road 4, and I leap out of the car and don't get very far before I'm kneeling in the emerging puddle of my breakfast. I return to the car a little improved, and Jonathan hands me a bottle of mineral water. I open the window and breathe in the clean air of trees but the smell of outside overwhelms me with nausea again and I hurry to close the window.

Ten minutes later I instruct Jonathan to stop again. This time I don't aim properly and stain my pants with the splash of carrot juice and bits of pancake. We head back to the city, stopping every ten minutes, even when there is nothing left for me to vomit. The stomach spasms continue. Jonathan looks at me with concern and drives on the old road so that it's easier to pull over, but the many stops and the stuttering road make the drive longer and makes my stomach churn more and more. My body is heavy and exhausted and I just want to get home.

"At least it's for a good reason," Jonathan says, and I am amazed, again, at his ability to ignore all issues and dress up reality according to his wishes. "It was a good vacation," he goes on, nodding to himself, as if trying to convince himself that this is the case.

I look at him and wonder if he means this or if he's really hoping that if he sticks to his version, reality will give in and be convinced.

"We barely spoke," I don't hold back.

"But we were together," he looks at me, hurt. "Don't you feel that we're together?"

I crawl into bed fully clothed, sweating but cold. I turn on the air conditioner, but the dusty smell coming out of it makes breathing difficult. I open a window and cold bursts into the room. Acidity is rising in my throat again and I close the blinds and the window and lie down in bed, depleted.

Jonathan quietly enters the room, sits on the bed and hugs me. I hug him back, but I don't want this hug for which I'll have to gather myself and swallow the pain and act like I'm not falling apart.

"Do you need anything?" Jonathan asks in a low voice that shakes me.

I shake my head, close my eyes and pray that he will leave so I can unleash my tears and the weight of my exhausted body, along with thoughts of Tomer, and Pinto, and Jonathan, and the promotion, and Weiss, and the baby. Instead he stays, saying, "I want to show you something that'll make you happy."

He leaves for a moment and comes back with his laptop, sits down too close beside me, puts the computer down on my thighs and opens it. On the screen is a sketch, and Jonathan looks at me expectantly.

"What is it?"

"His bed," he lightly touches my belly, "or hers," he adds, carefully, as if it's careful to rest his laptop on me now.

My whole body stiffens, and I'm hot and the AC remote is too far and I am trapped under the laptop.

"Isn't it a little early for that?" I try to speak calmly.

"It is, but I want to make it myself, and the changing table, too. I'll need to work on it at night, and I don't know how much time I'll have, so I should start early, no?"

"They say it's bad luck to bring stuff into the house for a baby that has not yet been born."

"Who says that?"

"People."

"Since when do you believe that kind of thing?" He asks. "I thought you'd be happy." He closes the computer, pulls it from me and looks at me with an expression which combines insult and determination not to allow me to spoil his happiness. I know that he expects me to be happy too. As if it's a choice and I'm just being stubborn, just doing it to spite him. Insisting on not being happy about anything, never happy, always finding something to complain about, never content with my lot.

"I need some air," I get up from bed despite the nausea swirling in my throat.

Jonathan is busy with his anger and doesn't stop me, and even though I want to get out of there, still I note this against him, that he lets me leave the house like this, sick and miserable. I slam the door hard behind me, quickly descend the stairs and arrive short of breath at the street. The tickle in my nose increases, but I don't want to cry. Not yet.

I try to hold in the tears until I reach some quiet, dark corner. All I want is a quiet corner to myself, but there is none. The street is bright and sparkling and busy, all the benches are occupied, the pubs are loud and smoky, and my eyes burn even more. Suddenly this bustling city life is too crowded for me, too intrusive, doesn't give me space. I can't cry in front of all these people, adults can't just cry like that in the street, they'll look at you funny, will think you're crazy. Everybody cries alone, secretly, as if they have something to be ashamed of. As if it's not crazy not to cry.

As I leave the neighborhood, a puppy approaches me and jumps on my leg with clumsy enthusiasm. Having no choice, I smile at its owner and then bend down to pet him. The puppy wags his tail, hungry for petting. His fur is so soft, his paws big and his body small and he trips himself up without even trying to walk. It's heartwarming but my heart stays cold. I straighten up and move on, looking for a dark corner.

Only when I enter a more residential neighborhood do the streets get emptier. I don't find a bench, and finally sit down heavily on the curb, letting go, letting the tears flow. The cold air feels pleasant and I cry quietly, calmly, at my own pace, finally managing to breathe; pain oozes out of me along with the tears. An orange cat rubs against my hip and winds around me, and my phone rings from my pants pocket. My breath stops at the sight of Pinto's name.

"No, you didn't wake me up, I'm fine," I sit up straighter, sniffing and clearing my throat, to get rid of traces of reality and phlegm.

"If it's not a good time we can talk tomorrow," he's quick to apologize, "I just wanted us to speak before you get back, so you'll be up to date, and also," he pauses a moment, "just to talk a bit."

He wants to talk a bit, the tears dry in my eyes and the nausea is forgotten. I stand up, "Okay, you want me to come to the office now?" I look at the time on my phone. It's 7. I'm still supposed to be mad at him but have a hard time remembering why.

"No, I had a short day today, I'm with the kids at the mall, eating McDonalds, wanna stop by?"

I do.

Two minutes later I'm already in a taxi across town. The roads are surprisingly empty, and within ten minutes I'm paying the driver at the mall entrance, but I have no idea where the McDonalds is. I miss the European order and planning, which make it possible to navigate easily even in streets you don't know. Apart from the order, navigating abroad has an additional advantage: I'm more focused when I'm there, less distracted, thinking less, less preoccupied with myself.

I make my way through the mall and finally recognize Pinto drinking coke from a huge plastic cup, dressed as usual in ragged, short T-shirt, his tan faded and nut-brown.

I look at him from a distance, and for a moment allow myself to imagine the two of us together. Here I am coming to meet him and the kids, they know me already and don't look at me with suspicion, and I stroke their heads naturally and Pinto's, too. How long will this last? How long until the excitement gives way to routine, which gives way to revulsion?

How long until it bothers me that he works until the middle of the night? Or that he writes messages with spelling errors? Or that his left front tooth is darker than the right? Or that he smells like black coffee all the time? Or that his car is always messy? Or that he speaks in staccato? Or that he's right-wing?

After all, it's only a matter of time until things dwindle and break. The goodness I long for doesn't really exist. You always have to compromise on something. Everyone compromises. But what if I don't want to be like everyone? What if I don't want to be reduced to Netflix binges, kissing with my mouth closed, sex while the kids are at daycare, nose hairs, masturbating in the shower, a sprouted avocado tree, a station wagon, a running club, an IKEA sale, sculpting fat woman with pa-pier-mâché, couples therapy, a women's empowerment week-end, red pasta, foot calluses, a mortgage, Corning plate ware, male breasts, a Dyson, strawberry picking, *The Drew Barrymore Show*, Adele, UberEats, NLP, Ali Express, osteopaths, or photos of the sunset?

"You're my dad's friend," I'm roused from my staring at Pin-to's nut-brown arms and find that his daughter's huge mocha eyes, like a Disney character, are fixed on me,

"I work with your Dad," I smile and sit beside her on the edge of the red seat, across from Pinto.

"But you're also his girlfriend," she asserts and pushes a handful of fries into her little mouth. On her hand is a sparkly My Little Pony sticker.

"Actually we've been friends since I was a kid," I smile at Pinto who smiles at both of us, amused.

"But you're also his girrrrlfriend," she insists, opening her little mouth and big eyes at him.

"They just said she works with him," Pinto's nine-year-old son looks up from his iPad for a moment and rolls his eyes at his sister.

"Could be both," she shakes her head at him, rolling her eyes back and taking another bite of fries, "Want some?" She holds the fries out to me.

"No, thanks," I shake my head and smile at her again.

"Are you on a diet? Our mom's always on a diet," the girl nods.

"Yali, that's enough," Pinto intervenes and crams a fistful of fries into his own mouth.

"Dad, you're finishing all of them!" Yali wails.

"I paid for all of them," Pinto shakes off the salt from his hand and winks at me.

Don't stare at his muscles. Don't stare at his muscles. Don't stare.

"What's up?" He turns to me, "How are you? How are we?"

"How are we?" I repeat after him, like I don't understand.

"We good? You aren't mad about what I said…" he reminds me of the conversation which feels like a lifetime ago.

"I'm fine, we're fine," I reassure him. I can't allow myself to be mad at him, I need him on my side, with me. And anyway, I can't stay angry at him.

"Great," he smiles at me with his eyes.

"Dad, I want money for ice cream," the boy is roused from the iPad once more, and Pinto hands him a bill.

"Ben, wait for me!" Yali jumps up, knocking over a half-full cup and runs after him, her gymnastics shoes flickering pink and green.

"Don't tell Orli that I'm not giving them sprouted quinoa for dinner," Pinto stretches, and once again I can see my favorite area on the side of his stomach.

Don't stare. Don't stare.

"We'll see, in the meantime I'm gathering incriminating information," I steal a fry dipped in ketchup from Yali's tray.

"Ah yeah?" He raises an eyebrow, "I didn't know you're on a recon. mission."

"My manager taught me to always be on alert."

"Your manager, huh?" He doesn't look pleased, squints his eyes while nodding slowly and letting air out heavily, "And what else did he teach you?" His mocha eyes, which his daughter got from him, look a bit sad, drooping, and then without looking away he reaches out a finger and wipes ketchup from the corner of my mouth. I hope he doesn't see the tremble that passes through me at the touch of his finger, and I purse my lips which tingle from the contact. His expression is charged and I'm trapped inside it, and I want him to say something, and I want to continue to be silent with him forever and tears almost come to my eyes because I know I can't.

"I got peanuts *and* chocolate sauce *and* strawberry syrup!" Yali declares and sets down a dripping plastic cup on the table. "That's cause you're gross," Ben spits. "You'll puke it all up, gross-y."

"No! Dad, tell him that I won't puke!"

Pinto shrugs, gives me a last look, and then holds out a packet of napkins to Yali and strokes her head, "Try not to puke it all up, Yali."

I want to go and sit beside him and for him to stroke me with his big hand too and I want to lean my head on his shoulder and forget everything for a moment but then he says that he wants to send Sharon to Rome in my place.

"You have to rest, and Weiss is totally on top of things," he says, and if he thinks that will reassure me, he's so very wrong. I am absolutely not about to hand this operation over to Weiss on a silver platter. If he wants to beat me, he'll have to work for it, "I don't need to rest, I need something to do," and distance from everything, I think, but don't say.

"You sure?" Pinto raises an eyebrow, "Maybe think about it another day or two."

"Nothing to think about. I started this operation and I will finish it. I'm not *disabled*, you know."

"Okay, as you wish," he says, and I look up at him to check if it's a hint, but he's already busy cleaning Yali ice cream off the table.

20

Women claim that pregnancy is not an illness, but not a day passes from the moment the egg is fertilized and they're already taking days off work. A blood test here, an ultrasound there, puking here, a few sick days there, not to mention bedrest. And guess who's left with all the work? Not that he's complaining, yeah? As far as he's concerned the operation could move ahead without Fishman. He does not need her getting underfoot, with her smart-ass, condescending comments, just let's not get confused with nonsense about equality and opportunities and affirmative action, which is one of the stupidest things ever invented. Just an excuse to let mediocre women take the jobs of excellent men. He doesn't say a word of this to Pinto, when Pinto informs him that due to Fishman's sick leave, Weiss will be flying to Rome with Yardeni. Roccelli asked to see him.

The Agency is concerned that the targets are starting to suspect Roccelli. They are asking more and more questions, want details about him and are investigating his background more thoroughly than expected. They were even spotted patrolling by his house once. Weiss, of course, should not pass any of this on to Roccelli, but knows that he must stand guard. He smells danger, all his senses are primed and he feels obligated to protect Roccelli.

"Why did he even ask to meet with you?" Yardeni asks when they are waiting for passport control.

"He didn't say. He's a bit needy," Weiss makes a face, then feels a little guilty, "He's not dumb, yeah? Just stressed and overly dependent, not the classic choice for an informant, not that we had any other choice."

"And you aren't worried that he's a double agent?" Asks Yardeni.

"This again? I don't understand why we can't just be glad he's providing valuable information? Why look for trouble where there isn't any?" Weiss rages.

"Because it looks a little too easy. The information just flowing freely."

"He's just doing good work," says Weiss, refraining from mentioning that it's him doing the work.

"I understand that it was Fishman's idea to recruit him," says Yardeni.

Weiss looks at him and wonders if this is an innocent comment or made intentionally to piss him off. Either way, he does not let on that it affects him and just says, "Yeah, you know, even a stopped clock..." He laughs, Yardeni laughs too and Weiss relaxes.

He schedules to meet Roccelli at the bottom of the crowded Spanish Steps. Yardeni takes a seat on a nearby bench and Weiss buys two ice cream cones from the famous tourist gelateria on the corner and arrives to the agreed-upon place. Roccelli is already there, waiting for him. Weiss hands him an impressive cone, packed with three scoops in different flavors, decorated with sprinkles and a wafer, and they settle on a bench beside a young couple taking continual selfies of themselves kissing. Despite the cold air, the ice cream melts and drips onto Roccelli's hand. Weiss hands him a napkin and he thanks him and clumsily wipes his hands. His mouth still has a smear of chocolate ice cream, which makes him look even more childish and pitiable than usual. When he's done cleaning up, Roccelli explains the reason he asked to meet, telling him that he intends to go visit his family in Naples for four nights next weekend, and see his sister whose health continues to deteriorate.

"Okay. Good you're letting me know. How is she?"

"Really bad," Roccelli shakes his head and his gaze grows distant, "The medicine stopped having an effect and the tumor keeps spreading."

Weiss sighs. "Can I help with anything?" He asks and looks into Roccelli's eyes; he really wants to help.

Roccelli looks like he's about to say something, but then he leans over to examine his hands, still sticky with ice cream. The couple beside them immortalizes themselves in one final selfie and get up from the bench, leaving them alone. Weiss can hear Roccelli taking a deep breath, letting the air out slowly through his mouth, and then speaking in a quieter than usual voice, "There is an experimental drug that the doctors say could maybe help," he continues staring at his hands and does not raise his eyes to Weiss.

Weiss doesn't look away and says quietly, "Talk to me, how much do you need?"

Roccelli clears his throat and says, "It costs five thousand euros. A month."

"Okay," Weiss says after a short silence. "Okay, that really is a lot, I'll need to..."

"I understand, I understand, I shouldn't have said anything," Roccelli says apologetically.

"Hold on," Weiss says in a measured tone, "obviously I can't commit to anything here, but I can promise that I will see what I can do."

"Really?" Roccelli glances at him and frowns, "Because I know it's excessive and you don't have to and..."

"Quit apologizing. We really don't have to, but we're

committed, I'm committed," he bows his head and puts his hand on the younger man's shoulder. "We work together, you and I, and I will do whatever I can to take care of the people who work with me, okay?"

Roccelli nods at him and mumbles, "Thanks."

"Don't thank me yet, I haven't done anything," Weiss says and stands up, "I'll be in touch," he says and leaves.

A few minutes later Yardeni stands up and heads up the street.

"Okay, well that's way too much," Pinto's sounds firm on the other end of the line.

"I know, listen, it doesn't have to be the whole amount, but I'm sure we could do something, scrape up something," says Weiss, trying to maintain a nonchalant tone. "It'll really mobilize him for the task. We'll get a lot more from this."

"I can ask for another grand a month, not more," says Pinto, "And even that will require a special permit."

"I know, I know," says Weiss, "just that if you're already asking for a special permit, maybe try for more? What do we have to lose?"

"It doesn't work like that, Weiss. This isn't a casino. You don't just throw random numbers around. I need to be able to stand behind my request," Pinto sounds impatient and Weiss resolves to turn down the pressure. He can't show how important this is to him, he can't even explain to himself why it seems so critical, so he just has to let it go.

"Of course, of course," he says to Pinto, "I trust you, whatever you think is right."

When he gets off the phone, he notices Yardeni on his single bed with his shoes on, looking at him questioningly.

"What?"

Yardeni props himself up on his elbows, "What's with the stress?" He asks.

"No stress," Weiss dismisses, "I'm doing everything I can for the good of the operation. The more relaxed the source, the better the chances of success."

"Yeah, you don't have to educate me about sources, Bro, it's just..." Yardeni says and doesn't finish the sentence.

"It's just what?" Weiss asks and wonders, as always, what's visible in him, what Yardeni sees. Sometimes he's afraid of the feeling of leaking, the feeling that he's not airtight, not sealed enough, like something he would like to imprison inside is escaping him.

"Are you sure there's nothing else?" Yardeni fumbles in a cautious tone that only annoy Weiss even more.

"What else?" Weiss raises his voice a little.

"I don't know, Bro, I'm just asking. I'm looking out for you, so you don't catch feelings on me."

"Catch feelings?" Weiss mocks Yardeni. "It isn't emotional, it's operational: We need the source with us, not just physically, mentally too. So there isn't other stuff bothering him, that's the way to do it, watch and learn."

"Okay, fine, Bro," Yardeni raises his hands in a gesture of surrender, "I trust you, I just wanted to make sure."

"All good, Bro," Weiss smiles at him with relief, "so long as that's the last time you suggest I'm emotional."

Yardeni grins and Weiss feels a sense of control return: They don't really *see* him, he's fine.

When Pinto calls the next evening to update that they were approved a grant for just five hundred euros, Weiss doesn't show any reaction. "Take it out of your account and you'll get a refund when you're back," Pinto tells Weiss, and Weiss confirms.

He makes a face to Yardeni as if to say, "Well, I tried," and leaves him in the hotel room as he heads to the nearest ATM to withdraw the amount. When he gets to it, he enters his secret PIN, and in the spur of the moment, he really didn't intend this, it's just how it turns out, he finds himself withdrawing not five hundred euros but a thousand which is the daily maximum. The next day it is intentional. While he and Yardeni are wandering around the city, a little after they get up from lunch at a local restaurant, they sit down to rest on a bench in Piazza Navona, in front of some street musicians. Weiss asks Yardeni to wait a few minutes because he wants to go back to the bathroom back at the restaurant. There, when he's outside of Yardeni's line of vision, he withdraws a thousand more euros from the ATM. On the third and final day in Rome, a little before his meeting with Roccelli, Weiss tells Yardeni that he wants to circle the block for a moment, in a routine tracking and surveillance move, and takes out an additional thousand euros at the last minute.

"This is what I was able to manage," he tells Roccelli and hands him the envelope of money. Roccelli takes the envelope hesitantly and scans its contents. "I know that you need more," Weiss goes on, "But..."

Roccelli looks up at him with moist eyes, "Thank you so much," he says and rises to his feet. "Thank you so, so much," he approaches Weiss and spreads his thin arms around him. His fluffy hair tickles Weiss who smells a whiff of something sweet and milky.

Weiss inhales the smell, and then is alarmed and stiffens. He claps Roccelli three times on the back, but Roccelli remains rooted to the spot, his arms around Weiss, and Weiss feels that he has no choice but to soften again and hug Roccelli back.

21

"I thought you were transferring to an office job," Jonathan gapes at me as I pack a bag for Rome, again. For a moment he stiffens, but refrains from further comment, careful not to get angry around me, afraid of provoking a fight in my state, afraid of my state. I feel like he's walking a tightrope between wanting to keep me from getting worked up and angry and risking the pregnancy, and wanting me to take a load off so I won't endanger myself and the pregnancy, and I wonder if he worries about me, too, amidst all these pregnancy concerns.

I put my always-packed toiletry bag into the suitcase, throw in a few shirts and pants and add scarves, hats, and wigs from the office wardrobe. "Yeah..." I mumble, "But it's not something that happens overnight, I'm mid-operation."

"You love me by night and leave me by day," he says, paraphrasing an old poem that he'd once read to me. How amazed I was then by the carpenter's son who talked stocks and then suddenly read me poetry. That was his way of expressing his feelings, and with each poem my heart opened to him more and more, overcoming the doubts, the criticism, the fear. In recent years, Jonathan doesn't read poetry and my heart returns to its closed state, but when things are good between us, he recalls poems and with them, a small aperture of hope opens. I don't want to close it back up, and anyway I don't think it would be helpful if I tell him that I could have had Sharon replace me on the trip but didn't even consider it.

While packing I come across a note that Tomer snuck into my hand while Jonathan was checking out at the hotel. "If you want to live life to the fullest," it said, along with a phone number. "I'm already filling up on life," I whispered, rolling my eyes, and pointed at my belly, but he had turned to leave. I mean to throw the note away, then hesitate and put it in my backpack's inner pocket, and just knowing it's there makes me feel more free, less trapped inside myself.

Jonathan doesn't say anything further about the trip, just waits for me to finish packing so we can go to bed together like we used to. He stretches out his big arms to me, and the more he stretches the more I shrink. I lie in bed, listening to his heavy breathing and wondering what's next.

When I fall asleep, I dream that the baby is born. He's a boy, like my mom wanted, and we called him Shahar, like my mom wanted, and he's cute and purrs like a cat, in his wooden cradle that Jonathan built, wearing overalls which read "I'm the boss" that Jonathan's mother bought him, and after nursing he falls asleep on me, his lips pursed in an upside down heart shape, his cheeks pink and drops of milk on his chin, which I wipe away with a kiss, and my milk is sweet, and smells like autumn air, and I smother him.

I wake up before the alarm, stricken and trembling, still feeling the texture of warm, soft skin under my fingers. I breathe heavily, sweating, my heart pounding. I sit up to cast off the night terror and get out of the bed quietly, so as not to wake Jonathan, but he wakes up and kisses me and reminds me to bring the hormones with me on the trip.

These are vaginal hormones, and I'm having trouble putting the applicator in place properly, when I hear Weiss' voice from beyond the door, "come on, Fishman, Roccelli is waiting for me."

"I'm finished, I'm finished," I call to him from the bathroom of the hotel.

He bursts into the room and sniffs the air suspiciously, then notices the Endometrin wrapper whose shape betrays the applicator inside it, "what's this? For hemorrhoids?"

"No, I have a yeast infection," I grab the package and shove him out. He makes puking sounds and I laugh.

We quickly leave the hotel, and I settle in the car and watch Weiss going into the cafe next door and sitting down to wait for Roccelli. Weiss' is breathing heavier than usual, but I don't have time to wonder about it because Roccelli arrives. I sit up straight and listen to their conversation through the microphone hidden in Weiss' ugly plaid shirt.

We no longer have any doubt that the targets are testing Roccelli's loyalty, sending him to perform different tasks for them at varying levels of difficulty. Roccelli also seems to be wondering about the interweaving forces from all sides, and sounded agitated in his last phone call with Weiss.

Since the Agency is not satisfied with the quality of the information collected from phone intercepts, at their last meeting, Weiss instructed Roccelli to enter the targets' apartment when they're out, and copy data from their laptops. But Roccelli is already unsettled. Two days after the last meeting he called Weiss and informed him, his voice trembling, that he's not sure he wants all this, he feels the commitment is too much for him, too great a risk, maybe he should stop, and if so, he would like to be done with it as soon as possible. Weiss was quick to schedule a meeting, and now his cold, measured voice is explaining to Roccelli that he doesn't really care what does or does not suit him, he made a commitment and he's in this now until the end and it would be a shame if the bank discovered that Roccelli got into the employees' personal data. He would lose his workplace, and there might even be a complaint filed with the police.

"You can't do that to me," Roccelli says, shaking.

"I have no choice."

There are noises on the line, and I can't catch what's being said, and only after several seconds do I realize that Roccelli is crying. Weiss faces him silently, waits for him to calm down, then hands him a napkin. "Enough," he says and pulls a few bills out of his wallet, "For your family," he adds in a gentle voice that I am unfamiliar with, "How are they?" In response, Roccelli's crying increases. Weiss sits in silence for a few minutes, and his breath heavy again in my ear.

"I know it's hard," says Weiss, "But we can't let you go now. You are too important to us. We need access to their computers, we need you. I trust that you will do the best you can, and the sooner you finish with this, the sooner you'll be free of it." He hesitates momentarily, then lays a hand on Roccelli's shoulder, "I've got your back."

When he leaves the cafe, Roccelli doesn't look back at him.

A few minutes later Weiss gets into the car without a word, throws himself into the driver's seat, starts the car, and drives away.

"You okay?" I ask him.

"Yeah, of course," he doesn't sound convincing, and I don't know if I'm imagining that he's upset or if he really is upset.

When I'm sad, I tend to project my sadness onto others. Through my sadness lens I imagine that everyone is sad, and maybe prefer to imagine that they are, to imagine that it's not just me having a hard time. There was a time when Maya believed in astrology, and even though I laughed at her, I kind of got it. There's something comforting in the thought that everyone with your star sign is experiencing the same challenges right now, or that Jupiter is in retrograde so it's not about you and your choices.

"You had no choice," I told Weiss.

"Of course," he says, and he really does look unhappy.

"He'll be okay," I try to reassure him. "He's just a bit stressed, that's normal."

"Why do you think I care if he's stressed or not?" He glares at me. "Who said I'm worried about *him*?" He snatches off his fake beard.

Right. I forgot about the lie detector. He has other concerns apart from Roccelli. If he fails the next test, he... actually I don't know what happens to someone who doesn't pass a third time. He's fired? Just like that? They tell him thanks, bye and take his badge. And it's over? Then what? Where would this thirty-something guy, who's been working this top-secret job that has no equivalent since he entered the workforce go from here?

"You'll be fine too," I try to match the warm tone Weiss used with Roccelli, but feel fake.

"Tell me, where exactly do you get the nerve to know everything all the time?" Weiss shoots at me, and flecks of spit spray from his mouth and land, glittering, on the glove compartment. His cheeks are flushed and he's breathing hard.

"I don't think I know everything," I try. "I'm just saying what I think."

"Yeah?" His voice is mocking, "And how do you know that it'll be okay?"

"Because I know you, Weiss," I tell him in a voice which I hope comes out congenial and calm, "You aren't a criminal and you didn't sell state secrets. If it's steroids then just stop taking them. I promise you will get girls even if you aren't so jacked."

He doesn't answer, and all I hear is a puff of air from his nose. He's facing the window, so I can't see him and I think he's snorting with contempt, but then see that his back is quivering.

"Weiss?" I call him, "Weiss? Gal?"

"You don't know anything," he sniffs and straightens up,

"You know how long it took me to get where I am today? Now it'll all be ruined."

"That's a little dramatic, no?" I ask.

"No," he says, his voice no longer trembling.

We continue in silence, following Roccelli's bus, eating sandwiches I bought for us at the cafe near the hotel. When Roccelli gets off the bus not far from the students' apartment, we slow down. He crosses the road, steps onto the sidewalk and looks over his shoulder, straight at us. He puts on sunglasses and we don't know if he saw us or not, but he looks for a long time, as if looking straight into our eyes, as if he recognizes us and wants to signal something. After a few long moments he looks ahead again, takes a deep breath until you can really see his chest rise and fall, and then he begins to walk quickly, with a kind of funny determination, his hands swinging at his sides.

"He couldn't be going to their place right now, right?" I ask Weiss who squints and peers at Roccelli with concern. "He's going for their computers now?" I ask again, and Weiss shakes his head to say he doesn't know, and looks at his watch and he's tense too and doesn't take his eyes off Roccelli. "You stressed him out," I say, "This is not good, I really hope he knows what he's doing. They're not in class anymore at this hour."

"This isn't like him," Weiss says and bites his lips," "Maybe I overdid it," he says quietly, and then adds in a rougher voice, "The last thing we need is for him to fuck everything up."

Roccelli moves quickly, and it's pretty clear that he's headed for the students' apartment. We pull over on the side of the road, parallel to the many stands that line the main street. I text Harari and Yardeni a status update and ask for the students' location. Roccelli is already passing the produce store beside their building and disappears behind the heavy front door. Yardeni texts back that they are headed our way on foot, and it's a matter of minutes until they get here. Weiss snatches the phone and calls Roccelli. He doesn't answer. Weiss waits, drumming on the armrest with his fingertips, and I hear the sound of dialing become a busy signal. Weiss swears and dials again, and then I spot the tall figure of Ibrahim Shakir walking past. He's wearing a thick scarf and his parka, his head poking up above the crowd in the street like an umbrella held aloft by a tour guide. Beside him, intermittently visible and hidden, walks Al-Saadi, his walk catlike in spite of his leather jacket and tight jeans.

Weiss, still holding the phone to his ear, hisses at me, "Get out," just as I say, "I'm going."

Harari and Yardeni cannot be exposed to the students, so we are the only ones who can stop them. I hurry in the direction of Shakir and Al-Saadi, who have passed our car and in a few moments will enter the building's front door. I go from walking to running, my body tenses, the stalls at the sides of the road blur in my peripheral vision, my body is bent forward. The wind is cold and hits my face, but I can't slow down. I accelerate more, ignoring the pain in my hip, closing the gap between us, until I run directly into Shakir's back and crash to the ground with him, overturning a display of colorful sunglasses. The fall is inelegant, and I twist my foot in a convincing way, rub it on the asphalt and let out an authentic cry. Shakir's elbow is jammed between my ribs, and we're both flat on the sidewalk. For a moment I look into his almond eyes, and he returns a penetrating glare, deep into my blue contact lenses. I shudder.

Shakir is strong and muscular beneath me, and he tries to move and push me off, but I don't hurry to get up, just open with a volley of hysterical, weepy apologies in English. I grasp my foot and screw up my face in pain and pull up the leg of my pants to examine the damage.

He manages to get out from under me with a convoluted maneuver, pushing me from him a little crudely and looks at me as if deliberating what to do with me now. After a few moments he holds out a big, tough hand to me, I take it, still not getting up. With my other hand I hold my foot and continue to wail and ask him if he can help me to a bench at the end of the street, in the opposite direction from their apartment. Out of the corner of my eye I see the front door to the building, just a few feet away, and pray that Roccelli gets out of there already.

Al-Saadi and Shakir exchange quick glances, and Al-Saadi raises his eyebrows as if to say, 'What can you do,' and holds out his hand to me. I hold out my other hand and when he bends toward me, a silver handgun pokes out from under his leather jacket, squeezed between his skin and his too-tight jeans. He catches my eye and glares at me, and a cold wave slices through my chest down to my feet.

The two of them hold me, one on each arm, while I'm still on the ground, and I let them pull me up. Once I'm standing on my own, Al-Saadi does not immediately let go and his hand still strokes mine, pinching the flesh.

That same moment I see Roccelli leaving the building at a run and disappear up the street. I muster a smile at Al-Saadi with the remainder of my strength and mumble, "Thank you, I'm okay now," but his hand still holds mine, unwilling to let go. I ignore the wave of pain that rises from my belly and force myself to look him straight in the eyes and then look away in embarrassment. "Thanks," I say again, this time in a softer voice, and cover the hand holding me with my other hand. Al-Saadi gives me a long look in the eyes, and I force myself to smile at him and blink, and breathe normally. When he releases me, I almost fall back to the bench with relief, holding myself with my remaining strength and walking slowly down the street.

On the flight back to Israel I recreate the incident over and over, asking myself if I could have done something differently, if I could have avoided being seen by them, and ultimately conclude that I couldn't. Weiss also tells me that we had no choice and we had to delay them, but it's easy for him to say, he's not the one that will have to endure a cooling-off period in Israel after being burned, and he's always nicest to me when I'm down.

My belly hurts and I wince. I think maybe it's from the stress and then remember that the medicine for strengthening the placenta can also cause stomach aches. I try to breathe through it and sit up straight, but feel as if my uterus is being scraped with a plastic knife and squeeze my legs up to my belly, moaning and curling into a ball. Weiss peers over at me, I must have groaned too loudly.

"Want water?" He asks, and I shake my head no and bite my lips and wait for this wave to pass. It doesn't. I bite my cheek, but the pain in my belly is overwhelming.

"Can I help somehow? Fishman?" Weiss asks, and I ignore him and try to focus on a black dot on the fabric cover of the seat in front of me. "Fishman," he continues, frowning, concern in his eyes.

"Mmmm," I groan in response, in too much pain to speak, my legs still folded to my belly.

"I think you're bleeding."

22

Shahar was killed in spring, just before I finished seventh grade, a little after Passover. There were a lot of matzos at the shiva, and Aunt Tammy, my mother's sister, said that we ate enough bitter herb for all of the Passovers to come, and Grandma Katya, who was still alive, scolded her that her little word games were not always appropriate, and Tammy said that it wasn't wordplay, but then she was quiet and just muttered, "tragic, tragic."

Everyone said that they were sorry for our loss, that Shahar would rest in peace, and that time would heal our pain and only the longing would remain. They were mistaken. Over the years the longing faded into a blurriness which I didn't really know, while the pain followed me everywhere I went. I was thirteen when I first learned that some things are just bad, that not every thorn comes with a flower, and sometimes life is not made up of lessons and lemonade, sometimes life is just the terrible thing that happened to you.

So now they don't have to tell me, the ultrasound says it all. Instead of the reassuring rhythm of the baby's heartbeat, all I hear is my own, consistent and infuriating. The technician's face pales and she insists on checking again and again, pressing the ultrasound device deep into my belly until she gives up and hands the device to the on-call doctor. He checks too, for a moment, dutifully, and then slowly hands me a paper towel to wipe the gel off my exposed belly and waits for me to clean myself.

"I'm sorry," he says in an expressionless voice, "the pregnancy failed." He scribbles a few notes in my medical file and hands it to the technician. "You'll stay here for follow up to make sure that the uterus expels any remaining tissue."

"I'm sorry," the technician whispers to me and frowns. "Try to rest a little," she squeezes my hand into a fist and follows the doctor out of the room.

The first thing to hit me is the guilt that splits my stomach and clutches my throat. "It's all your fault, it's all your fault, it's all your fault," a voice in my head repeats in a monotony that is almost calming. Jonathan was right. This work really does put me at risk, endangers the fetus—actually, there is no longer a fetus. I am no longer pregnant. My pulse speeds up as I think of Jonathan and my mother and remember them crying. I'm not crying, not speaking, not trying to move. I'm trying to understand what I'm feeling but no feeling comes, just emptiness.

A sharp pain stabs me in the now-empty belly, and I wince. Through the waves of pain that wash over me I hear the sound of doors slamming, someone calling Dr. Pharan to come quick, someone sighing, and birds chirping outside my window. Even after Shahar was killed, I heard birds chirping. I remember sitting on my bed in my clothes, amazed that they let me get into bed with clothes, and I noted that to myself as evidence of the tragedy. I was worn out from the crying—my own and my parents,' and I just wanted to hide in my room and not hear anyone, but I heard the birds. In books, the chirping of birds symbolizes a bucolic, calm atmosphere, but for me it signals that nobody cares about your pain, that the world carries on, despite what happened to you.

"Vishi..." Jonathan whispers to me. Jonathan. I almost forgot that he's there. After the technician leaves, he hurries over and strokes my cheek. His eyes are shining, mine are dry.

Before he hugs me, I notice the loose skin beneath his eyes and the new wrinkles on his forehead. He looks exhausted and sad. I let him wrap his arms around me and his tears to fall onto my shirt and I wonder why he's hugging me. How could he not realize that this is my fault? The fall was my fault, and the drugs, and the medicines that I didn't make sure to take at the same time every day, and Tomer and the dream. He'll probably figure it out any minute, he'll probably leave again now, when there's no reason to stay.

On the way home I look at him, trying to grasp what he might be thinking. He's looking straight at the road, and I only see a small muscle involuntarily twitching at the corner of his eye. I look down at my belly to see if it's still there, but it was never really there, and it hurts and I wince with a sharp, stabbing pain.

When we get home, Jonathan and my mom take turns taking care of me. Jonathan sports a small, sad smile and I don't know if he's sad about me, or him, or us. He dims the lights and brings me water and pills and oranges, and my mom tucks the blanket around me, puts a hand on my forehead, mumbles something and sighs. I don't say a thing, just lie in the dark with my eyes open and stare at nothing. They enter every now and then to check on me, and my mother replaces the bowl of oranges, which I didn't touch, with a bowl of strawberries. Jonathan suggests a book and strokes my cheek and furrows his brow. I just close my eyes and they leave the room or sit beside me in silence, or whisper amongst themselves in loud whispers until I sigh aloud and they go out. I drift in and out of sleep, and each time re-remember and swallow the pain and another feeling that I am afraid to call relief, and the two together mix and make my empty belly turn.

It seems to me that a full day has passed and now I'm bleeding less. My dad also comes to visit and flutters a big but weightless hand on me, and I might have actually spoken to him but he doesn't say a thing and leaves. My mom stays and serves me onion quiche that she bought, urging me to eat. I'm not hungry but she tells me to eat anyway and I manage to swallow a few bites and she's pleased. Later Jonathan comes in and brings me tea and I drink a little and he smiles encouragingly. I feel a little stronger and sit up, leaning on the pillows. Jonathan sits beside me in bed and looks at me, waiting for me to say something, and I know that for him to stay I need to give him what he wants, it's time to give him what he wants. I tried, in my way, and now all that we are left with is his way.

"I will reduce my workload," I say and try not to recoil. "You were right, I can't do it all."

"We don't have to discuss that right now," Jonathan says and hugs me hard and whispers, "I love you," and rests his head on my shoulder and I hear him breathe into my hair. It sounds like a sigh, and now I'm crying.

The next day I feel better, at least physically. I have more strength and I want to get up already and I fight with my mom who insists that I stay in bed, when Weiss turns up at the door. He stares at his sneakers, one hand tucked in his jeans pocket and his face nervous. It's a little funny to me and I smile at him and he tries to smile too, cracks appearing around his blue eyes.

"Your husband let me in. May I?" He asks.

I remember the panic that struck him when he realized I was bleeding, his hand that squeezed my shoulder in a clumsy but supportive way, conveying his good intention. He was the one who alerted the flight attendants and took care of me until the landing and used all of his personal charm to make sure that they let us off the plane first and that paramedics were waiting for me at the exit. He didn't leave me until I was let in at the hospital, and only then, after ensuring that Jonathan was on his way, did he go.

"Come, let's sit in the living room, I'm suffocating in here," I tell him and get up from the bed, to my mother's displeasure. In the living room, Weiss eats from the quiche that my mom serves us. She makes tea and Jonathan stands aside and examines Weiss with a frown and looks at me, as if seeking confirmation. I nod to him that I'm fine and he stays in the kitchen, supervising the conversation from a distance.

"I hope it's okay that I came," Weiss says, and it's the first time that I've seen him embarrassed, "I just wanted to check on you. You freaked me out back there with all the drama," he looks down and plays with the button on his gray shirt, with three buttons open, exposing light chest hair.

"I'm okay," I nod. "Thank you, I mean it, thank you for everything, I didn't have the chance to say it then."

He looks away and makes a dismissive gesture. "Forget it, you'd have done the same thing if I was bleeding from my..."

"Okay," I stop him with a smile before he goes on, "how's work?" I look at him, eager for updates, wanting to get a sense, catch up, be in the loop.

Weiss shrugs, "the usual, busy, you know," he stands and I wonder if he's being vague on purpose, if it's convenient for him to keep me at arm's length. I stop myself from asking again and seeming needy. "I really have to get back," he says. "Don't worry, everyone's working, everything's under control, you focus on getting better."

"Yes," I feel a door closing in my face. "Thanks again."

I ask Pinto to schedule me for managerial work for the next while, which works out with the fact that I also was burned with Shakir and Al-Saadi and that I need a two-week cooling off period. I still don't feel ready to ask for a permanent transfer to a back-end role like Jonathan and I had agreed, preferring to postpone this conversation.

Jonathan is really trying, as if he senses that this is his last

185

chance, that he can't screw up now, that everything has to go perfectly. He makes me breakfast with a too-salty omelette and over-chopped salad and onion which I don't like. But his look is warm and his arms are around me and stroking my hair or cheek and the saltiness of the omelette doesn't bother me. He tries to work less, and suggests that we go to a movie or the beach, even though it's winter and he hates sand. At the beach cafe he knows what I will order and I lean my head on his shoulder, breathing the familiar scent of fabric softener. I feed him popcorn or wilted french fries that the wind has seasoned with sand, and he kisses my fingers and doesn't say a word about nutritional values. A flock of birds overhead makes a V-formation like an arrowhead over the sea, and we look at the sun which paints the sky pink and at a child W-sitting and digging in the sand and a lone guitarist plucking out a melody, and Jonathan kisses my neck making me shiver pleasantly which I haven't felt for a long time. We return home and Jonathan, as ever, hurries to the shower to wash off the sea, but this time he pulls me in with him. He gathers my hair beneath the flow of water and kisses me and tells me that he missed me and that I'm beautiful and for the first time in a while I feel calm, or maybe anesthetized.

We don't discuss what happened or what will be, but I feel that Jonathan is worried about the moment when everything will blow up and reality will slap us in the face again, so when he takes my hand gently and we go to the routine blood test, I try not to linger on thoughts and consequences, just be, just walk, just do without thinking. And when, nevertheless, a twitch of something else creeps in, Jonathan notices and squeezes my hand, pausing to ask if I'm sure I'm okay. I nod quickly and say, "let's keep going," letting him lead the way. And there is something pleasant about this surrender, this giving over. I don't have to fight for anything anymore, just accept what is happening and what will happen. If I can.

23

Fishman's bleeding caught him off guard and he was genuinely worried. The intensity of his empathy surprised him, then filled him with an unfamiliar satisfaction with this proof of his own generosity and nobility. He accompanied her to the bathroom, supported her by the arm, waited patiently for her to come out. In the meantime asked the flight attendant for water and pads and maybe some of those hot towels that they hand out at the end of the flight, maybe she would like to put one on her forehead or somewhere else, to ease the pain. He got into the role, he was dedicated, he was gracious, and he loved it, at first. But as the minutes ticked by, other thoughts took over. What if the bleeding gets worse, if something goes wrong, not even something dramatic, just dramatic enough to move her out of his way? He watched her face and noticed every spasm of pain.

They were the first to deplane, into the open maw of the ambulance waiting for them on the runway.

"Ugh, you didn't need to," she mumbled, pale-faced and embarrassed, and he helped her into a stretcher and sat down beside her and wondered if it was really necessary. He went with her to the hospital and stayed until Jonathan arrived, and waited for updates and preferred not to think too hard about what updates he was waiting for.

But now, he wouldn't admit it out loud, he kind of misses her at the Agency. Something about her pushes him to be better, and in her absence his successes are less satisfying. Not that there are a lot of successes lately. For now, the operation isn't going as planned, and the managers are putting pressure on Weiss, monitoring him closely, which is new. Especially Pinto, who's been chewing through pens faster than usual, fidgeting restlessly in his office chair, and stands up and sits down much more than necessary. This is his final operation in this position and he wants to end his tenure with success. The covert surveillance of the students' phones failed to yield sufficient information, and the attempt to extract information from their computers failed, so they are in the dark about the date of the planned attack. The only option left was to install listening devices in their apartment. Following Roccelli's failed entry attempt, it was decided that this time he would bug the place while they were home. When Roccelli heard this, he panicked. Weiss breathed in and out with him for long minutes before beginning the gentle and patient work of persuasion. He held his arm and told him that he trusts him, that he can do it, and assured him that he would be right nearby, would watch over him, would be with him, not leave him alone for a moment.

Now, as Roccelli attempts installation, Weiss can hear him panting heavily into his earpiece and feels the stress affect him too. Weiss breathes deep, measured breaths himself, as if to convey to Roccelli to calm down, but Roccelli, who came to help the students with their homework, is stammering in Weiss' ear in shaky, muddled sentences. Weiss hears Shakir and Al-Saadi's voices getting impatient, until Roccelli apologizes to them, says something about an upset stomach and runs out of the apartment sweaty and agitated.

Weiss sits him down on a broad sofa in a far-away cafe, looks deep into his eyes, which refuse to look back, and rests his hands on Roccelli's narrow shoulders which won't stop trembling. He hands him a Clonex and waits for the trembling to subside. Then he assures him that he'll be with him the whole time, in the building across the street, won't take his eyes off him and will look after him. The next day, armed with an additional Clonex, Roccelli returns to the apartment, and Weiss notes to himself that this time he was pleasantly surprised. Roccelli manages to install the listening devices exactly as they had agreed, stays in the apartment for another hour helping the targets with their homework with only the slightest tremor in his voice betraying the storm raging inside.

But when Roccelli hears that Weiss has to leave and disappear on him again, his body resumes trembling and he grasps him physically, preventing him from leaving the cafe.

"I can't do it alone," he says, looking wide-eyed at Weiss.

Weiss lays his hand gently on the younger man's and takes his other hand. He slowly sits him back on his chair, orders another coffee and cinnamon pastry for him and says, "You won't be alone, trust me. Even when I'm far away, I'm always with you."

He stays with him, holding his hands, not taking his eyes off of him, until the look in Roccelli's eyes grows sharp, and Weiss extracts a promise from him that he will be alright. Roccelli nods weakly, his face still pale and his smile weak, and waves goodbye. Weiss waves back, knowing that Sharon and Yardeni will keep an eye on Roccelli from up close during his absence, and still, for the first time in his life he feels that it's hard to leave his source behind, and returns to Israel with a heavy heart.

But there are other worries. His third polygraph is booked for the next day and Weiss is terrified. He knows that this is it, his last chance. He can delude himself and hope that this time he'll do it, that this time, unlike the previous times, he will outsmart the machine and the checker. Orr not, and then so be it. Or he could tell the truth, and maybe manage to not lose everything. And he hangs on this *maybe*. On the small chance that there is a way back, some atonement. Let them understand that he made a mistake, let them forgive and forget, let him remember that he is still him, despite everything.

He sits absent-mindedly facing Pinto, who pats him firmly on the back, saying that Roccelli is doing a really good job and that the surveillance devices have already started to pay off, and there's some issue with a commercial vehicle that the students instructed Mansour and Aziz to buy or rent, and that could be very relevant, but Weiss isn't really listening.

"Okay, where's your head at?" Pinto asks.

Weiss takes a long breath and says, "I have to tell you something."

"Out with it," Pinto leans back as if to give him space.

"It's about the lie detector," Weiss says.

"I'm listening," says Pinto and nods.

Weiss sighs. Pinto grows serious and attentive, his chin resting on his hands and his eyes penetrating. Weiss takes a few deep breaths; he knows there is no way back from here. There is no way back from what happened. He swallows and feels like with it he also swallows his pride, his honor, everything he has been until now, and begins to speak.

"But promise not to stop me in the middle," he stops a moment before beginning.

"Promise," Pinto nods seriously.

"And to still be my friend after this."

"Of course," Pinto smiles.

"And not to judge me."

"So, are you going to talk today or should I tell Gidi to book us a follow-up meeting?"

"Okay, okay," says Weiss, shrinking a little as he exhales. "Okay, so in early September there was an end of summer party at 'The Clinic.' Don't give me that look, it's a club. What, you don't leave the boundaries of your suburb? Anyway, I went with my friend Gabi, remember him? From basketball? And his friend Amos who I didn't know. Looks like a real man's man, we had a good connection. Anyway, it was a crazy party. Everyone was fucked up, and a DJ from Moscow and tons of wasted girls, just waiting for someone to take them home, and I drank like a fish, we did shots and went hard for three hours or so, like me, if I'm drinking, you know I don't allow myself to drink often so I might as well, so I went wild. At some point Gabi started to lose it, puked like crazy and could hardly stand. He was always a little weak. We put him in a cab and stayed, just me and Amos. While we were dancing, some girl starts dancing up on me and teasing until she's fully grinding on me. It was clear that if I wanted I could screw her right there, and she's hot and ready, and I drank a ton, you know. Zoe doesn't make a big deal about that kind of thing. Anyway, my hands are already up her skirt and in her underwear and I feel that she's totally shaved and wet.

"I know you don't need all the details, I'm just explaining what happened. You want me to go on?

"Anyway, I don't know what went through my mind, Bro, suddenly I lost interest and stopped. Afterwards I drove myself nuts, like, why didn't I just do her there on the spot? She wanted it. I could have taken her to the bathroom and taken care of it and it would have saved me a lot of trouble afterwards.

"So why not, actually? Maybe because she seemed too eager. I need the chase, Bro, to feel like I'm getting first prize, not the participation ribbon that everyone gets. To feel like I'm special. I want a protected flower, not a wild one. So, I sent her off and stayed with Amos and we kept going hard, partying and drinking and we were having a good time. We finally left at three in the morning, completely wasted, flashing lights still flickering in my eyes, and we started walking home. That fifteen minute walk took us forty minutes. And on the way Amos asks me about that girl at the club, what happened with her, and what about Zoe, and tells me, 'I get it, the way you look they're probably falling all over you.' He was really talking me up, it was great.

"When we got to my place, I was barely walking and struggled to get up the stairs. Amos touched my face, noting how pale I was, and his hand was warm and my face was cold, and he asked me if I want him to accompany me upstairs. I said yes and he helped me slowly and held me and came in with me." Weiss stops for the first time.

"And...?" Pinto is waiting.

"And that's it," Weiss says in a small voice and lowers his eyes.

"What do you mean that's it?" Pinto tries again.

"That's it," Weiss raises his eyebrows and drops his chin.

After a moment of quiet, Pinto asks, "Did you sleep with him?"

"Yes," says Weiss almost in a whisper, not looking at Pinto, not looking at anything.

"What are you, stupid?" Pinto suddenly raises his voice. It's the first time Weiss has heard him raise his voice. And he looks up at him with red eyes in a panic. Here, this is how everyone will react. This is what everyone will think of him.

"You're going to throw your whole career away just so we wouldn't know that you slept with him?" Pinto continues, almost shouting.

"Shhh..." Weiss turns to make sure that the door is closed.

"Seriously, why didn't you tell me this until now?" Pinto's voice is calm again.

"I was afraid," Weiss casts his eyes down.

"But who cares who you slept with?" His voice rises a little again.

Weiss lets out a voice that is meant to sound like a chuckle, "Come on, Pinto, who cares—everyone cares. The branch will have a field day. Everyone will talk about it. They won't go near me in the locker rooms. My father will die of shame."

"I trust your father will get over it, and anyway, whose life are you living? Yours or his?"

Weiss swallows and his windpipe rises and falls.

"It's not that simple," he says finally.

"No one said it's simple."

Weiss' phone rings and displays: "DO NOT ANSWER."

"That's him, right?" Pinto asks, jerking his chin towards the phone. "It's him calling you all the time."

"Yeah," Weiss grits his teeth.

"You met again since that time."

Weiss' eyes grow wide, "How did you know?"

"I assumed. He wouldn't push so hard if you didn't give him an opening."

"I appreciate you not following through with the joke there."

"It wasn't easy."

Weiss sighs again, "You know what they say, first time it's a mistake; second time it's idiocy."

"Bro, one could call you a lot of things, most of them I have already said to your face, but an idiot you are not."

"So what am I?"

Weiss notices the smile sneaking across Pinto's face. "Come on, say it, I see it's on the tip of your tongue," he gives in and smiles and Pinto's smile widens, "What am I?"

Pinto's smile turns into a subdued laugh trapped between his lips.

"What am I, Pinto?" Weiss raises his voice.

"A faggot," Pinto's laugh rolls forth, shaking the office.

Weiss looks at him and an involuntary smile rises to his lips, while tears of laughter fill Pinto's eyes.

"Not funny," mutters Weiss.

"Sorry," Pinto tries to catch his breath. "You're right, it really isn't funny." He wipes his eyes.

Weiss smiles, the conversation with Pinto reassured him a bit. He told him and nothing happened and the earth has not swallowed him and Pinto is still Pinto and he isn't rejecting him. Still, when he leaves the office, the whirlwind attacks him once more and the room spins, and Weiss feels unable to stand. At first he scolds himself, that he finally made the shift to gay, and why is he getting so worked up over a bit of dizziness and a headache. In the hallway, he almost falls on Sharon, who looks at him startled and asks if he's okay, and he hurries away without answering and realizes that he should go home.

At home he closes the bedroom blinds and gets into bed. He's cold. When he has already burrowed into the blankets, he wants to take his temperature. His hand inches toward the dresser drawer beside his bed but he doesn't have the strength to reach it. He just gazes at it with moist eyes.

He looks at his phone, reaches out and goes through all the contacts. Lots of women contacts. More than a few men. But none of them would be happy to hear from him. He can't call Zoe. Not now, maybe never. For a long time now he hasn't had friends, not real ones anyway, maybe since high school, or the army. He had long ago convinced himself that he doesn't care, that friends are for people with too much free time. But now, from the depths of his bed, he acknowledges that he is lonely. It's a strange feeling, isolation, a lot of air but he's suffocating. He could call his mother, but he never calls her. She would think someone died. He could call his brothers. No, he can't really. He has no one to call. He could call...

He dials the number hesitantly, intending to hang up. But the ringing stops. "Am I bothering you? No, 'cause it's not so urgent... just... I'm a bit sick... and I don't have medicine at home and I can't get out of bed. It's probably nothing, I'll manage, sorry I called... yeah, fine, Abarbanel 3, apartment 1, okay, bye."

Good thing he left the door open because he fell asleep and wouldn't have managed to get up to open the door anyway. He awakens to the touch of a cold hand on his forehead and trembles.

"Wow, you're burning up," Fishman says, handing him a glass of water and an Advil. She put a big glass of orange juice and a vegan sandwich on the nightstand.

He's trying to make a comment about how hot he is or she or... ok, it's too hard. He gives up and obediently takes the glass of water and the pill from her outstretched hand.

"How long have you been like this?" She looks at him with compassion and Weiss is afraid she knows. It didn't take Pinto long to spread the news, huh? Of course. He was always on her team. It's not that he didn't know that he couldn't trust anyone, but what choice did he have? And now he will start to pay for his mistakes. He notices Fishman still waiting for a response, and doesn't remember the question.

"Did you talk to Pinto?" He barks at her, as much as he can without air.

"What?" She's confused. That's already good, she shouldn't look so smug.

"What's your deal?" He's irritable.

"What is wrong with you?" Fishman looks more puzzled than angry, "You asked me to come here, remember?"

"Oh right," his head sinks into the pillow, already less heavy than before, "Thank you for coming."

"You're being really weird today."

"Yeah, ah?" He chuckles wryly, "and usually I'm super normal?" The sounds of his laughter become fragmented until he chokes and falls silent.

"What's going on, Weiss?" Fishman asks. Her softness is hard for him and he looks away.

He's quiet. Fishman is quiet too and sits on the edge of the bed. He's still silent. After a few moments he takes some air and says, "Okay, I should just tell you since everyone will know soon, so better you hear it from me."

He sees Fishman straighten up and tense, her face grows serious, and he realizes that she thinks it's about the promotion. She probably thinks he got it. With his remaining energy, and the still-lucid space in his mind, he manages to enjoy the momentary power, but the pleasure quickly dissipates. What does that matter now?

"You already know I failed two lie detectors," Weiss begins, and Fishman nods vigorously and waits for him to go on, "So it's not steroids, I know you were concerned," he smiles weakly.

"So what did you do?" Fishman asks.

"A guy," he says almost defiantly.

She looks at him questioningly.

He takes a deep breath and says quietly, "I slept with a guy," he says in a firmer voice, "One. One too many."

Fishman's eyes are bigger than ever, it looks like questions are running through her mind like the credits at the end of a movie. She doesn't ask any of them but blinks her eyes back to their normal size. "Okay…" she says, "And… that's it?"

"Don't pretend it's fine. Tell me what you really think," he snaps.

"What I really think?" She asks him.

"That I'm an idiot, that I ruined my life, that I ruined my career, that I lived a lie, that I'm a gay guy disguised as a womanizer, that I'm a joke," he shoots in one breath.

"That's what I think or that's what you think?" The psychologist tone annoys him.

"That's what everyone will think. You know the consequences of something like this?"

"A life sentence?" Fishman raises her eyebrows.

"I'm not joking with you."

"Me neither. What do you think the consequences will be?"

"Fishman, you know what's worse than being a woman at the Agency?"

"Are you afraid they'll stare at your chest?"

"Come on, I'm serious."

"So am I," she straightens. "Are you afraid that they'll suspect you of sleeping your way to the top? Are you worried that they'll suggest you're not as professionally qualified as your colleagues? Or only assign you to missions where they need a female partner? Or that they'll say that you aren't qualified because your ass got big? Or that they'll ask you to organize team evenings and bring Shabtai his coffee and order pizza when we're pulling an all-nighter? Or they'll ask you what you'll do when you have kids? And why don't you have kids yet? And how many kids to you want?"

"Fishman, my life is ruined," Weiss says in a broken voice which alarms her.

"Your life isn't ruined because you slept with a guy once," she says firmly.

"Twice," he quietly corrects her.

"You're being very honest today," she smiles at him.

"I don't know what to do."

"What's done is done. Now let them decide how they'll handle it. My bet? They won't do anything. They won't even stare at your ass," she doesn't look especially convinced, but he appreciates the attempt.

"I'm going to stay in bed forever," he says and burrows under the blanket.

"Forever is a long time, make some space," she takes her shoes off and lies beside him on top of the blanket. "So, tell me, how was he?"

"How was who?" He pulls the blanket back towards him.

"The guy. I've never had a gay friend, let me enjoy it a little. How was it? How did you meet?" She takes a sip of the orange juice that she brought.

"Fishman, what hit you in the head? Do you *actually* think we're going to have this conversation? And get your filthy feet off my bed, you want to make me even sicker?" At the edge of his consciousness he starts to feel a little better, the pill is probably taking effect.

"Fine, what's your problem? You on your period?" She smiles broadly at him, and he snatches the glass of orange juice from her and takes a big sip.

"Thanks for coming," he hisses.

"Thanks for asking me to."

24

Jonathan and I are running late to his office Hanukkah party. Since I had stayed longer at Weiss's than expected, I got home behind schedule, and now I'm standing in front of the mirror deliberating, wondering what kind of impression I want to make on his colleagues and if this is how it'll be from now on; is "Jonathan's wife" my main identity now? Hanging from his arm at office events? In protest, I wipe off the lipstick and pull my hair back. Jonathan doesn't rush me or glance conspicuously at the clock, and doesn't sigh or click his tongue at red lights. He just smiles at me every now and then and holds my hand and hums along with the radio, drumming on the steering wheel.

We park in the south end, next to the event venue "Zenith," located at the top of an old office building with a creaky elevator.

"I feel like everyone is looking at me," I hiss to Jonathan as we enter, touring between the gyoza and kebab stations. I try to determine if those are looks of pity about the miscarriage, or because of the unsuccessful fertility treatments, or if they're wondering whether I am or am not currently pregnant. I try in vain to suck in my stomach.

"They've just never seen you at a company event before," says Jonathan.

He's right, on my few free evenings in town I prefer to meet friends or rest, and Jonathan's company events were low on my list of priorities. It's the first time that my schedule is so empty that I don't need to prioritize. When I told Jonathan that I'd come to the party with him, he smiled broadly and marked the date in the calendar that he brought from his office.

"We almost never go out," he said as he got ready in front of the mirror and smiled at me. "Let's make a date of it."

He's wearing tight, but not too-tight jeans, sneakers and a black polo shirt and looks particularly good. His hair is a bit longer than usual, the ends of it covering his forehead, making him look young and almost wild. When I stood beside him in the mirror, I felt like I was trying too hard, with too much makeup on even without the lipstick, in my nicest black dress and heels that I never wear.

"You look gorgeous," he hugs me from behind and whispers in my ear as he looks at our reflection in the mirror, "Look how good we look together."

I feel too fat in my tight dress and am busy failing to suck in my stomach, but still I'm encouraged by the warm touch of Jonathan's hand on my back. He doesn't leave me alone, but proudly leads me among random people, ignoring or not noticing, as usual, women's eyes following him, scanning him. He parts his way through the crowd with confidence, greets acquaintances and never forgets to introduce us: They work in the marketing department, these guys are our analysts, this is the CEO of the provident funds, these are the bankers who work with us and "Hey, isn't that Nili who we met at that hotel two weeks ago?"

Yes, that's Nili, cute and round, her curls dyed in shades of brown and blond bouncing around her friendly face, now beaming at us, and coming up behind her with two glasses of wine and his smile widening as he notices us—that's definitely her husband, Tomer.

"Right, hey, what's up, Nili? What are you doing here?" I force my face into a smile and feel my pulse accelerate with the looks Tomer is giving me over Nili's shoulder.

Jonathan is standing beside me so I can't covertly examine his face to see his reaction at the sight of these two.

"My whole department was invited as part of a company collaboration. And wherever there's good food and a childless evening, I'm there," Nili takes the glass of wine from Tomer. I'm guessing it's not her first glass this evening.

"Yes, the food looks great," I mutter.

"They got really highbrow catering, the chef from some cooking program made the menu," says Jonathan. He smiles congenially at Tomer, and I let out a breath. He doesn't know.

"Anything that's not hot dogs and alphabet-shaped noodles is a luxury to me," Nili giggles, the wine swirling in her glass.

Tomer still hasn't said anything, just nods his head at Jonathan, then looks at me, scanning me slowly up and down. I feel like I'm blushing and am careful not to return his gaze. Instead, I pull in my belly with all my strength, thread my arm through Jonathan's, and leave them in a hurry, pulling Jonathan after me.

After visiting all the food stands, we sit down at a side table with heaped plates. I reach for the bottle of wine in the center of the table and pour our glasses. We clink, and Jonathan doesn't make a face at the sight of my glass and doesn't say that maybe it isn't worth it, just smiles and insists, as always, on prolonged eye contact before taking a sip, and we look each other deep in the eyes while a young woman suddenly sits down beside Jonathan, swiping a piece of calamari from his plate and putting it in her mouth. I look at her in surprise, and Jonathan turns to see what I'm staring at.

"Hey Ofer, what's up?" He smiles and moves the plate closer to her.

So this is Ofer, I think to myself. When Jonathan mentioned Ofer from work, I imagined a pale girl surrounded by file folders and Excel tables, who changed her name from Ofra to Ofer in hopes of gaining some imaginary appeal. The real Ofer, who I'm no longer sure was originally Ofra, is all elastic skin, a small tattoo on the shoulder, an ear-fold piercing, black hair in an asymmetric bob and perky boobs.

"So you're Avishag," she smiles at me congenially when Jonathan introduces us. "Nice to finally meet you. I'm Ofer, Jonathan's date."

I must be looking at her strangely because she suddenly smiles uncomfortably and explains, "No, that sounds bad, just I'm the only one in this crazy company who's not partnered." She raises her hand and gestures around. "It's like Noah's ark around here, the race to bourgeoisie, so I kinda stick to Jonathan in these events, just so I don't find myself completely alone, counting my eggs or something," she smiles at me again.

She's nice, and I smile back at her without even meaning to and ask, "Are you bummed about that?"

"Just when I'm in human company," she smiles again. "You have a uterus, right? So you know that people think it's a public resource and that they should express an opinion about it."

"I am quite familiar," I smile and feel Jonathan squeeze my hand under the table.

"Ugh, people can be so tactless," Nili, who sat down beside us too, joins the conversation. "Don't let anyone tell you what to do. Only you decide when to have kids."

"Actually I'm not really sure if I even want kids," Ofer shrugs.

"Ah, like... at all?" Nili stutters, and I feel Jonathan tense beside me.

"I haven't decided yet. Maybe not."

"Ah, that's... sure, that's your choice," I see Nili searching for words, "But aren't you... that is, aren't you afraid you'll regret it?"

"Aren't you?" Ofer asks, then smiles and turns to Jonathan, "Were you at the investors' summit yesterday?" They're instantly engrossed in conversation and Ofer laughs and throws her hair back in one of those graceful, feminine moves that I could never pull off. I ask myself if she's flirting with him, if she finds him attractive, if he finds her attractive and how is it to work together, do they get excited to see each other every morning, do they talk about me, is she jealous of me or dismissive or does she pity me for not know something I should know... And I ask myself if I'm jealous of her, if I'm jealous of him, and look inside myself for that envy that would calm something in me, that would confirm something, but I don't find it. I don't find anything.

The HR manager gets up on stage in a puffy, festive dress, with that same smile that has been on her face since she shook our hands on the way in, hitting the black microphone which squeals in response, and asking everyone to take their places so they could start with the evening's show. A moment before the CEO rises speak, Tomer appears next to me, of course, and takes the chair beside mine. His gaze moves past my face and focuses on Ofer's sharp features and suggestive cleavage.

"So how do you all know each other?" Ofer asks.

"Nili and I did our BA together," I supply the explanation. "And we happened to be on vacation at the same hotel at the same time..."

"Great hotel, eh, Avigail?" Tomer interrupts her and rubs his hands together like a fly.

"Avishag," I correct him. "Yeah. Great hotel."

He doesn't stop staring at me with that look of his and I look at Nili, but she is concentrated on the CEO who's just going onstage. He welcomes everyone, seasons it with a joke about Hanukkah bonuses, lights the enormous menorah, insists on faking the song "Maoz Tzur" on the microphone, then hands the mic over to the main act, a stand-up comedian who was recently kicked out of the *Big Brother* house.

Nili is hypnotized by the show, following the comedian with

203

her eyes, back and forth across the little stage, and laughing aloud at his jokes which are mostly about his overly intimate relationship with his mother. Tomer sips slowly from his glass of beer, leans back and spreads his arms on the backrest of my chair. I look at him, raise my eyebrows and look at his arm as a hint to move it, and he does, changing position and leaning with his elbows on the table, as if focused on the show. He isn't touching me, but I can't shake off the tension or catch my breath, and I stand up, whispering to Jonathan that I'm going to the bathroom.

The bathroom has an industrial citrus smell, a row of black sinks on a white marble counter, above them a mirror the whole length of the wall and above each sink an industrial lamp too dim for the dark space. I enter a bathroom stall, also dark, and then wash my hands at a black sink. Jazz music masks the sounds of the show outside and the door opens.

Tomer appears behind me in the mirror, his eyes reflected in it looking straight into mine. "So this is where you're hiding," he says quietly.

I turn to face him. "Am I meant to hide?" I ask.

He takes a small step toward me and I feel the air between us diminish. "You tell me," he says, not taking his eyes off me. There's something in his expression that raises the temperature in the room, that melts the air, and I think it's clear that I am hiding.

He takes another step and is very close to me and my breathing stops and I'm scared—I don't know if it is of him or myself. The sink juts into my back, and he rests his hands on both sides of my body and I smell beer and cigarettes wafting from him and see that he has fine wrinkles at the corners of his eyes and that his stubble is sprinkled with gray. He doesn't touch me, but if he moves a little more we'll be pressed against each other and suddenly I'm disgusted by him or maybe with myself, and

I try to move, but he puts both hands on my arms and tells me quietly, "You can stop me at any point."

"So stop," I say, and hope he won't notice that I'm shaking, "What happened?" He pulls back a little, his hands still holding me. "I thought we had fun."

"Nothing happened, I'm just not interested," I say and pull my arms out from under his. "Could you move, please?"

He frowns and squints his eyes into two narrow slits and a vein sticks out on the side of his forehead and looks like he's considering his next move. He scares me and disgusts me and still a part of me doesn't want him to move, a part that wants him to decide for me, to free me from the responsibility and the price I will pay for every choice I don't make. But then the door opens, and he steps back quickly, spreading his hands to the sides, and I pass through the space that opened up between him and the marble, and Ofer who emerges from the direction of the door smiles at me and my heart skips a beat. I don't know what she saw, but she makes no indication that gives anything away, just heads for one of the stalls.

After the bathroom doors slam shut behind me, I allow myself to stop and take a few deep breaths. Tomer passes by without looking at me. I wait for my heartbeat to slow down, then walk calmly to our table and whisper in Jonathan's ear that I've had enough and want to go home.

25

He tells the interrogator everything, facing him, straight-backed, down to the tiniest details, ignoring the chill up his spine and the sweat at his temples. He clears his throat and speaks clearly, explaining as much as necessary, not hiding a thing, recalling more and more details, things said, phone calls he answered or ignored, until the interrogator stops him and says, "Okay, that's enough," and the whirlpool in his belly takes a few more spins before slowing down.

Then the lie detector test. Same examination room looking out at those towers, same uncomfortable chair, same needle that rises and falls at the rate of his speech, same shiny forehead of Alon, squinting at him and wrinkling his nose without a word.

Fifteen minutes into the polygraph, Alon straightens up and shakes his hand.

"Okay," he claps him on the back, "All good."

Weiss looks at him confused, "That's it?" He asks.

"That's it," Alon smiles at him for the first time. "Take care."

Weiss stares for another moment, then nods without replying, gathers his belongings and hurries out, searching for relief or fear, but he doesn't feel anything. He presses the button for the parking level, but when the elevator opens on the ground floor, he is expelled into the lobby, breathless. From there he spills out onto the street, hoping that there he will be able to suck enough air into his lungs, to breathe freely at long last. He sits down on a dirty bench, buries his head in his hands and tries to listen, to understand what he's feeling, to sense the change, the release, but feels only exhaustion, like the end of a long journey which is less a celebration than a collapse.

In the evening he joins Yardeni, Hadad and Harari for a game of pickup basketball at the elementary school next to Harari's house. He hopes that the sore muscles and sweat will defeat the anguish that fills his stomach and won't leave. The night is clear and the big, round moon shines above them. The squeak of shoes on the rubberized court and the shouts of his friends echo in Weiss's head. He is not with them. He runs from one end of the court to the other, with Alon the tester before his eyes. He no longer sees hostility on his face, but pity. This is how he interprets any gentle treatment. The interrogator's voice echoes in his head, softly repeating the words "homosexual intercourse." After so many repetitions, the words almost lose their meaning – almost.

Hadad is guarding him closely. Weiss feels his body heat, his chest pressed to his shoulder and his arms spread to his sides, fluttering, almost touching. Weiss wonders if Hadad would guard him so closely if he knew. He continues dribbling, tries to evade Hadad, he's doubly motivated now, but cautious and hesitant, not striving for contact as always. He loses the ball and curses. Now he should be guarding Hadad, but lets him rush forward and sinks a shot. Weiss bites his lip in frustration and rises back to the attack. He has to get a grip on himself, now and in general. He must put what happened behind him. That's it, he came clean, the saga is over. It's time to return to himself. The ball sails towards him and hits him in the head.

"Dude, what's up with you today?" Calls Yardeni. "Not defending, not attacking, you here to play or to jerk off?"

He looks at his friends who look back, scanning him, and

wonders, again, what they would say if they knew, what will they say when they find out, and maybe they already know, and why are they looking at him like that? Hadad gives him a teasing smile and whispers something to Harari who is standing beside him and raises his eyebrows. What was so interesting? What did he tell him? Even Yardeni, who has never spoken to him so dismissively, looks at him and rolls his eyes.

Weiss feels his forehead where the ball hit. The area is hot and throbbing and his pulse is pounding in his ears. He forces himself to disconnect from the pain, and his thoughts. Nobody will know if they don't see it on him. He needs to carry on as usual. Nothing changed as far as they're concerned and he can't allow anything to change. He picks up the ball which rolled off the court and passes it to Yardeni.

"Come on, start playing and quit whining like a little bitch."

The next day he's summoned to a meeting in Shabtai's office and he tenses. He wants to put the whole matter behind him already and avoid further conversations about it, along the lines of: "We're good and you're good and everything is totally good between us and of course it won't affect anything, we're such an enlightened, liberal organization. Everyone here is evaluated solely based on their qualifications." Then they will smile too broadly at him and shake his hand too hard and clap him on the shoulder too many times, as if to say, 'You're still one of us.' They will leave the conversation smiling and pleased with themselves and how open-minded they are and how they treat everyone the same, even "them." He does not want to be one of "them" and he does not want risk-reduction conversations whose whole purpose is to make them feel better, and leave him with the horrible feeling that he's not like everyone else, he's one of "them."

When he gets to Shabtai's office, he finds Shabtai and Pinto sitting at the round meeting table. Pinto, as usual, is rocking his chair back and forth and gnawing on a pilot pen while Shabtai spins lazily in his fancy executive chair. Liat from human resources is sitting beside them, eying the pages in front of her. When Weiss comes in, she straightens and runs a hand through her straight hair as if out of habit.

"Weiss," Shabtai stands when he enters the room, "Come, sit, how are you doing?" He asks with uncharacteristic formality and gestures to a glass of water that was poured before he came in. "Want something hot to drink?" Shabtai offers.

Weiss casts himself onto the solitary leather chair on the other side of the table, rolls up his sleeves and replies, "No, all good."

Liat smiles at him with a closed mouth hand asks with a head tilt and in a low, indulgent voice, "How's it going, Gal?"

Her tone annoys him and Weiss looks at Shabtai and then at Pinto, seeking someone to roll his eyes at, but their faces are stony and they look at him expectantly. The room is quiet.

"It's going great, how are you doing?" Weiss leans back in his chair, whose leather makes a squeaky sound. Otherwise, the room is silent. Liat smiles at him again without opening her mouth, takes a long breath, nods to Shabtai and Pinto and says, "Look, Gal, we wanted to speak with you today following the... personal matters that arose in the security clearance."

"Personal matters," Weiss repeats after her with a mocking nod.

"First of all, it's important to say," Liat goes on, "That we have no issue with the subject. None. The Agency recruits and trains the best agents, and does not interfere with its employees' personal choices." She looks at him and slows her speaking, "As long as," she emphasizes, "As long as there's no information security risk."

He closes his eyes with exhaustion, struggling to hide his impatience. What's with the speech now? Of course there's no information security problem. Does she think he's a child? He could teach her about information security. Sitting there with her lists of salaries and her closed door as if she's sitting on the nuclear secrets.

"The thing is," Liat goes on, growing slower and more hesitant, "that because of the concealment issue, there may be a concern here, as in, you are more exposed to situations of... you could be..." she struggles to find the words.

"You could be blackmailed because you're gay," Shabtai cuts her off and breaks into a phlegmy cough.

"Yes, that's..." Liat resumes stammering, "Like I said, we have no reservations regarding sexual orientation itself, but when not everyone knows, it puts you in a ... vulnerable position."

"Are you for real?" Weiss is stunned, looking from one to the other. None of them meets his eyes. Liat shrugs almost imperceptibly and nods. Shabtai scratches his belly, Pinto sighs and leans in, "Weiss," he says and finally looks him in the eye, "Listen, we're on your side, we'll give you our full support, we know that it's not simple, what we're..."

"It's not simple, what you're...?" Weiss mimics Pinto, "Do you understand what you're asking of me?" He feels the room growing smaller and the walls closing in.

Pinto nods, "I understand. It puts you in a position..." he shakes his head, "I can only imagine what you must be feeling."

"Why imagine," Weiss cuts him off, "Let me describe exactly what I feel. I feel like you fucked me. Forgive the irony, yeah? I feel like this Agency, where I invested my whole life, literally my life, is throwing me to the dogs," his voice begins to tremble but he doesn't stop, "I feel like you," he points at Pinto, "you lied to my face and strung me along. Why did you pressure me to tell, huh?" He feels his voice starting to break, "to get me into this exact situation? Press my back against the wall? Either I lose my job or my life?"

"I didn't know, Weiss," Pinto leans over the table towards

him, "I promise you I didn't think that they would make this demand."

"You didn't know. Great," Weiss mutters and doesn't look at him again.

Shabtai was one thing, that man would sell his mother if that's what the Agency required, but Pinto—he wanted to think that Pinto was different, that he actually cared, that he would defend him, that they were friends. But apparently there's no such thing. Like everyone else, he's just covering his own ass, and maybe Fishman's too.

"Okay, let's all calm down," Shabtai raises his voice slightly. "Weiss, we all love you and all of us are on your side, you know that, but we have a situation," he raises his hands in a gesture of 'what can you do?' "It's a complex situation, and you have to understand that our hands are tied here, this is a directive from the Information Security Unit. You have to tell your immediate circle what came up in the examination," he spreads his hands again. "I'm sure it's unpleasant. I'm also sure you'll get over it, you've overcome greater challenges, you're made of strong stuff."

Leaving the office, he feels like he was kicked in the gut. From one step to the next, he fills with rage and wants to abandon everything, the Agency can go to hell, may they all go down in flames, the operation included. They're giving him conditions? An ultimatum? No problem, he's good at arm wrestling, let's see how they manage without him. He feels like his whole mind, its entire contents, are coming to a boil and beginning to overflow. He wants to destroy them, he wants to teach them a lesson, he wants them to hurt like he's hurting.

He's hurting. People pass by him, waving, but he looks through them, doesn't notice them. His body is heavy and all of his resources are focused on walking, not letting his legs fail him. He is fighting his body, commanding it to advance, step by step, head high, back straight, face impassive, not to give anything away. But inside he is all wincing, hurting, walking slowly as if to avoid further jolting his body. He feels that everything is fragile, every incorrect move, every incorrect decision, could bring everything crashing down upon him, everything that he built, everything that he hoped. He asks himself what he'll do now, not from a desire to build an action plan, but out of the great void inside him. He is unable to imagine his life as they are demanding that he live it. Being closeted isn't hard for him, he's used to it, it's the exposure which he doesn't know if he will be able to overcome. The truth is that he didn't choose it, he didn't want it, and still it is threatening to crack and smash everything. He knows how to play characters, how to get into their world, to create their patterns and characteristics and even their inner world and ambitions, he doesn't know how to enter his own character. That is a door that he has been struggling to keep locked for years.

"You look like shit," Fishman appears out of nowhere, as usual.

"Fantastic," he replies, still dragging his feet.

Fishman matches his pace and looks at him. "What's with you?"

"I'm in deep shit. Didn't we cover this?"

"Care to elaborate?"

"Horse shit."

"Okay, you don't have to tell me," Fishman stops.

Weiss stops too, looks at her for a moment, then asks, "are you coming to the balcony?" And without waiting for her reply, goes outside.

Fishman hurries to keep up and walks beside him. On the balcony they sit at a table with an ice cream wrapper with vanilla residue on it and an overflowing ashtray. Fishman puts her feet up on the chair in front of her and trains her gaze on

Weiss. He looks out at the view of yellow sand dunes dotted with green that surround their offices, and does not look away from them even as he says, "They told me that I have to tell."

"Didn't you tell them already?" Fishman asks.

"Not the interrogator. They want me to tell everyone."

"Everyone-everyone?" She raises her eyebrows.

"Everyone, including my father, including my girlfriend."

"Oh, shit," Fishman says softly and thinks for a moment, "So you can't be blackmailed?" She asks.

"Apparently everyone figured that out ahead of time and no-body thought to give me a heads-up," Weiss hisses.

"I didn't figure it out ahead of time, unfortunately," says Fishman, "Would you have done something different?"

"You know what, I don't know, but I like to make decisions with all of the information."

"Yeah," says Fishman. "What'll you do?"

"Do I have a choice?"

"There's always a choice."

"I already told my managers."

"You don't have to tell whoever you don't want to."

"That means that I can't keep working here."

"Right."

Weiss glances over and nods slowly as if a new insight is dawning on him, "So that's your angle?"

"What angle?" Fishman looks confused, but for Weiss, the penny dropped. She won't confuse him with her innocent face. He was fooled once, that won't happen again. What happened lately that everyone thinks they can put one over on him? He doesn't know what he's giving off, but it ends here.

"You just want me out of your way, huh?" He sneers, leaning across the table. "You want me out of the competition, that's your only chance of getting the job," he leans towards her. "I'm sorry to disappoint you, but that's not happening."

"Weiss, are you serious? You think that that's why..." Fishman tries but Weiss won't let her, he won't let anyone mess with him or manipulate him anymore.

"Drop it, Fishman, don't even try. I'm in this system for twelve years, eight fucking years I've been at this job, waiting for a promotion, and you think I'll just give it up like that?"

"All I said was..." Fishman starts and thinks better of it. "Weiss, I'm on your side."

"So get back on your side," he stands. "We're finished." He heads back inside, leaving her alone on the balcony.

26

I don't know if I'm worried for Weiss or I just want to prove to him and to myself that I'm not threatened by him and the competition. Either way, I decide to seek out Pinto and talk to him, maybe there's a way around this, to save Weiss the complete emotional exposure that management is asking of him. After all, nothing good will come of it. It's something he has to decide for himself, not be forced into, it could completely undermine, even crush him.

Pinto isn't in his office, nor is Gidi, and I head to the conference rooms and the balcony and finally find him in the operations HQ, sitting, frowning at one of the dozens of screens that fill the room. Nofar is leaning over him, close, too close, her hand resting on the armrest of his chair, her straight hair falling onto his shoulder, and I can almost smell her sweet perfume which I've seen her spray behind her ears and on her cleavage numerous times.

"It has musk in it," she told me when she saw me watching her, one of those times, "It arouses desire."

"How exactly?" I asked.

"It recreates animal body odor, but with appealing additives," she smiled at me and rubbed her wrists together, after spraying the perfume on them too, "it also has pumpkin, lavender and liquorice. They encourage blood circulation to the penis."

"Okay, now you're just making it up."

"I swear, it's scientific," she laughed. "Want some?" She held the little bottle out to me and I want to say that I refused and did not look for it on the shelves at the drugstore later, cursing myself for not asking her for the name.

Now she and Pinto are focused on the screen, her arm rubbing his every so often as she points at something on the screen, and I pray that Pinto is congested. When I approach the two of them they greet me with smiles and look back at the screen. I take a chair and sit beside them. On the screen is a map of Rome, with different routes marked, like in the running app I use.

"This is a graphic report of all of the targets' waypoints and recurring routes," Pinto tells me without taking his eyes off the screen. "Like we saw in the material that you collected, the Great Synagogue appears to be a central destination, but it's not the only one."

"I'll try to cross-reference all the places and see if they came up in our other sources' conversations," says Nofar.

"Great, Nofar, that would be awesome," says Pinto and finally turns to me. "What's up?"

"I need to talk to you," I tell him.

"Okay," he nods, and waits for me to go on.

"Not here," I get up.

"Shall we go to my office?" He stands and turns to Nofar, "Thank you, Nofar, great work today."

"Of course, Hon, I'll talk to you later," Nofar shakes her hair as we walk away.

"Hon?" I ask him in the hallway on our way to his office. Pinto laughs and says nothing.

"What's up, Shagi?" He asks me and after we sit down in his office, "What's so classified?"

"It's Weiss," I say.

"What about Weiss?"

"He told me what you all are making him do. That's crazy.

216

You have to help him. There's got to be another way. Do you understand what you're asking him to do?"

"Since when are you and Weiss such good friends?"

"Let's not get carried away. But I still don't want him to get screwed like that."

"Look, I'm not crazy about it either, and it really sucks that it had to go like this," he sighs, "but what can I do? You tell me."

"You can talk to Shabtai, you could talk to Kiki, you could *all* go to the information security unit, you could do something!" I cry.

"Come on, are the two of you new here?" Pinto starts to lose his composure. "There's no chance we allow a situation where someone's hiding information that could expose him to blackmail. Not from his family and definitely not from us. We could come down much harder. It's actually because it's Weiss that we were so gentle here. At the end of the day we are asking him to clean up his own mess. These are the rules."

"Rules, rules, stop being so uptight," I exclaim, "there's no rule that's never been broken."

"Did you just call me uptight?" He smiles.

"If the stick in the ass fits," I don't let myself smile even though he's still charming, even when he's being a douche.

"Okay, that's enough, Fishman," he's serious now. "I think we've exhausted the subject. I wouldn't want to think that a candidate for a managerial position treats rules as a joke," it's less sexy, how he's talking to me now.

"And I wouldn't want to think that a manager at the organization is throwing an employee, when he's at his most vulnerable, to the dogs," I retort, "Management is not just marking targets for attack."

"Okay, Fishman, we're done here," says Pinto, "I do not need your management tips."

I stay facing him for a few more moments and he doesn't look at me, so I stand up with a loud squeak of the chair and turn to leave his office, pausing a moment to give him time to soften and stop me, but he does nothing and I slam the door behind me.

I know that as a manager he has play by the rules and tow the party line and uphold the system, but is the system anyway? He's part of the system. His automatic aligning himself with procedure makes me wonder how he would act if I was in a similar predicament. Would he bend the rules for me? For better or worse, I'm not sure I want to know the answer.

27

His high school teacher was called Ilana Gershon. She was short and had dark, cropped hair and glasses with black plastic frames which she only wore when she was reading, and which hung around her neck on a beaded necklace the rest of the time. While most teachers went by 'Teacher' or their first name, she insisted on the formal "Mrs. Gershon." insisted that students call her "Mrs. Gershon" and not "Teacher," or "Ilana." Weiss gave her the nickname "Mr. Gershon" which he wrote in large letters over top of a caricature of her that Roey, the class artist, had drawn. When Mrs. Gershon discovered it she summoned Weiss's parents for a meeting, not for the first time. He sat with them, mentally prepared for whatever was to come, ready to pay the price for making his friends laugh, to divert the outrage away from himself. But Mrs. Gershon did not dwell on the nickname he had given her. Instead, she spoke of Weiss's potential and his leadership abilities, alongside his tendency to bother others.

"He is very sensitive," she told his parents as if he wasn't in the room. "The question is how he will choose to use it." She lowered her eyes and turned to him, "I know that this is not an easy time, teenagers can be mean and you need a protective shell: Just be careful that it doesn't grow too thick, because you might not feel your skin anymore."

If she had just scolded and punished him it would have bothered him less than this, as if she saw something in him that he was trying to hide. He rolled his eyes at her, and when they got home he added a mole with three hairs growing out of it to the cartoon and ignored his mom's requests to explain what Mrs. Gershon was talking about. Growing up, Weiss learned to keep his struggles to himself, even from his parents. He did not feel they were on his team. He always knew how to look after himself, knew that his problems were his own, and did not want criticism from his dad or reassurances from his mom, who always complained that he didn't tell her anything. She did not understand that if he expressed his feelings or troubles to her or anyone else it would make them more real, the pain would show in his eyes and be tangible, so he chose not to share. Over time, his mother stopped asking, got used to him being that way. And he has been this way for years, the tough guy, impenetrable. People can't see when he's struggling, because he isn't. He's a rock, anybody could lean on him and he never needs to lean on anybody else. He does not bend, or need, or crack, or at least does not reveal the cracks, but plasters over them until nothing can be seen.

And now he is being asked to peel layer after layer, to scrape and dig until the foundations show and he will stand naked before everyone. They are asking him to break in, mix the outside and inside, to disturb the order that he worked for years to establish, to destroy the fence that he built.

He reminds himself that he does not have to tell, that the choice is his to make and he can still keep things to himself. The people in his life don't need to know everything. He can decide to leave the Agency, which is hard, but the question is what will be harder on him, what will turn his life upside down, which choice is reversible and which isn't.

It's only work; as satisfying as it may be, it is not his whole life.

He can still give up the career that he's made for himself, give up who he's become, give up the future that he wanted for himself and hand it over to Fishman. How happy will she be if he just gives up on the competition without a fight! She'll probably feel like she's proving her superiority, proving that she's better, more stable—she'd love to see him fall.

Losing the competition alarms him more than anything else; it shows weakness and inferiority, everything he wanted to refute. No, he won't go without a fight, he's good, if not the best, and he will not give up his place at the Agency. It's that fighting spirit that drives him forward, step by step from his car to his childhood home, and toward his parents.

"Gali!" His mother opens the door to him, and her face lights up. She is wearing a thin burgundy sweater, matching the color of her hair, a black button-down shirt underneath and brown pants. She hugs him and kisses his cheek. He smells soup powder and talcum and home.

"Hey, Mom," he says.

"Come in, I'll take your coat," she hurries him inside and closes the door behind him.

Weiss steps inside. The living room is small and dark, lit only by the flickering lights of the television that hangs above the heavy wooden sideboard. Across from her is the old couch, a checkered wooden blanket in brown and beige draped over it, and beside that a brown leather armchair, which the whole family bought his father for his sixtieth birthday. His dad is sitting in it, watching a replay of a soccer game.

"Come in, Honey, I'll make you tea," she hurries to the kitchen.

"No, Mom, thanks, I don't want any," he calls after her.

"I want some," his father's voice issues from the armchair, "Leave the teabag in, sit down. What are you standing for?" He addresses Weiss for the first time since he came in.

His mother returns from the kitchen with a floral-printed mug, hands it to his dad and turns on the living room lamp. She looks at Weiss with a smile, "You look great. So, what's the latest, how are you?"

"Actually I have to tell you something. Come, Mom, have a seat," he holds his hand out to her.

"You're getting married!" She exclaims with a clap, a spark in her eyes. "I knew he would marry Zoe, well, why didn't you come together? We haven't seen her for a long time, what a charming girl."

"Mom, I'm not marrying Zoe," Weiss tries to interrupt.

"Really?" His mom stops and looks at him wide-eyed. "That's a shame, Gali, she's such a sweet girl, how is she?"

"We split up," Weiss replies.

"Really?" She cries again, "Oh no, what a shame! She's such a good girl. Okay, Gali, it's okay," she says, and Weiss wonders if she's comforting him or herself, "You'll find someone else, you're such a smart, handsome man, and you've got your act together, who wouldn't want to snatch you up? You'll see, it'll be fine."

Weiss waits for his mother's flow of speech to stop, then says, "Mom, I didn't come to tell you that we broke up."

"Ah, no? So what is it, Gali? What happened?" His mom approaches him and fusses with the collar of his polo shirt.

"Mom, can you sit down a moment? Dad, can I have a sec?" He turns to his dad who is still watching the players running around the screen,

His dad looks away from the screen impatiently and says, "Okay, what?"

Weiss waits for his mother to sit as well and opens his mouth, his dad stealing glances at the television, his mom gently tapping her thigh, and he looks away again, "Well what is it? Speak!" His dad booms at him.

"Okay, I'll make it quick," Weiss stays standing, too anxious to sit, his pulse is in his temples and he blurts the news out in a hurry, "The reason I broke up with Zoe is..."

"No!" His father blurts and gestures at the TV, "Nooo what a miss!"

"Dad, can you please— just one moment?" Weiss raises his voice slightly.

"Yes, sure, I'm listening, it's a shame they missed that free kick, some goals are practically handed to you... I'm listening, shoot."

"Gali, you started to tell us why you broke up with Zoe," his mom helps him, her eyes expectant and her forehead creased.

"Yes, I know Mom," Weiss replies impatiently, "So the reason that I broke up with Zoe is that I met someone else."

His father unglues his eyes from the TV screen, and now both of his parents are looking at him in protracted silence until Weiss manages to find his voice again. "A man," he says. "I met a man." His eyes are fixed on the floor, but he can hear his mom's breathing stop.

When he dares to look up, he meets her wide eyes. A moment later she seems to shake it off, nods her head a few times and comes to hug him. "That's nothing," she mumbles quickly and strokes his head as if to forget, "Nothing happened," she pets him as if he were five years old and fell off his bike. "Everyone makes mistakes, Gali, it would be a shame to ruin such a good relationship."

"Mom, I don't love her," Weiss says.

"Okay," his mom seems to relent, "So some other girl will come along."

"And what if I don't want another girl?" Weiss blurts out and does not know why he said that, he wasn't even sure if it's true until this moment.

"Come on, Gali, that's nonsense," his mom says curtly. "Doesn't want a girl. So what do you want? To be alone? Not to have children or a family? Is that what you want?"

"Mom, I really don't know what I want. I just wanted to tell you," he says, choked.

"Why?" She asks suddenly reproachfully,

"What do you mean, why?" Weiss asks, and it's hard to breathe with the lump in his throat, it's too much for him, he can't handle this.

"Why did you feel the need to tell us that?" His mom rebukes him. "What good did that do?" She looks different to him, her soft voice replaced by a sharper, cutting one.

"Dalia, that's enough," his dad says in a low voice, his eyes fixed on a point in the distance.

"It is hardly enough, he barely ever comes, hardly speaks to us, always in a hurry, and this, of all things, was important enough for him to tell us? This?"

"Would it have been better if I'd said nothing? That I continue not to tell you anything? Is that what you want?" Weiss spits, and regrets it immediately.

He didn't want to hurt her feelings, she's the only one who always was on his side, he can't lose her now, especially, when he is going to lose everyone. But she's already left the room, slamming the bedroom door, and with her goes his protective net against his dad. He never managed direct communication with him, as much as he tried, he always needed his mom or his brothers to intercede for him, soften it for him.

Weiss looks at his dad who's looking at the sneakers on his feet. The TV is flickering in the background, but he's no longer watching. He bends over, unties a loose knot on his right shoe and reties it. He does not look up and does not say a thing.

"Say something," says Weiss.

"What is there to say?" His father replies in a quiet, halting voice.

Right. What is there to say indeed? Weiss just revealed the biggest secret of his life, his life which is turned upside down. He's just standing before him in his most vulnerable moment.

What is there to say? And what did he really expect? That he'd throw his arms around him? He didn't really expect comfort from his dad. He didn't even get it from his mom. He could at least say *something*, respond, acknowledge what just happened here, what he said, who he is, even shout at him, that would be better than this silence.

"What's on your mind," Weiss tells him, "Just say it. That I always disappointed you and I continue to disappoint you," says Weiss.

His dad looks, raises his head and his mug of tea. He drinks slowly and when he returns the mug to the table, his hand is trembling. "That's what you think?" He asks.

"Yes, that's what I think," Weiss squints. His heart is pounding.

His dad shakes his head from side to side, "Then you're a bigger idiot than I thought." He leans back heavily in his chair which groans under his weight, "Sit down already," he waves his hand toward the sofa.

Weiss hesitates, then sits on the edge of the couch. They sit for a few silent moments, not looking at each other.

"It's good that you told us," his dad says.

Weiss looks at him in surprise, "Are you serious?"

"Don't get me wrong, I'm not thrilled about... this. But for the first time in your life you're enough of a man to tell the truth, not just trying to impress. The first time you're taking responsibility. It's good, Gal. You're growing up."

"Ah," Weiss manages to mutter.

"Mistakes happen. I wouldn't hurry to break up with Zoe," says his dad, turning the volume back up on the TV. "She really is a good girl."

225

28

As the days go by, it's harder and harder for me to gear down at work. Nofar is tired of seeing me in the operations room, and Jonathan is back to raising his eyebrows at how often I exercise, but I need to be in motion. When I run I detach, my head clears, my breathing expands; I control the pace and calm the storm. The people around me blur and sharpen, the wind hits my face and the heat of my body beats the cold outside.

When I was a kid, Girl Scouts filled my days and my soul, filling the cracks that life had opened up. During my military service, at the remote intelligence base, I volunteered for extra shifts, which endeared me to my team and protected me from myself. It was only after my BA that I found myself, for the first time, completely free, too free, free of direction and burden, and although I tried to be a waiter seven days a week, there were many off-hours and the feeling of emptiness only grew. Looking back, Pinto's job offer saved me from myself, but evidently, even years later, that emptiness has not filled, just waited quietly, lurking for the moment when my mind is no longer distracted to come back and swallow me up. People yearn for freedom: I escape it. And now it is grasping me tightly. How am I supposed to handle a whole life in my own company?

It's too much to go to the operations room on a Saturday, but the thought of staying home another day, trying to find myself between its walls, turns my stomach. I suggest that Jonathan and I take a day trip to Udim to visit Maya and Asaf for a change of scenery.

As we approach the little village, the landscape turns from gray to green, diverting my mind and soul from the everyday hustle. We enter Udim, bouncing along the generously distributed speed bumps, forcing us into the slow village pace and allowing us a long look at the yards of the empty, well-maintained houses. Here and there some dog, freely wandering, barks cheerfully and chases after the car until it is swallowed up into one of the yards.

Maya and Asaf's house is the last one on the street. There is no gate at the entrance and we drive straight into a huge grassy meadow crossed by a wide stone path. Wind chimes hang from a distant tree, swinging in the light breeze, and I wonder how they survive a storm. There's a deck on the far side of the yard, dangling strings with pine cones. Three little bicycles are lying nearby. At the edge of the grass is a small vegetable bed with "cauliflower," "lettuce," "carrot," and "beetroot" signs labeled in childish handwriting, and between them stands a scarecrow wearing a "Clementine Kindergarten" shirt. Delicate pink flowers bloom along the sides of the path.

"Those are Vinca flowers," Jonathan whispers when he sees me examining them. He looks charmed by the garden, and there's an old, familiar spark in his eyes. We head to the front door flanked by a photogenic jumble of potted plants of different sizes, paint peeling off in pastel aesthetic. I overcome my reluctance and let Jonathan take my hand. Maybe this is what we need, the simplicity and quiet, far from the rat race and all the noise, and Tomer, and Pinto, and the voices that enter our home and my head and dictate what we want and how we want it. Here it is, in Udim, this simplicity, with a glimpse of fields and no city smog.

But as we get closer to the front door, the serenity is broken.

Voices are coming from the house and if I didn't know better, I would say that we are standing at the gates of hell. A mix of laughter, wailing, screams and the sounds of objects breaking intermingle and hurt my ears. The door opens, and for a moment I think we are about to be sucked into the furnace; the terrible noise gets louder, but it is only Maya, opening the door to us in a tunic, her bralette sticking out where there used to be cleavage. She smiles an exhausted smile at us, and something viscous sticks to the ends of her hair which she tucks behind her ear. Her face is thinner than I remembered, maybe because of the veganism, and on her leg hangs Tuli, her two-year-old, crying bitterly.

"Her Anna and Elsa cup broke," Maya explains the crying and stretches to hug me and then Jonathan, and I see the shock which he tries to hide behind a polite smile.

"Koreni and Goni broke it!" Tuli squeals accusingly.

Behind her, Koren and Goni are passing a soccer ball back and forth, Koren commentating hoarsely while Goni keeps screaming that he has to pass to him already, he's open, Dad, he's not passing the ball to me! Asaf presides over all this, responding calmly, his bass voice only adding to the cacophony as he gives his sons one last chance to calm down for the third time since we arrived.

I scan the beautiful house that Maya designed herself. Soldier figurines in khaki and olive green lie in a jumble on the Indonesian carpet, along with a Barbie with her hair cut and wearing war paint. There are handprints across the Belgian windows, a stained Hello Kitty blanket on the vintage armchair that Maya has reupholstered, and water guns on the couch that was made to order by a Druze artisan.

"Coffee? Rescue remedy? Coke?" Maya smiles at us and lifts Tuli into her arms.

"I'll get it," I head to the kitchen with Maya after me.

"I'll give her something to eat—she's always cranky when

she's hungry," she apologizes, and Asaf adds in his bass voice from the living room, "and she's always hungry."

Maya ignores him and turns to us, "meanwhile, tell me all the latest with you guys."

"I actually wanted to..." I start, but another scream cuts me off. Tuli wants to eat from the pink bowl, not the red one. The pink one is in the dishwasher, but that does not concern her, and she keeps screaming until Maya washes the dirty bowl, wipes it and pours out chocolate cereal.

"Sorry, it isn't always like this," she smiles a tired smile and sits down beside Tuli, "Or rather, it is always like this, but I'm not supposed to say that, right? I'm supposed to say that children are a joy and the suffering is all worth it, right?"

"That's what she's eating?" Asaf appears behind Maya, setting his eyes on Tuli's meal and then smiles, kisses me and gives Jonathan a friendly smack on the back.

"Yes, this that's what she's eating," Maya snaps in a tone I don't recognize, "But feel free to make her a colorful salad and a buckwheat quiche if you want. I'm sitting down. For the first time since this morning, by the way."

"Right, because I've been in the basement hitting the bong all morning," he says with a bitterness that's unfamiliar to me and pulls a towel off the armrest of her chair.

Asaf was always the ideal partner. Not just for Maya. He was like a universal plug that fits every kind of socket, meeting a partner's needs perfectly, whatever they were; handsome, thoughtful, sensitive and good in bed, from what I heard. But I haven't heard anything in a long time.

Asaf drags Jonathan to play basketball with the boys in the yard, and the house is quiet, disrupted only by the chewing sounds of Tuli who is eating with her mouth open.

"You look good," Maya tells me, "I guess some rest is good for you, huh?" She says after I make a face.

"I'm going nuts at home."

"Well, you're just not used to it, you need to get used to good things too. You'll have more time with Jonathan now, to work on your stuff, it'll be good for you, you'll see."

I look at her with her direct, knowing expression, and wonder if her certainty would waver if I told her about Tomer, and Pinto, and my heart which feels so far from Jonathan, and from me, for so long. I'm not even sure it would matter to her. Some people always seem to know exactly what's right, and follow their decision no matter what happens along the way.

"You're just stressed now, Babe. Which is normal, now that it's getting more real. Obviously rest will help you guys with the baby."

I nod. Sure it's normal to be stressed, sure. My head starts pounding hard, the too-sweet drink that she poured into a green plastic cup burns my throat, and I drink and chat about types of succulents and nature parties and can't find a crack in our conversation to insert truth or frankness, feeling increasingly distant as the conversation goes on.

When Jonathan suggests that we get going, I am quick to accept and to escape back into the walls of my home where I won't risk revealing my secrets with no hope for forgiveness or redemption.

The next day I'm eating lunch in the cafeteria with Sharon who's just back from a week of surveillance in Rome. We eat pea soup and exchange updates on the operation and Weiss and the van that the targets rented, and about her kid and my pregnancy and miscarriage. She's mad that I didn't tell her until now and I say that I didn't tell anyone, but she had heard about the miscarriage from Weiss and was really offended.

"He was with me on the plane, I couldn't exactly hide it from him," I try to appease her.

"Fine, forget it. How are you?" She lets up.

I open my mouth to answer but my phone rings and it's Shabtai's secretary. He wants me in his office in half an hour.

"That must be the appointment," says Sharon. "They probably want to tell you that you got the position," and before I can respond, she adds, "Or that Weiss got it."

My mouth goes dry and my whole belly fills with desire and fear and reluctance. I don't know if I'm more scared of Weiss getting the job or me, and how he'll react if I get it? And how I'll act if he gets it? Or how I'll respond if I get it...

"Why so quiet all of a sudden?" Says Sharon.

"I'm stressed," I reply.

"Well, in half an hour it will be behind you," she says. Or ahead of me, I think.

"Come on," she says and lifts her tray, "let's smoke a cigarette."

We clear our trays, I grab an apple and we leave the cafeteria. On the bench beside the vending machines, Sharon lights a cigarette and hands me one, "You look like you could use it."

I reach for it and take the lighter from Sharon. It's been months since I smoked and the first inhalation fogs my head with a soft, pleasant dizziness. I blow out a thin coil of smoke and look at the tech building in front of us, its hall lights flickering and irritating the eye.

"Six hundred engineers and nobody knows how to change a lightbulb?" I hear Sharon say out of the fog of my mind.

"Head of operations," I repeat to myself. Would I do job training with Pinto? Would it last long? The thought of working closely alongside Pinto fills me with a warmth that flutters up to my heart a little, but only a little because I instantly consider the alternative—Weiss sitting with Pinto at meetings, whispering with importance, sitting in his place at the table. He would probably replace Pinto's simple chair with a fancy one like Shabtai's and fill the liquor cabinet with imported whiskey. What would it be like to work under him? Could I even stand it? I feel like we got closer lately before he flipped again and I can't predict his reaction and whether the promotion would go to his head. If he gets it. But it could still be me.

"Come in, Sweetie, have a seat," Shabtai shouts at me as I stand just outside the room.

I sit down at the table full of binders, papers and wooden brain teaser games. "How's it going?" I ask, and my heart pounds again.

"Want something to drink?" He asks, and without waiting for a response presses his intercom and shouts, "Morani, two cappuccinos." I don't understand why he needs an intercom.

"I heard you took a cooling-off period from the op, I hope you'll get back to it shortly, yeah?"

"As soon as possible," I nod and realize that I mean it.

"Great, great, we need a little feminine energy around here, ah?" He winks at Moran, his secretary, who comes in with two cups of coffee, "Thanks, dear," he thunders in her direction and turns back to me, "So what have you been doing with the free time?"

"Not too much," I admit, "Mostly exercise."

"That's very important, staying in shape, very important," he says and pulls the waistband of his pants over his bulging belly, "Well, honey, you don't think I called you in here to talk cardio, do you?" He makes a phlegmy throat-clearing sound, which sounds like a chuckle. "No no, we're here to discuss much more important matters. Your future," he raises his eyebrows and nods, and I tense even more.

"So this round of promotions is finalized, and I have a very interesting proposal for you," he smiles, and I can't sit straight any longer, my whole body tenses and I stop breathing and wonder why Pinto isn't here, when Shabtai says, "How would you feel about being the new head of HR?"

I look at him stunned, wondering if he's messing with me. Human Resources is not an operational position, it's not a professional role, that is, not of the intelligence professions. It has nothing to do with the core work I've been doing at the Agency all these years. It's not even a job that I applied for, can they just give me that kind of appointment?

And of course, it's a woman's job, not a field position, not dangerous, compatible with motherhood. Should I consider this an opportunity? Is the universe trying to tell me something? Is this how you balance a career and family life?

"Haaaa..." I hear Shabtai choking and snorting with laughter before I manage to answer, "You should have seen your face, I'm joking, sweetheart, I'm joking. You're replacing Pinto."

I feel like cymbals have been clashed over my head, and for a moment it's as though I'm hovering in the air, light and free, sparks of joy and excitement flashing around me. I'm replacing Pinto. Me. Not Weiss. Me. There's a relief in this affirmation. They want me. I'm good enough. As good as them.

But gradually, other feelings creep in among the sparks of joy, occupying more and more space in my mind. I think of Jonathan, and the pregnancy, the treatments which will continue—or not, and how they will affect the job, and if I can even say no to this job, and why would I say no to everything I had hoped for in my career? I think of Weiss, too, and this additional blow for him, perhaps the hardest in a series of blows that he has gotten lately. Still, none of this erases the satisfaction that makes me hold my head high.

"Fishman, are you following?" asks Shabtai.

"Yes, yes, I'm digesting," I reply and smile.

"Well, digest quick, Sweetie, we're on a tight schedule here. We have to get you back to business as quickly as possible. Weiss hasn't been at his best lately—left you that job on a silver platter, as they say."

"Ah," I'm bummed to hear this but I already knew that Weiss was Shabtai's preferred candidate. That's legitimate, I don't need everyone to like me equally, nor for them to be happy with my choices. But I need to be happy. And I am. I am very happy they chose me, and I realize that I have to choose, it's time.

I thank Shabtai and promise that I'll speak to Pinto, and wonder again why he isn't here.

"Well, good luck," Shabtai concludes, "And of course, this stays between us, until the official announcement. I don't want the rumor mill starting up."

Sharon is sitting on the hallway floor outside the office and jumps up as I come out.

"I got the job," I tell her.

"Congrats, Queen," she hugs me.

I hug her back, but she pulls away and asks, "What's the matter? Aren't you happy?"

"I'm happy, but..." I frown, trying to articulate my feelings, "I'm not sure I can take the job," I finally say.

She looks at me with eyebrows raised, "Come again?"

"Because of the treatments," I say and drag her to the balcony.

"What do the treatments have to do with anything?" Sharon asks me on the way.

"I can't start a new job and then get pregnant right away. How will that look?" We sit down as far away as possible from the younger employees sitting and smoking.

"Okay, so postpone the treatments a little," says Sharon.

"And then what? I'll be free to work nights? And weekends? And be fully available?"

"And if you don't take the promotion?" Sharon asks, "What'll you do then?"

"What do you meant?" I ask.

"Well your current job—our job," she points her finger at me and herself alternately, "is no less demanding than Pinto's. Sure there's more downtime and we remember what our house looks like, but half the time we aren't in the country. How did you think this would work with a kid?" Sharon had been in the fighters' course two cycles ahead of me, and when she got back from maternity leave she continued from exactly where she left off, resuming trips and absences. "It's possible," she tells me and nods, "but I won't tell you it's easy, or that there aren't times when I feel like a terrible mother or wish I could just quit work or retire from motherhood. Yes, that too," she adds when she sees my face twitch.

My head starts to hurt. It's possible. Sharon is living proof that it's possible. She is also an example of the price I might have to pay. And anyway, Jonathan won't agree to postponing the treatments, he'll go crazy if I so much as bring it up. He won't understand, he'll be angry that my priorities are twisted, he'll feel like I deceived him, lied to him. I think he'll leave me and I think that I don't want to give up the job and I think that I have no choice, and I want to be happy about this accomplishment, but the ambivalence overshadows the excitement and I think that maybe it would have been better if I had not gotten the job and then I object. Here I am, again, allowing those closest to me to minimize my achievements and determine other goals that I should be aiming for, instead of being happy for me and my achievements, instead of being happy with me. No wonder it's hard for me to be happy.

29

He is sprawled on the sofa in sweatpants that smell of fried food and sweat. The room is stuffy, the blinds are shut and the usually spotless stainless steel sink is full of sticky plates and foul-smelling water. He's engrossed in a British crime show that he doesn't even know the name of when Shabtai calls. Weiss stares at his name flashing on the screen, debating whether or not to pick up, audibly scratching his overgrown stubble.

He knows he won't be able to ignore his bosses much longer; it's both impossible and unprofessional. But just for a few days, he would like to not think about it, not to deal with them, not to face the world. He needs more time to gather himself, gather strength. He needs to be reminded who he is. Or forget.

Weiss clears his throat, takes a deep breath and then answers the phone. On the other end, Shabtai demands to know how he is, his booming voice unusually quiet. After exchanging niceties, it's quiet. Weiss wonders if he should say something when Shabtai sighs heavily.

"Gal-chuk," he says, and Weiss' stomach flips. "It's not official yet, but I wanted to update you personally."

Weiss knows instantly. He should have seen it coming. How could he think that Shabtai was calling just to check up on him, still believing that someone might care—no. Shabtai tells him in a low voice that Fishman got the job and emphasizes that it was important to him that Weiss hear it from him first; it's not that he isn't an excellent, valued employee, otherwise they wouldn't have been encouraging him to apply. And the fact that they did just shows how much they admire him and see a future for him in the organization, but only one person can get this job and it's not his time. Fishman deserves it and there will be other opportunities. No reason to lose hope, on the contrary, he should keep working hard because opportunities are just waiting to come along. Good things happen to good people. Think positive and good things will happen.

A force within him grows and strengthens, like a wave that increases and swirls into itself, rises to his throat before retreating, collapsing and sinking. He feels like he's drawn inward, gathering and shrinking, while Shabtai praises him for "taking it like a man." He mutters noncommittally in response, as hammers pound in his head, and the call ends. It's over.

What was all this shit worth, and what price will he still have to pay to preserve the one place where he felt safe? He had kept his place but become a low-level player, not taken into account, back to underdog status after working so hard to move up. Apparently it wasn't enough. He hadn't changed enough, he's still him.

He seeks signs of rebellion within himself, a willingness to fight for something which was almost his but taken from him. He looks inside for the urge to convince, to explain, to repel, to kick in every direction and use all the resources at his disposal, the kosher and the less kosher, to get the upper hand. But he finds mostly emptiness, a kind of resignation that startles him more than any fit of rage, aggression or sadness he would expect to find.

He doesn't know how long he's been sitting like that, stunned and empty in front of the frozen TV screen, how long he feels nothing but a weak chill stroking his back, cold drips down his arms and legs, how long it takes him to notice that someone is knocking on the door... His heartbeat speeds up and his mind races, mapping out potential threats. Maybe Fishman is here to comfort him, a reluctant, false comfort, her face sad and her soul jubilant, or maybe Pinto, coming to check that he didn't hurt himself, since all the lines have been crossed and there's no way of knowing what he's capable of. Maybe it's his mother coming to talk; it's been a week since their conversation, the longest time they have ever gone without speaking.

Weiss remains sprawled on the sofa, not caring who might be at the door, who bothered about him in vain. He won't get up. The knocking continues and now his phone comes to life too, but he doesn't reach out or check the caller ID, just waits for the ring to subside and leave him alone, to surrender to the chill that is enveloping him.

Finally everything quiets, his body relaxes and his heartbeat slows, but then there's a rattling at the lock and the door opens. Weiss straightens up, looking anxiously at Zoe, who is standing in the doorway. The look in her eyes is a little surprised, mostly sad, and Weiss looks sadly at her too. She didn't deserve all of this, she was always good to him.

"Babe," she whispers, beautiful even without makeup, her skin golden and smooth and she comes over to him, not saying a thing about the jumble of clothes on the sofa, just making space for herself and sitting down on its edge.

"What are you doing here?" Weiss asks softly.

"Babe, I don't want it to be over," she says, tears hanging from her long lashes.

"Zoe," Weiss sighs.

"I know, I heard you, and it's fine with me," she hushes him, sitting tall and determined. "You know that I'm open about these things, you know I never imposed limits on you," she stops for a moment, and Weiss thinks she's waiting for his confirmation but he doesn't answer and she goes on, "Sure I was a little surprised when you told me, but I thought about it and I'm fine. Really. I don't think it should ruin things between us," she nears him a little, her knee brushing against his, and he fights the urge to withdraw his leg and only slowly changes his position to put some space between them.

"Zoe," he says again, looking in her direction but not in her eyes, "I am not sure that I can give you what you want."

"I want you," she says and tears are now streaming down her cheeks and she hugs his neck, hanging from him, her head sinking into the hollow of his shoulder, "Do you love me?"

"I," he hesitates, but he can't continue to hurt her, "Yes, I love you. But..."

"So that's it," she silences him, "I don't need more than that," and she kisses him and he is still and she continues, planting kisses on his neck and the hollow of his shoulder. He sighs again and hugs her tight and she grips him and whispers, "stay with me." Her whisper deepens the void in his chest and the cold in his hands and he does not say a thing and his thoughts are far away, but his arms remain wrapped around her, despite or because of the chill, and she stays for the night. They don't sleep together, just lie quietly next to each other until he reaches over and turns off the light. Some things are easier to bear in the dark.

In the morning she stretches out and her movements are long and languid, and she rests her cheek on his, rubbing her face against his overgrown bristles before slowly getting up and going to the bathroom. She washes her face, does her makeup, drizzles some of his cologne on her wrists and the neckline of her shirt as she always does. Then she makes them both coffee and two slices of whole wheat toast for him, as she always does, her things already spread around his apartment again, as if they had never been gathered up and taken away, and she kisses him goodbye as she always does, but her eyes are sadder and her kiss is longer and softer, as if trying to stop herself from crying. Weiss wants to say something but she looks away and hurries to take her leather bag, her big sunglasses and the keys to lock the door behind her.

30

It's been two days since my conversation with Shabtai and I still haven't talked about it with Jonathan. Or Pinto. He tried me a few times until I sent him a message that I'm not at my best and promised I would get back to him soon. He replied with a voice message saying, "I want to see you," and his deep, hoarse voice gives me chills every time I listen to it. I want to see him too, but I'm still not sure what to say. I feel the walls closing in, knowing that I have to decide but don't know what that decision should be.

I live in a culture that exalts freedom of choice as if it's a good thing. But what's good about it? After all, every choice requires a concession, there will always be an option I rejected, somewhere else I could have been. How do you choose what to give up? How can I choose who I will not be?

"You aren't choosing who you won't be, you're choosing who you *will* be," says Maya when I call to tell her the news, while wandering the supermarket, pensively loading up my shopping cart.

"It's the same thing," I say and try to remember which cereals Jonathan has not yet vetoed.

"And the opposite," she says, and I want to say that I'm not sure if I have the courage to find out who I want to be, but I have to cut it short because my mom is on call waiting.

"What, Mom? What's so urgent?" I transfer over to her.

"Hello, Mom, how are you, Mom – I'm fine, trying not to complain," she spits.

"And how's that going for you, Mom?"

"Listen, Shagi," my mother is the national champion of ignoring sarcasm, "We urgently need to organize Dad's sixtieth birthday party, we don't have much time."

"We?" I emphasize.

"Yes, we," she says, "He doesn't want a party, and I can't seem to persuade him myself."

"Mom, if he doesn't want a party, maybe don't throw him a party?" I try, despite knowing it's a lost cause. If my mom has decided something, God himself, were he to come down and reveal himself to her, could not convince her to change her mind.

"He doesn't want anything. If I give in every time he doesn't want something, he won't take his pills or shower."

"There's a difference between making him take his pills and celebrating his birthday when he doesn't want it, Mom. Give it up, poor guy," I try.

"If I let it go, he really will be a poor guy," she sticks to her guns.

"Fine, so leave me out of it, I have more urgent things to worry about," I say.

"What's more urgent than your father's birthday?" She retorts.

"I got the promotion," I tell her without meaning to, and as always, I regret it as soon as the words are in the air.

"What do you mean you got the promotion?" My mother stops for a moment and adds, "Ido's job?" My mother is the only person who calls Pinto by his first name. As far as I know, even his parents call him Pinto.

"Yes, Mom," I say. "Ido's job."

"Wow, Shagi, good for you, that's great, really, but how will you do that now, in the midst of fertility treatments?"

"That's precisely what I need to figure out."

"What is there to figure out? Tell them it's very flattering and good for them for giving a woman that kind of responsibility, but there are more important things on the line right now."

"I need to decide what is most important for *me*," I say calmly and feel a little stronger.

"Sure you need to decide, of course, just you also need to consider your age and that..."

"Thanks, Mom," I cut her off in a light tone, "I need to get off the phone, I'll be in touch with you about Dad's birthday."

After groceries, I go to the gym at the office to think a little somewhere quiet. Pinto doesn't like gyms. He prefers to run on the beach, no matter what the weather.

"It's the only legitimate place to run shirtless," he once told me, leaving me with that image engraved in my brain. And yet, just as I reach the seventh kilometer on the treadmill, I see him come in. He is scanning the people training in the afternoon until his eyes land on me, and he walks over and onto the treadmill beside mine, even though he's wearing jeans and Blundstones— his presentable attire. He must have a meeting at headquarters today. He matches his running pace to mine, and we run side by side in silence for a few minutes, but I'm distracted by his presence. instead of focusing on my breaths I am focusing on his and eventually I slow down and say, "You'll get blisters."

"All good," he replies, slowing to my pace and into a light jog. "What's up, Shagi?"

My nickname in his mouth makes me smile against my will. He seems to misinterpret the smile, and asks, "So you're pleased?" My smile fades.

"What?" He asks.

I stop the treadmill, panting, sit down on a bench and wipe my sweat with a towel.

Pinto gets off his treadmill, sits beside me and asks again, "What, Shagi?" His soft voice makes me melt inside; on the outside, I just shrug my shoulders and sigh.

"How foolish will I look, from one to a million, if I don't take the job?" I ask.

"You don't want the job?" He asks in a quiet, neutral voice, not clear if he's angry or empathetic.

"I want it more than anything but..." I cut myself off. "You know..."

"Fertility treatments?" He asks.

"Fertility treatments," I confirm. "And Jonathan. And you're the one who told me that family should come first, before everything else, right?"

"But you don't have a family yet," he says, "So the timing is actually good, no?"

"I have Jonathan," I say.

"True," he says carefully, "You have Jonathan. But you're not thinking of giving up the position because of him, but for your future child, no?"

It's a package deal, Jonathan and the child—I'm not sure there will be one without the other—but I do not want to indulge these thoughts so I don't answer, just sigh again and close my eyes and touch my head to his shoulder for a moment. I don't lean on him, just make contact and feel the soft fabric of his shirt and smell the coffee and apple-hookah and a little sour sweat mingling in my nostrils, and I hold back from taking another big inhale. Instead I straighten up. Pinto smiles at me, gets up and says, "Anyway it's yours, Shagi. You got the job, so whatever you decide, let yourself enjoy it." And I am happy, but sad, too, and I don't respond and a moment later he leaves.

In the locker room, I peel off my sweaty workout clothes, shower in boiling hot water and mumble to myself, "let yourself enjoy it," and continue to roll my tongue around the words even as I emerge from the thick steam on, get dressed and go home. Jonathan is not there, and I take off my coat and tall boots and lie down on the sofa in my long, thin dress. My muscles are tired and sore, and my thoughts gradually blur into a dream in which Pinto and I are running in the sea with bare feet, and behind us, like groomsmen who lost their way, lots of small children in white clothes are running, leaving little footprints on the wet sand and a trail of pink and white petals.

When I wake up, the smell of salt still in my nose, Jonathan is leaning over me, kissing my belly, holding my hips with both hands. I wake up slowly, stroke his head with my hands and think to myself, "Let yourself enjoy it."

Jonathan whispers, "Hey," and continues to kiss me slowly, descending, his tough hands rise up my thighs and roll up my dress. He used to wake me up like that in the morning, a few minutes ahead of the alarm clock, snatching quick morning sex before the start of the day. I lift my hips and he pulls down my underwear and spreads my legs and kisses me up my inner thigh, drawing spirals with his tongue and nibbling gently. I tremble and raise my hips, but he takes his time, strokes in circles, faster and stronger until I can't take it anymore, and he hugs me tightly as I tremble in his arms. As I come down, he kisses me on the neck and behind the ear, whispering, "I love you," and lays his head on my shoulder. I hug him and say, "Me too," and don't manage to tell him about the promotion.

"You've been kinda gloomy these past few days," he says and strokes my hair.

"I'm going nuts at home," I tell him.

He raises his head and looks in my eyes, "I know. Maybe we should consider another solution. That won't put you at risk, or drive you crazy."

"I want to go back to the op," I hear myself saying.

"That will put you at risk," says Jonathan, but then adds, "It's up to you. I don't want you to be miserable."

My eyes sting with tears, and the effort of not crying hurts in the bridge of my nose. Jonathan runs a finger up the length of my spine, and I shiver and hug him tight, so he won't see the tear rolling down my face.

31

He enjoys a few moments of grace before it all comes crashing back to him, a few moments when everything feels normal. He wakes up in his well-designed bedroom, partly covered by a satin, mocha-colored sheet, sunlight moving across Zoe's golden skin; she is beautiful as she sleeps, her hair spread across the pillow and her leg resting on his. Everything is good.

But then, like a wound, its scab torn off too soon, the pain floods back and he winces, the beauty of the room, and of Zoe, fade in light of reality. His limbs are so heavy he doesn't know if he can get out of bed. He doesn't want to. He wants to tell Pinto to shove the op up his ass, or Fishman's, if she's so eager to replace him. He wants to shake it all off, the responsibility, the concern, all the trouble is not worth it. But that's not his way, he won't give in to these impulses. He's a professional, and there's Roccelli and the country's security and his pride, what remains of it, and he can't just run away.

With great effort he gets up, takes clothes out of the wardrobe without even looking, drinks an espresso from the new machine and gives Zoe a small kiss on the cheek. Avoiding his own reflection in the mirror, he grabs an energy bar on the way out the door. Arriving at the Agency, he walks down the corridor with his head held high and face relaxed, entering the briefing room a few minutes early as it slowly fills with people.

"... so then she tells him, it's an extra fifty from behind," he hears Danino finish a story, groan with laughter, "it's more expensive. Because you only paid for one hole. It's extra, see?"

"Okay, enough, you overdid the joke, Bro, you milked it dry," Yardeni calls over to Danino, "you just tweaked its titties and..." he raises his head and notices Weiss in the doorway, "Hey man," he grows serious and nods at him. "What's up?" The laughter around him quiets down.

Weiss sits down in an empty chair with a thump, looks around the faces staring at him, wide-eyed, and doesn't respond. So this is how it's going to be? They don't even get that quiet for Fishman.

As if hearing his thoughts, Fishman enters the room, tells Yardeni that he needs a haircut and smiles a small smile at Weiss before sitting down at the end of the table. Weiss wonders if she's sitting there on purpose, close to Pinto, if it's part of the training, if it's official already, if the quiet conversation that she's having with Pinto is about the job, if Weiss is already out of the loop.

When the meeting begins, he tries to focus on Pinto's updates about the targets, who rented a van a few days ago and frequently discussing "the wedding" in a week and a half. "It sounds like the real thing. A tracking device has already been installed on the vehicle, and we're moving up to the highest alert level," says Pinto. "We won't let them win."

The room buzzes with bustling and excitement, tension rises, procedures sharpen. Weiss hears everything as if from a distance. It's like when he's tracking someone and hears their voices through the earpiece, but the images are far away. He feels like he's no longer there, no longer with them. He tries to wake himself from this daze, to reassure himself that everything is okay, or—almost okay, and it's just a matter of time until he's totally back on track, he still has his job, and Zoe, even his father is acting as if everything is normal, and his mother will calm down, he's not worried about her.

But something deep and dark in his stomach insists, pulls him down, passionate and vibrant, bubbling and refusing to be ignored. If everything is so okay, why isn't he fighting for this promotion? Why did he not appeal their decision? Why won't he claim what he deserves, what he has fought for so long, what he wants more than anything else? Could it be that he lacks the strength he thought he had? Maybe he no longer wants it? Or maybe this desire was always there to hide other, bigger, more burning desires, that are now out in the open? But instead of relief, he feels defeated, tired, and more trapped inside himself and his choices; not only the promotion but the dream of promotion was taken from him, that ambition that had defined him for so long, that had marked a path. He feels like the only thing keeping him invested in the operation is Roccelli. This boy who fell into the op without meaning to, without wanting to, who is risking a lot, unaware of the consequences, who has entered Weiss' heart far deeper than intended.

Weiss looks at all the people around him writing notes in their little notebooks with the symbol of the unit, alert and buzzing with anticipation, gazing at Pinto as if he could help them with something, as if he could save them from their pathetic lives. But nobody can.

"Furthermore," Pinto continues, "Regarding the source, from the information we have collected, we have a suspicion, insufficiently substantiated, for now, that he will serve as an unknowing asset. That is, that the targets will use him to carry out the attack."

Weiss straightens up, "What do you mean?"

"I don't know exactly," Pinto shrugs, "But they're probably giving him some role. We're still looking into it."

"As a collaborator?"

"A collaborator or executor," says Pinto.

"You understand what that means?" Weiss feels his blood boiling

"Yes," Pinto says without further comment.

"I don't think you do," Weiss raves, "We could be sending one of our sources to his death."

"As I said, the information is still uncertain, and anyway we aren't sending anyone to his death because we are planning to stop the attack, remember?"

"I remember. I also remember that for every operation, all possible scenarios must be taken into account."

"And we are accounting for all possible scenarios," Fishman suddenly intervenes, her voice inflaming Weiss even more.

"I don't think that the death of a source is a reasonable scenario. I propose that we consider ending his involvement in the operation," he says, channeling all of his energy into keeping his cool, not to catch fire in front of them, not to reveal the extent of his concern for Roccelli, not to be suspected of anything other than concern for the operation's success.

"Weiss, think about it," Fishman tries to cool him down. "How will it look to the targets if he suddenly disappears? They'll suspect something, and we'll never manage to get our hands on them. They'll just disappear and pop up somewhere else and all of our work will be for nothing."

"We know how to be discrete. We could think of a cover story, we could organize a suitable excuse, we can," he tries.

"Back to the operation." Pinto cuts him off, and Weiss takes a deep breath so he won't let him have it. Now is not the time to break all the barriers he set for himself.

"In conclusion," Pinto continues as if Weiss is not going up in flames right before his eyes, "all of the indications show that we are nearly there, I need you all sharp and focused, not doubting, not sentimental," he looks at Weiss, who narrows his eyes and a chill passes through him. He had never before been suspected of sentimentality. Calling him sentimental is like saying he's weak and now the burden of proof is on him. He hardens his expression and his jaw, and doesn't respond or show a hint of the flames burning in his chest.

"Are the Italian authorities involved yet?" Fishman asks.

"That's a good question," he smiles at Fishman, but Weiss no longer cares. "Not yet. We are waiting for the exact right time to involve them. In the meantime we are bringing in reinforcements," he continues. "Fishman and Weiss will join the two teams already in the field—day after tomorrow."

"Fishman's coming back?" Yardeni asks.

"Fishman's coming back," Fishman replies.

"What about the cooling-off period?" He asks, and Weiss objects too. He had hoped to finish this operation alone, it's his responsibility, he owes it to Roccelli.

"Given the urgency we shortened the cooling-off period to a week and a half. We need her there," Pinto smiles at Fishman again, and she actually smiles at Weiss, a friendly, condescending smile, but Weiss looks away. All of this thoughts are on Roccelli, and he's certain he's the only one in the room thinking of him. He bears sole responsibility for the kid's wellbeing. Even if he doesn't get hurt he could be arrested, or accused of collaboration. If that happens, the Agency will help him, Weiss reassures himself, they must. But what if they don't?

At the airport, Fishman keeps giving him pleading looks. They arrive separately, close to boarding, but she soon locates him at a small table by the fountain, despite the hundreds of people patrolling the area, awaiting flights.

Fishman buys an overpriced sandwich and coffee for each of them, places the refreshments on the table, takes a seat beside him on a cold metal chair and asks gently how he is, her eyes fixed on him, awaiting a response. She doesn't rush him even when he says nothing, gives him time, to re-gain his trust, but he won't fall for that again, he won't reveal himself before her, won't give her the satisfaction. Who knows what she told

Pinto, and who knows if that had anything to do with the promotion decision. He won't be tempted by her again. He'll go to Rome and do his job like the professional he is and maintain minimal contact. He won't say any more about his concern for Roccelli, won't show weakness or give them another chance to underestimate him and take him out of the game.

"Well, at least eat the sandwich," says Fishman, holding out a ciabatta sandwich in plastic wrap. "It's whole wheat flour and tuna, just how you like it." She's right—that is what he likes— and he takes it from her and tears angrily at the saran wrap.

A group of foreign flight attendants pass by, dressed in blue uniforms, with skirts barely covering their knees, their heels are high and their hair is tied back. Fishman turns her head after them and then looks back at Weiss.

"Well? No comment on the blonde?" She asks. "Her buttons hardly closed over her chest."

"That's objectification," he retorts.

Fishman bursts out laughing. Weiss tries to keep a straight face, but to his dismay, his mouth curves into a small smile. Fishman gets serious and looks at him with sad eyes.

"Come on, enough of that cocker spaniel look," he says.

"What kind of look does a cocker spaniel have?"

"Look in the mirror," says Weiss.

"I don't have one. Can I use yours?" She smiles at him sweetly.

"Stop it, Fishman, let me hate you in quiet," he says in a low voice.

She nods, "You're allowed to hate me. But just promise me that you'll be done with it eventually. It will be pretty boring in Rome without your offensive comments."

"How about a quickie in the bathroom?" He says tiredly.

"You're just saying that to make me feel better," she says with a smile.

Weiss gives another small smile, "alright, let's get to our

gate—so your nonsense doesn't make us miss our flight."

"When I replace Pinto, we'll only fly first class," she winks at him as they stand at the boarding gate.

"Okay, shut up, the line is moving," he hurries her along.

They get to the hotel in the late morning, giving Weiss two hours to prepare for his meeting with Roccelli. Originally they had scheduled for the following day, but the day before the flight Roccelli called Weiss, demanding to move up the meeting. He sounded upset again, and Weiss didn't argue, just promised he would do his best. They managed to get an earlier flight, and now he's sitting across from him at the cafe that has just opened, the elderly owner of the place bustling around them, placing a large blackboard menu by the door, and hurries back to them, straightens the tablecloth, takes their orders and fills glasses of water. Only when she gets farther away does Weiss give Roccelli a penetrating look and ask quietly, "So what's troubling you, Kid?"

Roccelli shifts uncomfortably, stroking the embroidered tablecloth, his eyes darting in every direction since they sat down, his hands shaking as he picks up his glass of water and drinks thirstily from it. A drop of water drips down his mouth and neck. When he finishes, he wipes his mouth with his hand, reminding Weiss of a young kid again. Weiss wonders what he knows.

"I'm sorry, I don't want to do this anymore," Roccelli says the words as if they're escaping from his mouth, before he can think twice. "It's getting too risky. I think they're onto me. I'm not a part of this, I want to stop."

Me too, thinks Weiss, but says, "I'm sorry. You know you can't back out now."

"I'll return the money," says Roccelli.

"It's not about the money," says Weiss.

"So what is it about? You have to release me from this," pleads Roccelli, his eyes reddening. "You have to, talk to your superiors, I know you aren't working alone."

No one ever mentioned the Agency, but Weiss realizes that Roccelli has some idea, he knows that Weiss has deceived him, but he still looks at him expectantly.

"I can't," Weiss replies quietly; the pain in his stomach grows.

"So I'll just stop!" Roccelli's voice rises. "You can't force me, and if they fire me from work over this, so be it."

Weiss sighs. "It would be unwise to stop right now," he forces himself to say. "You have your family to worry about and your sister, believe me that you want me on your side," he says and hates himself for it. "Up until now you've managed to break the law more than a few times. It's not just your job that's at risk, but your scholarship too. I doubt you'll even be able to keep studying if someone finds out what you did."

"Why would anyone find out?" Roccelli looks at him with big eyes.

"Sometimes things get found out. Especially when one refuses to cooperate," Weiss sighs again. "As you said, I don't work alone and I don't make all the decisions, certainly not the big ones. This thing is bigger than the two of us and sometimes I regret involving you, but it's too late for that. Let me help you as much as I can, don't go against me."

Roccelli looks down, his shoulders slump forward, his head hanging between them. Weiss waits a beat before saying, "promise me you won't do anything impulsive, okay? And I promise that I'll try to get you out of this as soon as possible."

Roccelli looks up at Weiss, "you promise?"

"I promise to do what I can," says Weiss.

"Okay," Roccelli says and nods, "okay."

Weiss nods at him, puts his hand on Roccelli's and says, "You'll see, it'll be over soon."

32

We are sitting in the car by the entrance to the targets' hotel. After his meeting with Roccelli, Weiss looks even more shaken, biting his nails, hardly saying a word. Now, as the big moment approaches, every move the targets make could be critical and we cannot take our eyes off of them. We document their movements, noting any suspicious activity around the hotel, every person entering or leaving, every vehicle that passes by, photographing every license plate.

A thick scarf is wrapped around Weiss' neck and chin as if he's trying to disappear inside of it. I hold out a bottle of water but he shakes his head and resumes staring through the windshield. Rain begins to fall. Two kids with colorful umbrellas pass.

"I hated carrying umbrellas around everywhere as a kid," I say, still observing them.

"And now?"

"Now nobody makes me take one. One of the few advantages of adulthood," I smile.

"Being a kid isn't so great either," he says.

"No," I say. "But they have hope that things will get better."

Weiss breathes in sharply. I wait for him to say something, but he doesn't, and I think maybe I shouldn't have said that. "Was it already there when you were a kid?" I ask, stammering, "You know, the boys thing?"

"Fishman, leave me alone, would you?"

"We can talk about something else," I say.

"We can also not," his head slumps into the scarf and his eyes look out at the distance.

After about two tense hours of waiting, including my failed attempts to make conversation, and unknown pop songs that I find on some random radio station, the targets finally emerge from the hotel. But instead of turning towards their usual bus station, they walk in the opposite direction to the end of the street where their rental van is parked. It's big and white, like a blank ambulance. Weiss and I are on alert. According to Yarden and Sharon's reports, the targets did not use the vehicle since renting it, and now they are starting the car with a loud noise. We quickly update the other teams, waiting until the van passes by us in a cloud of gray smoke before tailing them.

We race down the streets of Trastevere, through central Rome, and beyond, to less and less touristic areas. On the outskirts of Rome, the targets slow down and enter a long street crowded with old workshops. They drive almost until the end of the street before disappearing into one of those old buildings whose front is wide open. We stop a few feet away, and Weiss dons a hat, a goatee and sunglasses, silently gets out of the car and crosses the street to photograph the place from a safe distance.

He comes back a minute later.

"It's a garage," he tells me and removes the hat, making his hair wild and fluffy.

"Okay," I take a deep breath, feeling my heartbeat accelerate and considering what this means. "Okay. We have to update the Agency and the other teams right away," I say. "We may need to act as soon as tonight."

"We have to check the listening devices to determine when they plan to come back for the van," says Weiss.

"Of course," I nod so he won't think he came up with something before me, or that I'm stealing credit for ideas. He keeps looking at me like a victim as it is.

We wait around twenty minutes, until the targets leave the garage without the van. Weiss hurries after them on foot, and a few minutes later he signals to me to join him at the bus stop two streets over. I park behind a bend in the road, providing a good view of the targets who are smoking at the empty station, waiting for the bus.

The owner of the garage, a Muslim Italian by the name of Belal Marai, is not known to the local police or linked to terror organizations, as Pinto informs us that evening. With two days remaining until the peak of the operation, our superiors in Israel still want to hold off on updating the Italian authorities until we've managed some further reconnaissance. This aberrant decision could be criticized, but it's meant to maximize our operational freedom.

Two days later, on the night of the reconnaissance infiltration, Weiss and I are black-clad in our break-in gear near the garage. The two other teams are stationed on both ends of the street to monitor and report on any suspicious movement. Once they confirm that the coast is clear, we approach the garage's closed gate, covered in colorful graffiti. The air is freezing, and our breath becomes vapor in the air. Weiss directs a flashlight at the gate's rusty lock and my anxiety sends a rush of blood to my trembling hands, but after a few attempts we manage to overcome the lock. Our silhouettes dance against the gate for a few moments, then it shifts up with a screech and we are swallowed up into the dark maw.

Inside it is pitch black and our flashlight beams search the garage walls, inspecting its contents. Rain starts falling, shaking the metal gate. Weiss aims his flashlight at the center of the space where it hits the targets' white van. There are a few tires in the corner, and from the center of the ceiling hangs a big fluorescent lamp. I deliberate for a moment, before locating the switch and turning on the light. The old garage is laid bare before us and I hurry to photograph it before scanning the place. A dirty door on the back wall leads to a tiny office. Dozens of rusty keys hang on a hook and we try each one of them to open the van doors, but they remain locked. Yardeni's voice crackles through the transceiver, warning us of t an unknown vehicle entering the street. I hurry to turn off the light, and we press against the garage walls until Yardeni confirms that the car is gone. Upon further inspection, we finally locate a bunch of keys in the desk drawer, which opens the van. We speculate that the owner of the garage installed explosives in the van. Our plan is to disable it and replace its sim card with one that we brought with us. This way the targets won't be able to activate the charge from a distance.

But when we open the trunk door, it's completely empty. We scan the vehicle, maybe something was attached to it from below, opening the engine cover, searching for openings in the upholstery, in the headrests, but in vain; we can't seem to locate the explosive. I start to sweat; precious time is running out and missing something crucial could have devastating consequences. I look at Weiss who is still busy carefully examining the front seats, and finally he looks up at me.

"It's all clean," he says, and I recognize the frustration in his voice.

I don't understand what we're missing, what we don't see or what made us miss something. I recall the Agency's suspicions about Roccelli and wonder if Weiss's intuition missed something here, if it's possible that Roccelli and the targets were collaborating, that they tricked us into coming here, but why?

The rain continues to hit the metal gate, thunder rolls in, and we check the vehicle again, inside and out, scanning the whole space of the garage once more, yet find nothing, until I finally say to Weiss, "okay, that's enough."

He nods silently. We close the van doors, return the key and leave the garage. The old gate closes behind us with a screech that can be heard clearly in the quiet street, and we get into the Fiat and drive away empty-handed.

33

Today is the day, the moment of truth, H-hour. He sits in the Fiat with Fishman, awaiting movement. Towards eleven a.m. the targets leave their hotel briskly and hail a taxi. Fishman starts the car and merges into traffic in their wake. The car is filled with a tense silence, both withdrawn, as they try not to let the stress cloud their senses. The tension grows as they realize that the route is leading them to the garage. The targets disappear behind the rusty iron gate and before long, emerge again in the van.

Weiss updates the operation teams and the local authorities, who are now finally in the loop and have taken control of the event. Even though they found nothing in the van the night before, Weiss and Fishman know that there's a good chance that it was booby-trapped afterwards. The event is classified as highly urgent, and since the early hours of morning, the Rome police have set up checkpoints all over the city.

At this stage, all agency teams go into passive status and receive constant updates from HQ in Israel based on local police reports. Tracing of the targets' vehicle shows that they are advancing through Trastavere towards the Great Synagogue. Sharon and Yardeni are surveilling the synagogue from Via Catalana, while Hadad and Harari observe from Via del Tempio. The area appears quiet. Sharon updates that a white Lancia is parked beside the synagogue and Weiss waits impatiently for her to finishing reading off the license plate number to free up the radio for more essential updates.

Now HQ reports that the van is approaching the synagogue, but a police checkpoint is supposed to prevent it from reaching its destination. All of the teams are anxiously awaiting an update from the checkpoint. They'll be stopped any moment now, thinks Weiss. The targets should be at the checkpoint already, but suddenly Nofar's voice on the transceiver says that they changed their route. Instead of turning at Della Rovere toward the Great Synagogue, they cross the Tiber River, heading North-East. The voices on the transceiver flare up as police stops are re-deployed. Weiss is frozen to his seat, listening to the voices on the two-way radio. The synagogue teams have not yet been evacuated; they must remain vigilant. The targets are traveling along the Tiber towards the city center.

"Where are they going? Are there other synagogues there?" Fishman asks.

Weiss' eyes narrow as he scans the map etched in his memory, all the synagogues and key points in Rome are mapped in his head and he says, "The Tripolitanian Synagogue is that way."

Fishman raises an eyebrow, he nods and hurries to report into the transceiver.

"We know," Pinto's voice confirms, "And the Israeli embassy, too."

He hears Fishman's breath stop, and Weiss struggles to take a breath, too. The Israeli embassy is secure and well-guarded, so the capacity to carry out an attack there is very low, nevertheless the thought of such an attack gives Weiss chills. It's not only the possible harm to such a significant site, but also the possibility that they screwed up, big-time, that he let his senses betray him, perhaps trusted the wrong person, and now months of surveillance went down the drain, leaving everything in the hands of the Italian police.

Nofar maintains an open line and updates them on the targets' progress towards another police checkpoint. Weiss' phone rings and Roccelli is on the line, despite their agreement not to have contact throughout the day. Weiss silences the phone but it keeps flashing in his hands like a ticking bomb. He tosses it aside.

The targets should be stopped any minute now, and this should be over, then he can get back to Roccelli and reassure him, tell him it's finished. But a minute passes, then two, then five, and there are no updates. Fishman looks at him questioningly and he looks at her; they don't understand.

If the targets realized they were onto them, they could accelerate and smash into the police stop. They could run over police officers or pedestrians, they could crash into any structure they chose and activate the possible charge in the vehicle. Weiss finds himself biting his nails and puts his hands down. Fishman shifts uneasily in her seat, they look at the clock again and again, waiting for news, when finally Nofar's voice is heard from the phone between them, "They've been arrested."

Weiss and Fishman exchange glances. Weiss wonders if this is it, if he can breathe a sigh of relief, when Roccelli calls again. He needs him. Weiss turns the phone over so as not to see it flashing. Nofar's voice comes in over the transceiver again, "They've finished scanning the van. It's clear and the targets have no weapons on them. They've been detained for questioning."

Weiss frowns, could this be how it ends? He hears Pinto on the line and turns up the volume.

"It's not over."

The teams around the Great Synagogue are on the lookout for suspicious movements. Weiss thinks he hears the wail of sirens in the distance, and his body stiffens, but it's just an ambulance somewhere. His nails dig into his palm. What are they waiting for? Why isn't it officially over yet?

"The forces are advancing towards the Lancia," they hear Nofar on the transceiver. Weiss has never been this eager for the end of an operation. He wants to talk to Roccelli, and tell him that it's all over, he's free. Maybe later on he can persuade Pinto to grant him a bonus for his involvement in the operation. Maybe they'll even let him meet the kid one last time to give him the money in person, say thank you, not apologize or anything, just show him that they weren't taking advantage of him, not treating him like a tool, to pat him on the shoulder and tell him he's proud of him, tell him that...

"Explosion by the Great Synagogue," Sharon's sharp voice zaps him from his thoughts, and Weiss needs several moments to understand what he heard, "I repeat, a car blew up a moment ago on the street by the Great Synagogue. No casualties among our forces. Casualties among the Italian forces. A license plate check indicates that this car belongs to our source."

34

He arrives at the airport in a daze, his eyelids red and swollen and the heart rate monitor on his watch reports abnormal readings following a sleepless night. He'd spent the night replaying their last conversations in his mind. His and Roccelli's. Antonio. He never called him Antonio. Probably nobody called him Antonio, but Weiss had never bothered to ask if he had a nickname. How little he knows about him. How he had trusted him and how he had disappointed him. It was a different kind of disappointment, deeper, more existential, than letting down the people around him. Guilt wound tightly around his neck, leaving no space for air or for forgiveness. Roccelli had depended on him, put his life in his hands, trusted him—he had no one else. And Weiss had abandoned him. He was dead because of him, there was no way to sugarcoat it, no escape from it. Weiss so loved to escape and now he couldn't.

He does not know how he got into the booby-trapped car, if he did it knowingly or not, if the targets threatened his family and he chose to sacrifice himself or they just gave him the vehicle and he didn't suspect a thing. Either way, it was clear to Weiss that he could not dodge his own guilt, nor did he wish to. He wanted to wallow in it, be submerged in it slowly, let it tighten around him, smother him—here, it's already happening—and make him disappear.

He leaves Fishman with the luggage in the check-in line and runs to the bathroom to vomit. When he gets back, he hears Fishman whisper-shouting into the phone at someone.

"So you just decided to keep us out of the loop? What are we, trainees?"

"No, don't tell me to calm down, do you even realize what happened here?"

"If we'd known, we could have done something, we could have tried to protect him."

"Oh please. We have good judgment, we wouldn't have done anything to risk the ..."

"We certainly will talk about this back home, you can be sure of that."

She gets off the phone, enraged, and he sees all the fighting spirit leave her body.

"They knew that Roccelli's car was booby-trapped," she tells Weiss.

"Yeah, I gathered."

"Motherfuckers."

"Yeah."

She puts a hand on his shoulder, and they walk silently to passport control. Weiss hands his passport to the ground attendant, trying to breathe slower, the voices around him muffled and intense at the same time; the commotion is dizzying. He continues on to the next queue without really paying attention. Fishman is beside him, pale too, touching his hand lightly and signaling to proceed. He bumps into the man standing in front of him, and his hard plastic suitcase falls to the floor with a thud. The man snarls at him, Weiss shrinks. Fishman reaches for his hand and squeezes it lightly but he withdraws it.

They sit silently on the plane, Weiss stares at the houses and trees growing smaller as the plane soars higher. The stewardess serves breakfast and Fishman passes it to him. The tray before him is steaming and smells like powdered eggs. He doesn't bother to open it, just drinks the glass of orange juice he had requested weakly.

Towards landing, the passengers are asked to stow their tray tables, and Fishman looks at Weiss and frowns. "Weiss, I know this is so, so shitty, but you have to remember it isn't your fault." His eyes burn. "Really," she goes on. "You did your job and you did it well. You couldn't have done anything differently."

"I could've," says Weiss through pursed lips as if holding back from a burst of crying.

Fishman shakes her head, but what does she know? Or maybe she gets it and she's just trying to say the right thing, or maybe she feels guilty too, after all, she is guilty too. They all ruined the operation together. They all sacrificed Roccelli. But Weiss in particular.

"They should have given us that update," says Fishman.

Weiss looks at her through narrowed eyes. What does she even care? Update or no update, she doesn't look shaken. She doesn't look like the world is collapsing on her. She doesn't look like she can't remember how to breathe.

On his own in the taxi home, the radio station, turned up loud, mixes with the noise of the taxi drivers' two-way radio. Weiss's headache grows stronger. He asks the driver to turn it down, not sure his voice is heard over all the sounds, and now his phone is ringing too, shrill and defiant. Weiss is startled, for a moment he expects Roccelli's name and his heart races. But it's not him. Weiss stares at the screen. After a long period of not calling, the display warns, "Do not answer."

"Are you going to answer that thing?" Grumbles the driver.

Weiss looks up at him and quickly silences the ring. A minute later, a message flashes on the screen. "I understand you don't want to talk. Sorry if I complicated your life. I won't call again."

He stares at the letters long after they fade away and lose all meaning.

"Here's your stop," barks the taxi driver.

Weiss looks up at him, startled, and realizes he's home. He pays, grabs his suitcase from the trunk and rolls it down the entryway to his building. His cellphone rings again and his heart pounds again, but it's just Zoe. He silences the ring and closes his eyes tight. His headache is pounding hard in his temples and he pulls the suitcase after him.

At home he swallows two Advils with a few sips from the whiskey bottle which has been left open on the kitchen shelf for longer than he can even guess, a mix he's hoping will cloud his consciousness. As the pain dissipates, he pours himself another round and the liquid burns in his throat. The phone rings again, and he silences it again, postponing Zoe again.

He needs not to think right now: Thoughts hurt him, or maybe those are emotions, but the alcohol doesn't erase the emotion, just blurs it, like a paintbrush drawn through the orderly thoughts, mixing them into a pulp and making space for other emotions, crashing over him in waves and whirlpools, flooding him. There is no dry land. He decides to let go, not to resist, to let the drift that swells in his stomach and chest take him. He closes his eyes. His cheeks are wet, it's raining outside, and he shivers and feels the sadness deep in his throat, grabs it and releases, grabs and releases. He reaches for his cell phone.

When the doorbell rings, Weiss puts down his glass of whiskey and stiffens. He stands, then sinks back down, snatches of thought flashing through his mind: He isn't sure what to do. The doorbell rings again, harsh and reprimanding. Weiss stands up again and hurries unsteadily to the door. He's still wearing his travel clothes—olive green Columbia cargo pants and no shirt. Just a long white cotton undershirt. He opens the door.

"You're here," a smile rises to his lips, then falls. His face is searching for the right expression and his heart is pounding.

"Don't call me just because you're drunk."

Amos is standing at the threshold, as good-looking and threatening as he remembers. He is tall and broad, his dark hair shaven and a black raincoat glistening from the rain outside. He unzips his coat and frees the black wool scarf, but still does not come in. Weiss wants to hug him, and wants to slam the door in his face, and is offended by his distant expression, but happy that he's here, and anxious, too.

"I'm calling you on account of the fact that I'm drunk," Weiss replies, his tongue heavy in his mouth, and he does not dare look Amos directly in the eye.

"That's the same thing," says Amos, the muscles of his jaw moving forward and back; obviously he doesn't accept that response.

"It's not," replies Weiss and pulls back a little. "I also miss you when I'm not drinking," he says and immediately regrets it, biting his lips in frustration. What did he just say?

"Okay," says Amos, quiet for a moment, considering Weiss' words, "But you don't allow yourself to say it," he says from his removed spot by the door, but something in his voice has softened.

"Well there, I said it," says Weiss, suddenly filling with rage. Who does Amos think he is? Coming here with his posturing, as if he could come and do whatever he wants with him, as if Weiss had given in.

"Sounds like you're still mad at me," Amos comes a little closer. Weiss feels his hands and the corners of his mouth quivering. His body is petrified, does not dare move. Every particle of him is aware of Amos's proximity, every particle screams 'Danger!' Amos does not touch him, does not violate the fine balance keeping the bodies apart, does not reach out to stop the shaking. He looks directly into his eyes, "What do you want, Gal?"

He wants to silence the voices; he wants everything to be light again, as if it were ever light; he wants to stop being afraid;, he wants to stop running away; he wants to not have reasons to run away; he wants to be like everybody else; he wants to be like himself; he wants to know who he is; he wants his father to be proud of him; he wants help; he doesn't want to need anyone ever again; he wants to hug Amos; he wants to forget that he ever knew him; he wants a way out.

He looks up at Amos. "I don't know," he says finally, "I really don't know." He feels the exhaustion in his whole body. "But I want to figure it out."

35

I get home, close the door and lean against it, trying to breathe; I've barely breathed for over twenty-four hours. I can feel the tension in my tired muscles loosening up. I leave my suitcase at the entrance and trudge to the bedroom, hoping to recharge, to escape my thoughts and the feeling of failure echoing through all of my organs, to escape from guilt and frustration. This was one of our biggest ever failures and I don't know how long it will take us to recover from it—how long it will take me, let alone Weiss.

I want to rest and breathe for a moment, but as always when I'm away, reality in Israel has not stopped and does not offer me respite. And so I encounter something blocking my way to the bedroom. It's a wooden cradle wrapped in a big, white gift bow, an exact copy of the plans that Jonathan showed me. There is even a delicate etching of a rabbit on the headboard. I smell the cut wood and the dizzying scent of fresh varnish. The varnish smell burns in my lungs and I push the cradle out of my way, and escape to the bedroom.

I get into bed, but the varnish smell sticks to my skin and my clothes, and the hammers in my head pound all the more forcefully. It hurts, I turn over and can't fall asleep. I lose track of the time until I hear the front door open, and Jonathan appears, leaning quietly on the doorframe.

"Hey," he whispers when he sees my open eyes and sits down beside me, "I didn't want to wake you."

"I couldn't sleep," I say, stretching.

"So, what do you think?" He smiles at me.

"About the cradle?" I recognize the anticipation in his eyes. "It's beautiful, Babe, really nice, thank you," I say and kiss his lips as they near me, and I am so far removed from that cradle, and from him, and I can't tell him about what happened, and I can't handle all of the things at once right now.

"It won't stay there," Jonathan sees that I'm bothered, "Obviously, but we don't have much space here. Actually I wanted to talk to you about a project that I saw," he says and hands me a glossy flier with a picture of two children lying on a green lawn, resting their chins on their hands and smiling at the camera.

I sit up straight, take the paper from his hands, and the caption "Ono Springs" shouts at me from the page.

"We could move to Kiryat Ono," Jonathan says excitedly, "How did we not think of that? It's just half an hour from your work and great value for our money."

I set the brochure aside, my headache increasing. "Wait a minute." I feel like everything is moving too fast, life is too fast and my mind is still in Rome, and Jonathan is busy with his plans, completely unaware of my mood.

"We haven't decided on buying yet," I say finally.

"True, but it's time we decided already. This is not a place to raise a child," he gestures at the apartment, "You said that yourself, there isn't even space for a crib in here."

"We don't have a kid yet," I say.

"But we should get ready for him," he says.

Get ready for him, I think, and wait for those words to awaken something within me, to move me like they move Jonathan, but it doesn't happen. I don't get excited by the thought of a cradle or a baby. This realization makes my heart tight and my lips quiver and Jonathan notices and gathers me into his arms and squeezes me to him.

"We'll get there," he whispers in my ear, "I promise you, it'll happen," he says, and his words pierce even more, and the smell of the varnish makes it hard to breathe, and his hug is too much for me, and the cradle is too much for me, and Kiryat Ono and the treatments and the child and Rome.

"No," I shake my head.

"I promise," Jonathan repeats and pulls me to him, but I wriggle out of his embrace.

"No," I shake my head again and take a deep breath, "Jonathan, I don't want to keep doing this anymore," I whisper, more to myself than to him.

"You want a break? We can take a break, maybe it'll help to cleanse your body of all the hormones. I heard about women who stop and then get pregnant." He keeps telling himself success stories, and I just want him to stop talking.

Stop talking, stop talking, stop talking.

"Stop talking!" Apparently I said it aloud because he falls silent and looks stunned. "I don't want to keep doing the treatments anymore," I say in a quieter voice and keep going before I lose courage.

"Things happened at work, bad things... good things too," I add after a moment, "I got the promotion," I stop, give him a moment to digest, then say, "And I want it." When I say this, something inside me breathes again. These words have been running in circles through my mind for so long, crashing into walls and are finally out and in their place comes a sense of relief.

Jonathan pulls back from me silently, tightens his jaw and then turns away. He takes the Ono Springs flier and folds it into two and then four, presses it tighter with his fingers and places it back on the dresser. He stands, straightens his ironed pants, adjusts the shirt which came a little untucked, then asks quietly, "you did it on purpose, didn't you?"

"What?" I ask, "Did what?"

"The miscarriage. You miscarried on purpose. You didn't want the pregnancy."

I feel as if he slapped me. "What is wrong with you?" I force myself back to my senses. "I didn't even know about the promotion at the time."

He looks at me and his face grows long, and his mouth opens a little, and his eyes are big, "And if you'd known?"

"I wouldn't have miscarried on purpose," I tell him.

"I don't believe that," he says.

Maybe I don't believe it either.

I watch him leave and don't say a word or beg him to stay and a moment later I hear the door open then close quietly.

Either the varnish smell disappears or else I grow used to it and I lie alone on my bed, listening to the quiet of the house, not knowing if Jonathan will come back, and what he might say if he does. I don't know if my marriage just ended, if we can overcome this, if we even want to. I'm waiting for the whirlpool that will turn my stomach, the doubts that will eat away at me—did I make a mistake?—but they don't come, and after a long time swirling between options, possibilities and counter-possibilities, I made a decision, I finally told him what I want, and with this thought I fall asleep.

When I wake up, it's dark outside. It's dark inside, too and Jonathan still isn't home. I reach out for my phone to call him but think better of it, giving us both time to consider what we want. I have a missed call from my mom who probably wants to talk about my father's birthday party which is in two days and I'll have a lot of explaining to do if Jonathan doesn't come. I'll wait a bit before reaching out to him, not to persuade, just to see what his plans are and if he'll come. In the meantime I get up and take care of the chores that my mother assigned me, a great distraction from everything.

I go over the long invite list that my mom sent, messaging each of them, asking that they RSVP, and coordinating with the singer who will lead the singalong that my mother decided to organize. On Friday I'm supposed to pick up the cake from the bakery, buy quiches, bread and cheeses. My mom is responsible for salads and for warding off any comments that "Nehama never serves hot food," and Jonathan is supposed to take care of the alcohol. It seems legit for me to contact him to check whether he's coming or not. I'll do it tomorrow so he'll have enough time until then to think about it.

But when I call the next day, Jonathan blows up at me.

"You go a whole day without speaking to me, and when you finally do call, all you're concerned about is whether I'll come to your father's birthday?"

"Babe, I really thought you needed time... I was giving you time to think," I stutter.

"And I gather that that time is over now that you need something from me."

"No," I say, "It's really okay if you need more time, I just need to know..."

"It's really okay? What exactly is okay here, Avishag?" He asks, venom in his voice. "Is it really okay that you suddenly decided you don't want a baby? That you choose your work over me again and again and again, *that's* really okay?"

"I'm not choosing it over you," I say.

"You are, however you spin it, but forget it," he says. "You're not even calling to talk, right? You just called to ask if I'm coming to the party, so, no I'm not."

"Okay," I breathe deeply, "And when can we talk?"

"I don't know," he says, "I'm really not up for it right now."

"We'll have to talk sometime, you know," I say.

"I don't know anything and we don't have to do anything, you've made that very clear."

"Jonathan," I say.

"What?"

I could tell him that I love him and want him to come home and that we will get past this and we'll work on what needs work and it's just temporary and our relationship is stronger than that, but I don't. I'm not sure it'll work and I'm not sure we'll get past this or that we're stronger than that and I don't know if I want it to be just temporary.

"Nothing," I say finally quietly.

"So goodbye," he says.

"Bye."

There's a work meeting this afternoon to discuss the lessons learned from the operation. Shabtai reads the data without moving a muscle in his face. Three people were killed in the blast including Roccelli, and four injured, medium to severe. Shabtai says that we aren't looking to lay blame but we all feel guilty, we all failed. There's no other way to put it. When there are specific intelligence indications and we're still unable to thwart an attack, the responsibility is ours, the blame is on us, and our source got killed.

Everyone seems to be in rough shape, but nobody looks as broken as Weiss. He's slumped in his chair, silent and only speaks when someone addresses him directly, and even then sometimes it takes several requests for him to shake it off and provide some laconic answers.

At the end of the meeting, I ask Pinto if he has a few minutes, and he directs me to his office.

"Are you still mad?" He asks after I close the door.

"Yes. But that's not what I wanted to talk about."

"Okay so let's actually talk about that for a moment. I made a decision and I stand behind it. You're entitled to think I made a mistake, but the decision is mine and so's the responsibility."

"Okay, so for the record I think it was a terrible decision that might have hurt the operation and definitely hurt Weiss when he's in bad shape as it is."

"You know that we took that into account, right?"

"Sure. Still."

"Fine, your criticism has been noted, for the record. How are you apart from that?"

"Not great."

"Some operations are like that," Pinto's calm voice does not try to reassure, but says things as they are. "In a long career there are painful slip-ups, but we cannot give up over it. We learn our lessons and move on. Tomorrow is a new operation."

"Of course," I force more formal behavior. I know the drill, licking the wounds while running toward the next target even if the wounds have not scabbed over, even if they're scarring, even if they're still bleeding.

"I hope that this won't make you doubt the position."

"Actually that's what I wanted to talk to you about," I clear my throat, "I wanted to inform you that I decided to take the job."

A smile spreads across Pinto's face for the first time since the discussion began. "I'm happy to hear that, that's great news. I'll ask Gidi to book training hours in the timetable. No need to wait for the official start date."

I nod, then look at him and say, "It'll be weird not having you around."

"I'll be really close by," he points as if towards Shabtai's office. "And I'll still be your boss."

"It won't be the same."

"Change is not a bad thing, Shagi," he tells me. "How did Jonathan take it?"

"Amazing," I say, raising my eyebrows for emphasis, "Just amazing. Speaking of which, do you want to come with me to my dad's sixtieth birthday party? A space opened up."

"Ah, I've actually got the kids tomorrow..." he starts.

"I'm kidding," I reassure him, "I was just being bitter for a sec. I'm so not in the mood for this party and I was hoping Jonathan would spare me the headache of buying drinks and setting up tables..." I stop. "Never mind, I'm just whining."

"Well that I can help you with," says Pinto.

"No no, I really wasn't saying that so you'd help me," I say quickly.

"I know you didn't say that so I'd help you, Avishag," he speaks slowly. "But I'd be happy to help."

I look at him, consider it, then say, "You know what? I'd love for you to help me."

He smiles, "When should I pick you up?"

I sit on the low cement wall around the courtyard, waiting. The time I spent choosing my outfit was a welcome distraction from the turmoil of recent events. I was entirely consumed with selecting the perfect jeans and sweatshirt – the tightest jeans and the softest, most flattering sweatshirt. I didn't bother with a jacket because it would have ruined the look, my hair is down, still damp from the morning shower and smells citrusy. According to the shampoo bottle, anyway.

"You'll get sick, weren't you taught not to go out with wet hair?" Pinto pulls up beside me with his car window open.

I get into the passenger seat and say, "I love the way you talk like my mom, it's sexy." I narrow my eyes at him, raising my eyebrows and pout at him exaggeratedly. He really is sexy in his threadbare cotton shirt, his stubble and morning hoarseness.

"So's pneumonia," he says, and adds, "you smell good."

"So it's worth the pneumonia," I say and swing my wet hair. Our first stop is the liquor store. Pinto helps me load the crates of drinks into the trunk and I try not to stare at his arm muscles. Next we head to a deli for cheese platters and quiches, plus four loaves of bread from the bakery next door. When I get back in the car, it smells of fresh bread and Pinto snatches the end piece off the whole grain loaf.

"You're gonna be in trouble with my mom," I warn as he reaches for a second slice.

"I can handle your mom," he says with his mouth full.

"True." My mother seems to like Pinto more than she likes me.

He manages to eat three slices by the time we get to the last stop—the pastry shop. My mother, blessed with dependably refined taste, ordered a dulce de leche cake with whipped cream and a picture of my father in the center, wearing a visor, squinting into the sun, and then a triple layer cake decorated with alternating pink macaroons and yellow meringues, and in the center a large chocolate slab of chocolate, sticking out of the cake cream and writing that reads: "Happy 60th birthday dear Avner" as well as a Mozart cake with whipped cream and cherries. The chocolate slab sticking out of the triple layer cake makes it impossible to close the box over it, so I hold it on my lap all the way to my parents' house.

When we arrive, my mom is in the midst of preparations. "Good, good," she says when I come in. "Put everything in the kitchen and we'll arrange it later."

"Ido-do," she cries when she notices Pinto and hurries to hug him. He sets down the beverage crates and hugs her back.

"Hey, Nehama, what's going on?"

"You can see for yourself—it's madness," she sighs, gesturing around.

And indeed, the house is crammed with balloons, birthday signs and shiny decorations. Our round dining table is now elliptical and has been moved to the corner of the room. A folding table will go next to it. The living room furniture has been moved aside and in the center is the sound system rented for the singalong. I set the cake down on the counter and urge Pinto out to the shed to get the folding table and escape my mom.

I remember there being a light in the shed, but I can't find the switch so I use my phone's flashlight to locate the table. I find it behind a ladder, ten flattened boxes and two bags of soil, and put away my phone to make my way to the table.

"Let me help you," says Pinto and moves the sack of soil aside.

"It's fine, I can handle it," I tell him.

"I know that you can do it," he smiles. "But I'm here to help you, right?"

I look at him and smile too, "Yes," I say, "thanks. I really appreciate it."

"Do you?" He smiles and approaches me and the flashlight lights up his side.

"Yes," I say, my breathing is heavy and I look him in the eyes and he does not look away.

"Good," he says and is now just inches away from me and as he continues to look me in the eyes, he reaches out and strokes my cheek and his hand is big and warm against my cold cheek. I shut my eyes and hold my breath as his hand glides down my neck and my legs are trembling as I close the gap between us and wrap my arms around him, gripping him tightly, and when I feel his arms close around me tightly, I slowly release the air trapped inside my chest.

A herd of horses is galloping in my chest and shaking my body from the inside out and his strong arms tightening around me press me close to him and I feel his heartbeat through his thin shirt, and the small hairs on the back of my neck bristle at the sensation of his exhale on my skin and that's the only air that I want to breathe from now on.

He loosens the embrace a little and now we stand face to face, nose to nose, breath mingling with breath, eyes half-closed, almost touching, but not quite, and I look at him and though I've known him almost my whole life, this closeness makes my heart leap and my skin hurt with anticipation. We are so close that I can feel the body heat radiating off of him, and I get chills, maybe because I am burning from inside, and I want to touch him so badly, it's just an inch or two between us now, but I can't seem to close this gap, nor does Pinto step closer, and the seconds grow long and he sighs deeply and pulls slowly away from me, and I tremble. He takes a deep breath, and steps back, clearing his way, then lifts the folding table and exits the shed, leaving me alone in the dark. I'm alone.

I wait for my heart to resume its normal rhythm, for my legs to stabilize, and then gather myself and a pile of chairs and go into the house, hiding my shaking hands behind lots of unnecessary movements. I open the table, distribute the chairs, adjust their positions, lay out table cloths, arrange plates, cups, cutlery, napkins, "It's still too early for that," says my mom, but I don't stop because if I stop they'll see everything.

Pinto observes my movements out of the corner of his eye, while my mother interrogates him about his children and scolds him for looking tired. My father is in a sweat suit by the counter making lemonade and he winks at me when I close the fridge door. I give him a kiss on his unshaven cheek, and I don't know if he feels something or not, when he puts two hands on my face and kisses me on the forehead, and I don't find anything else to do so I hurry to get going. Mom tries to coax us into staying for tea, but I tell her that Pinto has to take me home before picking up his kids, and she lets us go.

Back in the car, everything is weird and the closeness we shared has evaporated completely. I am unsure what to do with my hands or what to say and we don't look at each other, even though I can see out of the corner of my eye that he is sneaking glances at me, but I don't return them. I hold myself back not to reach for him, but I am not ready to risk further rejection; the insult burns deeply in my belly and throat as it is. I want to get home already, and don't want this trip to ever end, as it is the only opening I have and it is closing.

Pinto drums on the steering wheel, irritably or distractedly.

When we stop at a light, he turns his head and looks out the window in contemplation, or to avoid my gaze, and when the light changes and we're moving again, a great sigh of relief or of difficulty escapes his lips. When we stop at my place, he cuts the engine but we both remain silent. There are many conversations happening between us in this silence, in the glances that we steal at one another, in the hands that we are holding tight to our bodies, in the mouth that opens and closes without a word. Finally he touches my shoulder with a fingertip, and when I turn to him, he says, "You know I will always be here for you," and I nod even though I want to scream.

36

The evening of the birthday party I get home, determined not to think about Pinto or the Agency for the evening, and focus on my Dad. When I arrive, the decorations are hung, the garden is lit with a string of tiny lights, there's pleasant music and well-dressed guests. I put the flowers I brought in a vase, fill it with water, wave to people I know, hug Aunt Tammy and search for my Dad. I find him sitting alone in his armchair holding a glass of wine; all he needs to complete the sad picture is a party hat. I approach him, kiss him on the cheek and say, "Happy Birthday, Dad," handing him his gift: a watch in a fancy, nicely-wrapped box.

"Shagi, my girl, good you're here," his face lights up when he sees me and he puts the box aside without opening it.

"How are you holding up?" I whisper.

"I think I'll survive," he winks.

"Give me a sign if you need saving," I say as my mom approaches.

"What, no hug for me?" She asks, holding out her arms, "where's Jonny?"

I hug her and say, "Jonathan's not coming."

She pulls away, astonished. "What do you mean, not coming?" She cries.

"Mom, let's talk about it later," I try to brush her off.

"Just—in a word—what was more important to him than coming to your father's birthday?" She doesn't give up so easily.

"Mom, I said *later*." I repeat, and she opens her mouth to respond, but luckily for me, a stranger interrupts, embracing my mom, then my dad, then me.

"You remember Miri," says Mom.

I don't, but nod and smile as Miri takes my hand and looks at my belly.

"How are you, Shagi? I gather from Nehama'le that you're still doing treatments."

"It's been half a year now," now Aunt Tammy wades in, "I believe that at this stage you move on to IVF, right?"

"Yeah... I'm not sure," I mutter.

"You should check with your doctor, you know, at your age, timing could be critical."

"Yeah," I reply, "excuse me, I have a phone call to make," I say and move away.

"A phone call on a Friday evening?" Miri wonders.

"You know how it is," Aunt Tammy says with a wink, "they don't observe Shabbat in Iran."

I go back to the table after the meal has started and sit beside Dad. Uncle Gideon loads his plate with more than it can hold, while Aunt Tammy pushes half of the food back onto the platter.

"Don't drink so much," my mother puts her hand on my father's glass of wine.

"Nehama, it's only my second glass," Dad tries to pull the glass back.

"I know you, you don't handle your wine well, and who'll have to drag you into bed at the end of the night?" Mom insists.

"Well, maybe that's why he's doing it," Uncle Gideon cries while Mom glares at him. "So you'll drag him to bed," he wants to make sure she understands his joke. She just gives him a penetrating look, as the smile peels off his face. Aunt Tammy pats his hand encouragingly.

"Stop it, Nehama," my father says quietly. "You don't have to drag me anywhere."

"At least eat some rice, to absorb the alcohol," Mom lifts the platter of yellow rice and piles it onto his plate. He pulls his plate back, but she moves it toward her and adds two slices of bread and some cooked vegetables.

"That's enough, just leave me alone," Dad raises his voice and the table goes silent. Surprised by his own outburst, he puts a hand to his throat as if checking for damage. Mom's chair screeches as she stands and leaves the room and Aunt Tammy is quick to put down her cutlery with a clattering noise and follows her. The quiet around the table is only interrupted by Uncle Gideon murmuring, "great roast."

Aunt Tammy is back and shoots Gideon a look. "What?" He looks up at her, "Have some, there's tons left."

The door at the end of the hall slams as Mom lopes back to the living room, her face flushed, "Just imagine," she waves her pointer finger at Dad, "just imagine what would happen if I really did leave you alone. Where would you be, hm? Would you even be, at all?"

My father gives her a quiet look—he's hunched as if all of the fighting spirit has left him.

But Mom does not back down, like a soldier doing a dead check, "Answer me, what would you do if I didn't tell you exactly what to eat and what medicine to take, if I didn't do the grocery-shopping and clean the bathroom after you? I'll tell you. You would have drowned in your own shit ages ago," Mom sniffs, the veins in her neck protruding, then crumples, exhausted, on an empty chair and Aunt Tammy puts her hand over hers.

Dad remains silent. He blinks slowly and with each blink

I wonder if he will open his eyes again. Finally he opens his mouth, I hold my breath, and he says, "fine, I'll eat the rice."

"Take some roast too," Gideon hands him his plate and takes a piece of roast from it onto my father's plate and praises the sauce. It's the first time that Uncle Gideon's lack of social graces is useful, and Dad looks grateful for something to busy himself with as he saws at the meat with great focus.

Conversation resumes and Mom starts talking too, at first in singular sentences and with a grim expression, but she gradually thaws and it seems as though everyone is making an effort to move past the embarrassing incident.

After the guests ate and drank enough alcohol, the singalong in the garden begins. I sit to the side by the back row of chairs, humming along with the songs, smiling at people who seek out my gaze, but my mind is somewhere else. I go into the house and check Pinto's WhatsApp status, just to check for signs of life from him, and when I see that he's online, something inside me calms down a bit. I clear the dirty dishes piled on the table to the sounds of "When I'm Sixty-Four" as my mother comes into the house to take another bottle of wine and some beer from the fridge.

"Are you okay?" I ask her.

"Yes, why?" She asks.

"Because of that thing with Dad earlier," I say.

"Ah that, forget it, I'm used to that nonsense. So will you tell me what happened with Jonathan ?" She asks.

I set down the salad bowl I'm holding and sigh, "I told him that I'm taking the promotion and want to pause the treatments for now."

"You did what?" My mother cries and sets down the bottles, "have you lost it completely?"

"No, Mom, I finally decided what I want, and then I said it out loud. Is that so terrible?"

"Shagi, you don't find a man like Jonathan every day," she

sits down at the table, "Think long and hard about what you're doing. Partnership is more important than work and career, and it's important that you listen to your partner's needs."

"Mom, stop meddling."

"I'm not being sexist, yeah? Don't get mad, that's just how you manage a shared life."

"Do me a favor, Mom, what do you know about shared life?" I cry and feel the blood pounding hard in my temples.

"Excuse me?" She gapes at me with her green eyes.

"What you and Dad have together is a shared life? You drag that poor man around from place to place tyrannizing him."

"And what do you, Miss, know about sharing a life? What do you know about making sacrifices for the good of your family?" Mom's cheeks are flushed.

"Not much, apparently," I shrug, "but I'm not sure you're the model I'd choose to learn from."

"I'm not the model? You should be ashamed of yourself. After everything I gave you?" Mom speaks in a low, furious voice, "I did everything for you, I put a good face on things so you would have it easy and comfortable and you wouldn't have to deal with all of the shit."

"Telling me that my father was depressed and impotent when I was 14 is putting on a good face and hiding the shit from me?"

"No. But not telling you at 17 that he tried to kill himself, that's hiding the shit. Not telling you that I'm keeping him away from medications and sharp objects, and that we aren't moving out of this big house that I'm dying to be done with and into an apartment, just because all of the new apartments have a balcony, that's hiding the shit from you."

I open and close my mouth a few times and can't find any words. Suddenly I remember the ambulance that rushed my father to the hospital. What did I think that was? Why would an ambulance race through the streets with a depressed person?

My mother examines her nails. Her face is tired and she looks drained. She is hunched and fragile. I reach out and touch her shoulder, and after a few moments she puts her hand on mine and returns a squeeze with her cold hand.

"Sorry, maybe I didn't have to say it like that," she sighs, "But believe me, Shagi, when I tell you, people need kids. I don't know what I would have done if I hadn't had you. I want you to have the best life you can. You know how much it hurts to watch your only daughter make mistakes over and over, and not be able to prevent her making the next one?"

"Who said I'm making a mistake?"

"Me."

"You," I make a face at her of 'now it all makes sense.'

"He has kids of his own, Ido," she smiles sadly at me.

"What does that have to do with anything?" I ask.

She smiles a small smile, "You may think I don't understand anything, but I still know a thing or two."

"Mom, believe me, this has nothing to do with Pinto," I say.

"So what is it about?" She asks.

"It's about me, what I want or don't want. I always did what others wanted and I've had enough."

"I think that you should do what you want," my father is standing in the doorway to the kitchen looking at the two of us. "We're out of beer," he says apologetically and heads to the fridge.

"Do you think it would be a mistake to stop the treatments?" I ask my dad.

He thinks for a moment, then shrugs, "You're a big girl, Shagi. You need to make your own decisions and not waste your life regretting what you didn't do."

I hug him and he's surprised, but then gives me a clumsy hug with two beer bottles in each hand. When I let go, he looks at me sheepishly and says, "I trust you to do what's best for you."

After Mom brings out the cakes and everyone sings a string

of birthday songs and ten men in their sixties insist on getting Dad onto a chair, complaining about their backs and then lifting him up six times and one more for good luck. I say goodbye to all of the guests, embracing Dad tightly and Mom too, and she whispers to me, "I just want you to be happy," as I leave. But not home.

I drive to Pinto's. My belly is flipping but I'm determined. Maybe I'm still charged with energy from the operation or maybe I'm unsettled and maybe I ran out of patience. I'm not twenty years old anymore and I won't sit at home wondering why he didn't call or kiss me. Why the hell didn't he kiss me? We will talk about it like the mature adults that we are, I will tell him how I feel and then he will tell me how he feels. Yes. Being Pinto does not exempt him from the expression of feelings, so he should express them already! Even if they aren't the right feelings, I can handle it, I think. I really need answers and unequivocal statements because this recent period has been so full of uncertainty, and I'm fed up already.

According to his WhatsApp status, he is still up, and I imagine him walking around, stirred up, alone in his home, considering all of the possibilities that have ripened all at once. I imagine myself showing up at his place, him a bit surprised but not really, because he hoped even if he didn't dare to believe I would come, and he'll take me in his arms again and this time without hesitation, but letting us both just be.

I knock quietly on the door so as not to wake the kids and hear the echo of his steps getting closer and the rustling of the key and my heart flutters. The door opens and Pinto is standing there in sweatpants, with tired eyes and bare feet, and I hold myself back from hugging him. He looks surprised and I search his face for something else but am unable to decipher it. "Come in," he says, and opens the door wide.

I enter the living room. There's a TV show on the frozen screen and a takeout box on the white Ikea table.

"What's up?" He sits on the black sofa, moves two cushions and gestures to me to sit down beside him.

Sitting on the sofa, I take a deep breath, inhaling the scent of soya sauce and shampoo and Pinto. Most of my courage has evaporated, and with the remainder of my strength I stammer, "I wanted us to talk about what happened today."

"Yes, we really should," he says, "I feel like I owe you an apology."

"It's all good," I reassure him, "It caught us both off guard."

"That wasn't supposed to happen," he says.

"What wasn't supposed to happen?"

"Us," he says, "I shouldn't have crossed the line."

"Is that what you're apologizing for?" My voice is squeaky.

"Absolutely, I was out of line and I promise it won't happen again."

I have to be brave. If I want something to happen here, I realize that I will have to initiate, otherwise he will blame himself for taking advantage of the power imbalance, that idiot. "And if I say that I want it to happen again?" I look at him, but he lowers his gaze and shakes his head.

"You don't."

"Excuse me?" My squeaky voice rises another octave, "Are you telling me what I want?" I rebel like a child, because that's how I get when I'm around him.

"Shagi, aside from our complicated relationship, you don't want people to think that you got where you are because you slept with your manager."

"Well, well!" I cry, "Who's this getting me into bed already in his dirty mind?"

This is the first time I've ever seen Pinto blush, and he looks even more charming than usual, but he's mistaken. We both know I deserve the job, regardless of my romantic connections and that's what I tell him.

"You deserve the job, yes," says Pinto, and I see that he wants to add something else.

"But?" I press him.

"It's not exactly a 'but,'" he furrows his brow.

"So what is it?" I insist.

"It's just that it's good that someone was there to fight for you," he says.

"You fought for me because you know that I'm the best candidate," I say, awaiting his confirmation.

"Yes..." he says weakly, then clears his throat, "Yes, of course I think you're the best candidate."

But I no longer believe him.

"Do you really think that I wouldn't have gotten the job without you?" I don't wait for his confirmation, "Stop living in the past. I'm not a kid anymore, I deserve this job. I'm worthy. You need to believe in me more and constantly worry less."

"I'm not constantly..."

"You are," I cut him off. "All the time. Don't get me wrong, I really appreciate it. You look out for me more than anyone, more than my family, at times."

His forehead wrinkles again as he chooses his words, "I didn't look out for you more than your family, Shagi. You're very important to me, yeah? You were Shahar's sister. But it was your mom who asked me to come," he says. "She told me you were different when I came over, I... let's just say I wouldn't have thought of it myself, there were things that interested me more at age twenty-one."

I feel my face grow cold.

"You're just saying that to push me away," I say.

"It's the truth."

"Okay," I try to ignore the wave of sadness that rises from my stomach to my chest. "Okay, that was when you were twenty-one. What about now?"

"What do you mean?" He asks.

"Do you love me?"

His eye twitches and he sighs, my heart pounds and my breath is short and what am I doing here? He could say no. He could say yes. Both options are terrifying.

"Yes," he says finally, and my breath returns, then sticks again. "But not like that. You mean a lot to me and I will always care for you."

"That's it?"

"That's a lot," he says.

"I don't believe you."

He shrugs, "I'm sorry," he says, his gaze distant.

I wait for him to say something else, to regret it, to apologize, to say that I misunderstood, but he doesn't, just sits there, slumped.

"Okay," I say and take a deep breath. "I think I should go now."

Pinto looks at me softly and nods, then rises and escorts me to the door. As he opens it, our hands brush, sending a wave of heat that he must feel too, no way I am alone in this. I look at him expectantly, but he just turns on the light in the staircase and says, "Bye, Shagi."

37

Weiss stares at his phone screen which buzzes with a short news flash. Despite trying to forget, to blur it from his thoughts, the events seep back into his consciousness. He usually enjoys reading these news updates, to receive some recognition of his work, even if impersonal, to know much more than everyone else without saying a word. But he doesn't want to read this, he already knows too much, and he

291

can't dodge it, can't escape as he always did into work, because it is his work that is pursuing him. It's as if he's lost the ability to escape, just when he needs to most.

"Think about it as much as you need," Zoe tells him.

"It's better you take your time and not do anything you'll regret later," says Amos.

Weiss isn't sure which decision Amos is more concerned about. He has always made decisions calmly, without batting an eye or second-guessing, but not anymore. He asks himself if he misses the old Weiss, if it really was easier then, and he doesn't have a clear answer. In fact, he's starting to get used to all this not knowing. It's scary not to know, but liberating, too.

His mother still isn't speaking to him. He hasn't tried to contact her either. Typically, he had no need to initiate contact with her. She was the one who always made sure to update and to ask, to check in and take an interest, to keep the embers of their relationship alive. But all that came to an abrupt end, and Weiss doesn't want to court or convince her of anything, and what is it that he should even convince her of? He doesn't want to make a case for himself, he doesn't want to justify or apologize, he just wants his mother to be there for him, as she had been up until now, as he thought she always would be, but she isn't. And with each passing day he is confronted by this realization. And to convey the gravity of the situation, it's his father who picks up the phone to ask if he's coming to Friday dinner.

"Don't be an ass, your mom wants you to come," he says after Weiss wonders aloud. "But it's still hard for her. Don't expect it to just go away. It took you time, too."

"So maybe I should give her time," Weiss says bitterly. "Let her take all the time she needs without me, what do you need me there for anyway?"

"Come on, don't get smart with me," says his dad, "Stop feeling sorry for yourself. Just come and act like a grown-up."

So he comes and tries to act like a grown-up, and he does not raise the subject, nor does anybody else. When he enters, his eldest brother Yuval gives him a friendly punch in the shoulder, and Peleg, the middle brother, briefly pauses in his cutting of a chicken breast to mention that he read about the terrorist attack in Rome.

"Bummer," he says, "Things probably would've turned out differently if you'd been there."

Weiss knows he's trying to be supportive, and tries to smile. He takes a piece of the sweet challah bread, stuffing it into his mouth as if to stop himself from speaking, to silence the bubbling in his belly, climbing up to his throat, to quench the strong desire to tell, today of all days, this story of all stories. He wants to get it all out, to puke the truth up from his innards out, and watch their expressions change. Maybe they'll understand something about him that they never understood before. Maybe they'll understand less, but would want to know more. He knows that this is a thread that could be pulled and everything would unravel, and he knows that he must hold tight and not say a thing.

"In any case, they deserve our appreciation," his father says. "It should be said, not just after successes."

Weiss looks up at his father in surprise. He isn't looking back, just loading potatoes onto his plate, and Peleg smiles and shrugs as if to say, I don't know what just happened.

Nobody asks him about Zoe, in fact, no one asks him anything. There is a lot of talk about not much; about the meatballs and the government and the coming spring, but not about Weiss, they hardly talk to him, apart from his nephews who ask him to demonstrate combat exercises for them again and to crawl on the floor as they ride on his back and for him to play 'carousel' with them. He throws them in the air and they spin and squeal with delight.

His mother remains silent throughout the visit, not addressing him and not looking when he speaks. She is busier than ever with the grandchildren and with the food, serving and clearing and standing and hopping around them, and it seems like she is trying to get away while staying in one place.

But a moment before he leaves, she emerges from the kitchen, wiping her hands on a towel and shoving a bag loaded with Tupperware full of food into his hands. He looks at her and she looks at him for a moment, before her eyes wander back to the countertop, and she just says, "Take these, so you won't be hungry," and turns to go. He says, "Mom," and she stops, still with her back to him, and he says, "Thanks." Her back arches and shakes as she takes a deep breath, exhales and returns to the kitchen.

38

It's not exactly a farewell, though that's what we named the WhatsApp group that we created especially for this evening, which was meant to help us navigate everyone's impossible schedules. It's not really a farewell, but we are seizing the rare miracle in which most of the branch are in Israel to get together at the Irish pub near the office around a table full of French fries, schnitzel and tall glasses of beer, to mark the occasion which is not a farewell.

I look at these people who have become my closest companions over the years, and with whom I have spent some of the best, worst, scariest, most satisfying and most frustrating moments that I have experienced in my life. I don't like when workplaces refer to themselves as a family, since it's usually a cheap manipulation to make employees feel more obligated without compensating them adequately, and yet, there is something intimate and unique in this fabric that connects us all. It's like a web of translucent threads stretching between us, thin and invisible, but strong and holding tension, guarding us, keeping us balanced, preventing anyone from falling.

Beer fumes rise from around the knights' table and the usual jokes are exchanged at a higher volume than usual. Yardeni is imitating Gross, the head of logistics, who loses it when he discovers an equipment order form filled incorrectly, Sharon imitates Kiki's expressions, who won't look her in the eye when she is displaying cleavage, and Hadad is singing the Palmach march with vulgar lyrics in a bass voice and drumming on Harari's belly. Weiss rolls his eyes at them. He is quieter than usual, but his back is straighter and his smile is smugger and seemingly back to his old self.

On the other side of the table, Pinto sits drinking Guinness from a big glass and looking at all of us with a big, proud, fatherly smile. He's the only person under eighty who can actually pull off that smile.

Pinto and I have started unofficial training. I accompany him to various forums and meetings, we consult on professional and human resources issues, discussing precedents, different operation management protocols and possible courses of action, and also conduct regular small talk, almost like we once did. But something in the delicate fabric between us has been unraveled and sewn back together with coarser seams. I don't know how satisfied he is with our current dynamic, and I occasionally wonder if he regrets anything, even if nothing in his behavior implies that. On the contrary. He is back to being friendly and caring and a little distant like he once was, and sometimes I wonder if I imagined everything that happened between us that evening.

Pinto sets down his glass on the table and stands up to speak, as is expected at such events. His sheepish smile reminds me how much he despises these kinds of situations, and he puts his hands deep into his pockets, shifting his weight from one foot to the other and clearing his throat. Most of the people go quiet and look at him, apart from Hadad, who is busy stuffing two long French fries into his nostrils and shooting them at Yardeni. Pinto looks at him patiently until he settles, and only then does he open his mouth.

"Okay," says Pinto, "You know me, I'll keep it short," he smiles.

"This is already longer than usual," cries Harari.

"True," Pinto smiles, "Anyway, there are some significant changes within the team and I feel it's important to say a few words," he grows serious, bows his chin and continues. "Weiss," he says and turns to Weiss who returns a serious expression, "You know how much I appreciate you, and how much you've contributed to our branch and the entire unit. You are one of our pillars here. Some of you may laugh at me," he glances at me for a moment, "But I see our department as a home, that's how I've tried to make it since I've been here, and no parent likes it when their children leave home. But I respect your decision, and I trust that you will excel in your new branch too."

Hadad puts both hands around his mouth and shouts, "Boo!" Sharon elbows him in the ribs.

"And really, you're not going very far," Pinto continues, ignoring the disturbance. "Fortunately or unfortunately for you, I'll still be managing you in the future, so you won't be rid of me so fast."

Weiss makes a "what can you do" gesture and there are a few chuckles, but he doesn't channel them into a joke like he usually would, just smiles at Pinto and approaches him and they share the awkward hug of two men who are unused to the situation.

As their hug lingers, I start to worry that the guys will make comments, but the quiet is disturbed only by the waitress who comes to check if everything is okay. Pinto and Weiss pull apart and Weiss returns to his seat with eyes a little shinier than usual.

"Ok, enough with the drama, I'm still on the same floor," Weiss says, reaching for the schnitzel.

"To Weiss," cries Yardeni, lifting his beer glass in the air and raising his pinky finger with a wink.

"To Weiss!" Cry Harari and Hadad with raised glasses and outstretched pinkies, and the commotion returns to the table.

As we exit the pub I hurry to catch up to Weiss who is a few meters ahead. I call his name, and he slows down, allowing me to match his pace, but does not say a word.

"You know, you could still change your mind," I say, "I trust us to figure out how to work together."

"I really can't," he shakes his head, "believe me, this is better for everyone."

"I really wish you'd reconsider," I say, "I really think we could..."

"Fishman," Weiss cuts me off in a quiet voice, "enough, let it go." We continue to walk towards the parking lot in silence.

"I'm parked there," I point at a distant row of parking.

Weiss cocks his head and looks at me seriously, "It'll be okay. You're the second-best choice," he says and winks, then pats me on the shoulder, "Give 'em hell."

I smile and reciprocate the pat on the back. He moves farther away and gets into the passenger seat of a black Mazda waiting by the exit with blinking lights. I can't tell who's in the driver's seat, just see a hand reach out to Weiss and stroke his head, and I continue toward my car. I start the engine, turn on the heat and the radio, but don't drive away just yet. There's no one waiting for me at home, and that feeling, apart from loneliness, feels liberating: an expanse of air and time.

"Good thing you didn't get around to having kids," the mediator said to us.

"Yeah, eh?" Jonathan smiled sadly at me. "Good thing."

He left our home quietly, with the mutual acceptance that we couldn't do it any other way, there was no way to fix it, and maybe we were no longer motivated enough. I truly loved him, in the wood shop and with his poems and ragged shirts and also his button-down shirts and broad, solid chest, the warm embraces, and the pursuit of goals, and the determination and insistence; and I wanted us to be, and I wanted us to have, and I wanted with all my might until it was no longer there. And he did too, maybe he still does, but understands that I can't give him what he wants, what he needs. And for the first time in a long while, there is no time pressure to choose, I can give myself the chance to figure out what I want, what I need.

I breathe deeply and begin to drive. On my way out of the parking lot I pass by Pinto's car. He is sitting there with the engine running, reading something on his phone which lights up half his face. I slow down and look at him, and he seems to sense something, looking up and we lock eyes for a few moments until someone honks at me and I drive away.

The end

Printed in Great Britain
by Amazon

57913817R00169